Like Bees to Honey

~bħan-naħal lejn l-għasel

Caroline Smailes

The Friday Project
An imprint of HarperCollins*Publishers*
77–85 Fulham Palace Road, Hammersmith, London W6 8JB

www.thefridayproject.co.uk
www.harpercollins.co.uk

This edition published by The Friday Project 2010

3

Copyright © Caroline Smailes 2010

Caroline Smailes asserts the moral right
to be identified as the author of this work

A catalogue record for this book is available from the British Library

ISBN 978-0-00-735636-2

Set in Book Antiqua by Wordsense Ltd, Edinburgh
Printed and bound in Great Britain by Clays Ltd, St Ives plc

Mixed Sources
Product group from well-managed
forests and other controlled sources
www.fsc.org Cert no. SW-COC-1806
© 1996 Forest Stewardship Council

FSC

FSC is a non-profit international organisation established to promote the
responsible management of the world's forests. Products carrying the FSC
label are independently certified to assure consumers that they come
from forests that are managed to meet the social, economic and
ecological needs of present and future generations.

Find out more about HarperCollins and the environment at
www.harpercollins.co.uk/green

MALTA GOZO COMINO   www.visitMALTA.com

Remembering, always, my grandparents
George Dixon and Helen Dixon (née Cauchi).

'You sent for me sir?'

'Yes Clarence. A man down on Earth needs our help.'

'Splendid! Is he sick?'

'No. Worse. He's discouraged. At exactly 10.45 p.m., Earth-time, that man will be thinking seriously of throwing away God's greatest gift.'

~*It's a Wonderful Life*, 7 January 1947 (USA)

Xejn

~zero

Christopher Robinson, born 20 December 1991.

I remember the exact moment when Christopher first realised.

We were standing together, in my mother's kitchen, in Malta. He had been unusually quiet.

I asked him, 'What's wrong Ciċċio?'

He looked up to me and whispered, 'Can you see the mejtin too, Mama?'

~dead people.

I looked at my five-year-old son, shocked, confused, thrilled.

'Dead people,' he translated. 'Can you see the dead people too, Mama?'

Wieñed

~one

Checking In:

Please allow ample time to check in. Check-in times can be found on your ticket, by contacting your local tour operator or your chosen airline. Our broad guidelines state:

Please ensure that you check in three hours before departure for long-haul flights.

Please ensure that you check in two hours before departure for European flights.

Please ensure that you check in one hour before departure for UK and Ireland flights.

I am focusing on the woman, the one in front of me, her, with the black high high heels. She is wearing tight white jeans. I think they call them skinny jeans. She is wearing white socks and black heels, her. My son, Christopher, is standing next to me. He will not speak. I am focusing on her. I am focusing on her calves and on her black shoes. The heels are caked in mud, dry mud, around the tip of the cone. The mud is speckled up the back of her, of her calves, over her white skinny jeans.

I wonder if she realises.

We are standing in the queue. We move forward slowly. I have wrapped my large shawl around my shoulders, I roll the tassels with the fingers of my right hand. In my left hand I am clutching a small clear plastic bag containing a lipstick that does not suit and mascara that is almost empty, beginning to cause flakes on my lashes.

As we reach the security arch, Christopher walks through, no sound, no signal, no attention is given to him. I shout for him to wait. People turn and look from me and then towards where I am shouting, screaming.

Nobody asks.

Christopher carries on walking, ignoring me, he is angry. I know that I have upset him. I am anxious to reach him, uneasy when he moves from my sight. I wonder if it will be the last time that I see him, I wonder if he will finally have had enough of me, of the way that I have become.

I am stopped.

I am forced to remove my boots, empty the pockets of my jeans, be frisked with a detector that beeps. I take off my belt, I take off my boots. I look to my feet. I notice that my socks do not match.

Airport security is tight, these days. I smile. I smile as they appear to have let through my son, unnoticed. I am still smiling as I slip back into my knee-length boots. I am still smiling as I move over to the conveyor belt, searching for my handbag. I do not think that the officer likes my smile; he holds my handbag into the air, accusingly.

'Is this your bag?' the officer asks.

'Yes,' I say.

I look to the officer in his black uniform, with his shiny shoes and his shaven head. I wonder if he is proud, I wonder if he holds his head up high as he fights to save Manchester airport from terror. I like him, I decide.

'Are you travelling alone?' he says.

'No my son's with me, he's...' I point after Christopher. The officer flicks his eyes to there and then to me.

'Work or pleasure?'

'Pleasure,' I answer. I stop.

◎

And then, I remember.

◎

Christopher is waiting for me when I walk around the corner, out from security. He is leaning on his shoulder, against the white wall. He still refuses to speak. I scold him; I shout and scream that he is not to leave my sight, ever, again. He remains silent. He stares down to his canvas shoes, his favourite shoes. He will not look at me. I wish that he would. I wish that he would speak. Tourists, passengers, they all stand and stare.

◎

Christopher waits for me to finish shouting. His cheeks look blushed. I am wagging my finger, my eyes are wide, my voice is shrill. I am embarrassing him; of course I am, he is sixteen.

Two security guards turn the corner. They stand still. Their legs are apart, their arms cross their chests. A third security guard appears, he is mumbling into a radio. I finish shouting; it has been one maybe two minutes. I do not like being watched.

I tell Christopher that I need a coffee. He walks off, still looking down at his canvas shoes, still silent. I follow. He is guiding my way.

◎

The airport is busy. I do not know why I expected stillness, a silence. It is 4 a.m., a Thursday, flights come and go all through the night. I know that. I do not know why I needed a silence.

or why I expected a hush, a hush hush.

~hu – sshhhh.

~hu – sshhhh.

Christopher is sulking, not talking to me and I do not have the energy to pander to him. I am trying not to focus on him, not to give him negative attention. Instead, I am listening.

to the grrrr.

~grrrr.

~grrrr.

of the milk steamer.

~grrrr.

~grrrrrrrrr.

~grr.

~grrrrrr.

The noises lack symmetry.

◎

The coffee shop is crowded. There is not much else to do, but to drink, to eat, to wait to be called for boarding. It is 4:20 a.m. I have purchased a coffee, nothing to eat, no thick slice of cake, no huge muffin, just a tall café latte, no sugar and a child's milk for Christopher. He hates to be called a child. There is music, unrecognisable. Looping notes with a tinny edge, what the Americans would call elevator music, I think. I wonder if I am right.

I used to dream of going to America, one day.

there is the whir.

~wh – irrr.

~wh – wh – irrr.

~wh – wh – irrr.

of the coffee machine.

then the grrr, again.

~grrrr.

~grrr.

~grrrrrrrrr.

of the milk steamer. There is the dragging scrape of the till drawer.

and the clink.

~cl – ink.

~cl – ink.

of the coins.

And then I realise that Christopher has gone. He has wandered off, again. He does that a lot, these days. I will not look for him. He will find his way, I reason. He will come back, he has come this far. He knows that he must take this journey with me, for me. He has been told that he has to escort me back to the island.

◎

I need to telephone Matt.

◎

I have left my mobile phone at home, in the kitchen, close to the kettle. Matt will have found it, by now. It is 4:30 a.m. and I know that I should not be calling my husband. He will be in bed, perhaps sleeping, but we have that telephone in our bedroom.

I find a payphone. I fumble in my bag, in my purse, for loose change. I lift the receiver, insert a 20p, press the number pads, wait.

9

It is ringing.

With the ring, I can see him stretching over the bed, I can see him in his sleepy haze, a panic, reaching his naked arm out, to answer, to grab.

'Nina?'

'Yes,' I say.

I can hear crying, sobbing in the background.

'She needs to speak to you. Will you speak to her?' asks Matt.

I do not have time to answer.

'Mama?' She is sobbing, making the word high pitched.

'Molly, Molly pupa. Stop crying,' I say.

~my doll.

I am trying not to shout. People are listening.

I am sure that, I think that, the grr.

~grrrr.

~grrrrrrr.

has stopped and the whir.

~wh – wh – irrr.

~wh – wh – irrr.

10

has stopped too.

People can hear me.

'Mama, you didn't kiss me bye bye.' Molly tries to stifle her heart, but I know that it is broken.

And then, suddenly, I am missing her too much.

And then, suddenly, my throat is aching and I need to cry and I need to scream and I need Christopher. I need for him to remind me why I have left my little girl, my four-year-old daughter, my pupa.

~my doll.

It is late, it is early, she will be tired and emotional, more emotional than usual. I am reasoning with myself, but I know, I know really. I know within that I have hurt my innocent.

I hang up.

I hang up on her sobs, leaving her to Matt. Her daddy.

◎

I need to see Christopher.

◎

I am walking around the departure lounge, searching, sobbing, snot dripping from my nose, tears cascading down my cheeks.

I find him.

He is squashed in between a couple, tourists, I presume. The woman tourist's hair is bleached white, she wears a short short skirt and I see that her thighs are fat and dimply. She wears blue mascara, it clogs on her lashes; her lips are ruby red and her skin is orange. I do not look at the man tourist. Christopher smiles, briefly. Then he squeezes out from in between and he is off, again, running.

I refuse to chase him. I turn to walk away.

'Are you alrite, pet?' the woman tourist asks.

'I'm fine,' I turn, I say. 'Thank you,' I say, I start to turn and walk.

'It's just you was crying like a bairn a bit ago. I says to me bloke, "Look at that lass crying."'

'I'm fine, honest, I thought I'd lost my son,' I say.

'Shit,' the woman tourist says. 'Have you found him?'

'Yes he's there –' I point, I turn, I walk away.

◎

I find Christopher, standing below the departures' board, straining his neck to read the listed times. The details for our flight have changed; we need to make our way to gate 53. We walk together, in silence.

◎

All of the tourists have crowded to the gate. Christopher stays close to me, intruding on my body space. We do not have a seat. I am leaning onto the white wall, Christopher is leaning onto me. I think that he is feeling anxious. I am still sobbing. I wonder if he fears that I will change my mind, that he will fail his task, again.

'Air Malta flight KM335 is now boarding from gate number… What gate are we?' The crowd of tourists laugh, ha ha ha.

'Yes. From gate number 53. Would all passengers please make their way, with their boarding cards and passports open at the photograph page.'

There is the usual scurry, the fretful rush of people desperate to claim their pre-booked seat. I do not move, neither does Christopher. I am standing, leaning, waiting for a realisation. I am waiting for some bolt of enlightenment, for something to enter into my head and to stop me from boarding the plane.

The bolt never comes.

The muffled sobbing continues, but still I am boarding the plane. I am leaving my Molly, my pupa.

~my doll.

I have no plans to return.

Tnejn

~two

Air Malta is not only committed to provide you with a comfortable journey, but also to give that extra personal touch…

The doors have been closed, security measures have been explained. I did not listen or watch. Christopher is virtually on my knee, squashing in between me and the passenger next to me. He is fidgeting, wriggling, annoying.

'Sit still,' I tell him.

He looks at me but does not speak. We both know that the plane is ready to lift us from that ground.

the engines are whirring.

~wh – hir.

~wh – hir.

~wh – hir.

and as my head falls back to the headrest, the engines whir some more.

~wh – hir.

~wh – hir.

then the plane darts forwards, upwards, it tickles into the back of my throat. I swallow, forced gulps.

I look out through the small oval window, the houses and cars become insignificant. I see the clouds. I am flying over the clouds. I am flying over a blanket of greying white that separates and joins. I am in the air, higher and higher.

And then I realise.

I am gone from his England.

I wrap my large shawl around my shoulders. I bring the two ends together, up to my face. The shawl has tassels, the tassels tickle me, annoy, remind me. I wore this shawl when Molly was a baby, before she began toddling. I can remember her curling into me, fiddling with the tassels, rolling them between her tiny plump fingers, pulling them up to her mouth.

I want the smooth material close to my face.

I am sobbing.

~s – ob.

~s – ob.

~s – ob – bing.

into my shawl.

I am dripping.

~dr – ip.

~dr – ip.

~dr – ip – ping.

snot and tears into my shawl.

The plane continues to move higher and higher above the

clouds. I continue to sob, muffled sobs.

I have become the flight maniac. I want to apologise to the passenger beside me. He is dressed in a casual suit, creased slightly; his shoes are shiny, polished and buffed. I want to tell him about my life and my loss, but I do not. Of course I do not.

I am the flight maniac.

telling him my story, loudly, over the sound of the whir.

~wh – ir.

~wh – irr.

whirling engine, would only make things worse.

And so I continue to stifle my sobs. And the passenger beside me turns away, his left shoulder protruding, twisting awkwardly.

◎

Christopher does not speak. I think that he may be sleeping.

◎

The seatbelt sign goes off.

the plane is filled with the click.

~cl – ick.

~cl – ick.

~cl – ick – ing.

of metal.

And within the minute, there is a queue for the toilet, four men and one woman line from the drawn curtain and down the centre aisle. She looks pregnant, the woman. Her stomach is large, egg shaped; her palm is resting on it. I wonder if she is having a girl or a boy.

I want to talk to her. I need to talk to her. She must be able to smell food.

I really should buy her food.

I grew up on the island of Malta, in a close neighbourhood, with open window and open door. The community liked to cook and the odours of our foods were rich. They decorated, they floated in the air, breads, sweet pastries, baking potatoes, spice-filled macaronis, soups that celebrated local vegetables. This meant that a pregnant woman, whoever she might be, would smell the food and that with that smelling her baby would feel a desire, a need. And so, in Malta, without request, all from the community would know to take a dish of any food being prepared to any pregnant neighbour. It was almost a law, I think. It is said, in Malta, that the food will feed the desire of the baby. If a pregnant woman does not have, does not eat all that her baby craves, then it is said that the child will be born with a birthmark, a mark with a suitable shape.

I remember that my mother had a notebook.

She would write down the names of our pregnant neighbours and I remember that when one of our neighbours was heavy with her fourth child, my mother, she told me, 'Nina, listen, take this to Maria.' She told me, 'I do not like her but her baby must have what it desires. Take her this.'

I remember looking down to see my mother holding a dish of minestra.

~a vegetable soup containing local or seasonal vegetables, potatoes, noodles.

We had many mouths to feed with our daily food, yet still we would feed a baby of a neighbour. The bowl was hot, my mother's vegetable soup sloshed as I walked down the slope to Maria's house. I remember that it was summer, the tall houses sheltered from the burning sun, the cobbles were cool under my naked feet, the dust swirled from recently brushed doorways. The smell of the minestra, so rich and sweet, danced and twisted up my nostrils. I remember the liquid spilling onto my fingers, burning and my longing to taste the food, but, of course, I would not, could not even. I had learned not to deprive a baby; I could not even lick my fingers. I remember walking the cobbles, slowly, slowly down the slope and I remember Maria answering the door.

She told me, 'I will not eat the food of your mama' and then closed her front door, with a slam. I knew better than to return home with the minestra and so I left the bowl to the left of her step, where she could not trip over it. And I shouted loudly, told Maria that her baby's food was outside.

Three months later my mother told me, 'Nina. Go look. Maria's baby has the mark of a broad bean.'

I stare at the swollen stomach of the tourist on the plane. The queue is slow. She is leaning now, against an aisle seat. I look to her face. She is young, she appears tired.

I remember how tired I was when pregnant with Molly.

I push Christopher off me, slightly; he continues to sleep. I stand, place my shawl onto my seat and walk to her. I do not like walking on planes. My feet seem too light, like I have marshmallows on the tips of my heels. I squish my way to her.

I reach her.

'Are you hungry?' I ask.

'Sorry?' She looks frightened.

'Can you smell food?' I ask.

'Sorry? No. Please.' She is frightened.

'You must eat whatever you smell,' I say.

I turn, I walk from her, squishing my marshmallow-tipped heels, not looking back. I find my seat.

I move Christopher to one side; I sit.

I look to the pregnant woman. She is talking to the man in front of her; they are looking at me. She is full of fear. I need to reassure her. I know that she is frightened, but she must eat.

I mouth words to her.

I mouth, do not worry.

I mouth, I do not have the evil eye.

I mouth, you must eat what you smell.

◎

I wonder what shape birthmark her child will have.

◎

and then I realise that I have started.

~s – ob

~s – ob

sobbing, again.

I really am the flight maniac.

I have woken Christopher with my moving about, with my sobbing.

'Iwaqqali wiċċi l-art.'

~you embarrass me/you make my face fall.

I stare at him, stopping my sobbing, allowing tears to trickle and snot to drip, but no sound.

'Iwaqqali wiċċi l-art.'

~you embarrass me/you make my face fall.

'Who taught you that? Who taught you that?' I demand.

'It's ilsien pajjiżi.'

~mother tongue.

'How? Tell me how,' I demand, again.

Christopher does not answer.

The small television screens come down, a graphic of a toy plane is edging slowly over the UK, heading South. The air steward tells us that headsets can be bought, the film starts. *Live Free or Die Hard*, I am glad that I cannot hear the words. Christopher is watching the screen.

A child, across the aisle, says, 'For fuck's sake.'

I turn. He is twelve, maybe younger. His mother smiles at me, briefly.

And I think of Molly, again.

>tears drip.

>*~dr – ip.*

>*~dr – ip.*

>again.

It is nearly 6 a.m. I think of her getting dressed. I wonder if Matt will send her to school. I think of her hair and of how Matt cannot manipulate bobbles, cannot bunch or plait. He may use the wrong brush, tug at her tats, not hold the hair at the root. I think of her crying out with pain.

I think of the mums in the school playground, of how the news will spread in hushed tones. I think of how they will fuss around Matt, eyes full of pity, of how they will never understand what I have done. I think of how he will have to excuse me, talk of grief, and how they will say that six years of grief is excessive.

And I know that they are right.

I think of Molly's pink sandwich box, of routine, of her tastes, her quirks. I think of Matt struggling to find clean uniform, to dress, to juggle his work and his Molly. I know that he will be late for work if he waits for her to be clapped into school from the playground.

My thoughts are confused, jumbled, whirling.

I can still hear her sobbing.

I hope that Matt keeps her from school today, just today. He will need to go in to see the Headmistress, or telephone her, or both. The teachers will have to be told what an evil mother I am, of how I have abandoned my daughter and run away to a foreign country with my only son. But I know that any words exchanged will be missing the purpose, the point, that they will never fully understand why. I know, I appreciate, that people will be quick to judge me. I would hate me too. But, still, leaving my Molly, leaving my beautiful girl is dissolving any remnants of my remaining heart.

I think of her.

And then, suddenly, I am missing her, too much.

My sobbing vibrates through my body; it causes me to snort snot from my nose. My sobbing causes tears to stream.

> and my shoulders shudder.

> *~shud – der.*

> *~shud – der.*

> *~shud – der.*

> beyond control.

I am out of control.

I pull my large shawl tighter around my shoulders. I bring the two ends together, up to my face, again. I bring the smooth material onto my face, until it covers my eyes, my nose, my being.

I breathe into my shawl.

◎

I wonder if my Lord is laughing at me.

◎

She wakes me.

'Would you like any food or drink?'

I forget; for a moment, I am unsure where I am.

'Would you like any food or drink?' she repeats.

I look at her trolley. I see tiny bottles in a drawer.

'Two whiskies, please,' I say.

'Ice?'

'No, thank you.'

'A mixer?'

'No, thank you.'

'Anything else?'

I look to Christopher, he is absorbing the film; I wonder if he is reading lips, if I should buy him a headset. He seems to be on another planet, not really with me today, an outline.

'Do you want a coke?' I ask him.

Christopher looks at me then shakes his head.

'Nothing else,' I turn, I tell her.

'Sorry?' She is confused.

'Nothing else,' I repeat, louder, almost a shout. She nods, takes the drinks from the metal drawer; she does not question me any further.

'That'll be five pounds.' I hand her Matt's money, as she pulls down the table clipped onto the chair in front and places the drinks before me.

◎

The whisky burns my throat but at least I feel something.

◎

I stare out through the oval window, watching, waiting.

I see the sea, the deep blue sea.

The seatbelt sign goes on.

> within minutes the click.
>
> ~cl – ick.
>
> ~cl – ick.
>
> ~cl – ick – ing.
>
> of metal is heard.

'Cabin crew, ten minutes till landing,' he says but we all hear.

And then, the plane is descending, rocking, bowing, dipping, shaking, swaying.

And then, I see Malta.

◎

I see my Malta.

The island looks so tiny. I look through the small oval window. I see white, grey, green, blue. The natural colours dance before my eyes, they swirl and twirl and blend.

And as the plane dips, the colours form into outlines, then buildings, looking as if they have been carved into rock, into a mountain that never was. A labyrinth of underground, on ground, overground secrets have formed and twisted into an island that breathes dust. An island surrounded in, protected by a rich and powerful blue. I know that there is so much more than the tourist eye can see.

Quickly, the plane bows to my country, the honeypot of the Mediterranean.

And then, the wheels hit tarmac.

Merħba.

~welcome.

I am home.

Tlieta

~three

Malta's top 5: *About Malta*

✳ 3. Location
The Republic of Malta is a small, heavily peopled, island nation. Situated in the middle of the Mediterranean Sea, south of Sicily and north of Tunisia, the islands benefit from the sunny Mediterranean climate.

I was born Maltese, in 1971, into a family that had been united through ages, through generations. Malta had first crumbled under the sun, then under siege, bombardment, invasion and yet each time it grew stronger. The dust, the ashes, it all formed into the labyrinths, secret passages that connect, divide, protect. The islanders have resilience, a determination, an acceptance of sorts. It is said that if you have been stripped to nothing, when you mend you alter, your aura changes, your purpose becomes clear.

My mother once told me, 'In-nies jiġu Malta biex ifiequ.'

~people come to Malta to heal.

◎

I left. I do not know what that means.

◎

In Malta, my people speak the language Malti.

~Maltese.

We have a Semitic tongue that developed from the language spoken during Arabic invasion and occupation. Later came French-speaking Normans, the Knights of St John with their Italian and Latin, then British occupation. And so Malti became a combination of all the languages that drove through the island, of all those who came and left. It was born a rich, a breathing tongue, one that voiced our history, our invasions, our identity. When Malta later gained independence, both English and Maltese tongues were offered official status and Malti became the national language of my island, of Malta. It is known that my people can speak with one tongue, with two tongues, some speak with three or even four.

I was born into the home that was shared by my parents, by my grandparents, by my sisters and by my oldest aunt. It was the way, then. Our family was sealed, a unit that leaked noise, anger, laughter, excitement, wild gesturing with arms and hands.

There were no quiet moments. We liked it that way.

I was the third, the youngest daughter to be honoured upon Joseph and Melita. I was the favoured daughter of Melita. She called me qalbi.

~my heart.

My mother used to tell all that I was a kind, a loving, a quick-witted child. She would describe how my eyes carried a mischievous sparkle that warmed her. When I was a child, I could do no wrong.

But from an early age my feet would shuffle. I wanted to

know more.

My mother would tell me that from the moment I could I would toddle out of the front door and down the steep slope that led to the harbour. My mother would tell me about frantic searches and screaming relatives dashing around the city. My mother would say that soon they learned to run to the harbour, that I would always be found standing on the same bench, waving at the boats.

And as I grew, my fascination with the atlas, the globe, the sphere, with the wide spaces and exotic names, grew too. No one could tell me of life off the island, no one had ever travelled to the distant, the bizarre-sounding shores.

I was restless to roam.

I longed for further than my island could give.

And so, as soon as an opportunity arose, I asked.

I asked my father if I could be educated away from the island, in England. Eventually, because I drilled and drained, my father agreed that I would travel, that I would be educated in the UK, but then I would return and marry a Maltese boy. I promised my father and then my mother that I would return. I promised them that they could choose my partner, I would agree to anything, to everything.

I promised.

My mother wept for twenty-eight nights.

One month before my nineteenth birthday, I flew to Manchester airport, and then climbed into a taxi to Liverpool University.

Four days later, I had found Matt.

I can, without any hesitation, avow that within four days on English soil I had met the man whom I was convinced I would spend the rest of my life in love with. Within four days, I knew that I would not keep my pact with my father, with my mother and that in doing so, I would break my mother's heart.

As I was falling into Matt, my mother wrote to me. She said that when I left the island that 'naqta' qalbi'.

~I cut my heart, I lost hope.

She knew.

It was as if she could always see into my spirit and then into my mind. My mother gave up hope because she knew, just knew, that when I fell it would be totally, all or nothing. And so when I left Malta, my mother lost hope and now I realise that without hope, there is nothing.

◎

I lost my virginity to Matt. I lost my family too.

◎

I remember.

'You make me lovesick,' Matt said; he turned his naked back, away.

'Is that bad?' My fingers brushed his shoulder.

'My heart is sick,' he spoke and his shoulders began to quiver.

'I don't understand. What have I done?' I feared the end of us. I remember that Matt turned to face me. We were squashed into a single bed, his student room, naked skin on skin.

I had known him for five days.

His fingers, his face, were covered in my scent.

I remember.

Matt stared into my eyes.

I remember the intensity, the strength, the drowning.

'I have fallen for you. I feel lovesick.'

'You mean you feel love?' I questioned.

'More than that.'

'Lovesick?'

'Lovesick,' Matt smiled.

The lovesickness was mutual, but I never told him. Those words were his. The concept, the depth, the languishing in lovesick moods. They were claimed by Matt. He left me wishing that I could find the language to express the extreme emotion that he whipped within me.

My sacrifice showed him what my tongue could never curl.

◎

I was naïve, perhaps dim. It was a tradition, a lesson, a belief, a thought that floated with my friends in Malta. There were rumours that if we went to the toilet immediately after or if we stood during sexual intercourse, then we would not find ourselves pregnant, it was our only control. I'd seen pregnant women, of course I had, but the connections that I made as a child didn't quite fit. In Malta, we were told that babies were bought in shops or sometimes they came by boat. Pregnancy and sexual acts didn't quite go together, somehow. A pregnant woman went on to buy a baby, not to deliver one, it made sense.

As girls, we were also taught, through generations, that a sexual act outside of marriage would pollute all those who came into contact with it, it would lead to catastrophe. I knew that.

◎

Seven months after landing in England, I found out that I was pregnant. I never talked of having an abortion, my faith was strong, my love secure. Christopher was growing inside of me.

I was naïve, uneducated in such matters. Within my family, sexual consequences were never discussed, not fully, not in practical terms. Pregnancy was masked. My mother had told me that I had arrived by boat.

◎

Matt and I decided to marry after the child was born, in love, not from duty.

We decided that I would stop my studies and we decided that Matt would continue his. We would live together officially; we would move in somewhere, rent a flat.

I was excited.

I loved Matt.

He thrilled my insides with words, with gestures, with his lovesickness. I wanted to grow old with him, happily.

And so, I telephoned my parents.

My father answered, he was so very thrilled to hear my voice.

And then, I told him that I was with child. I told him that I had a baby growing within me and that I understood the sexual facts of life. I told him that everything made sense now, that my coming to them on a boat must have been a lie. I even laughed, ha ha ha.

My father told me, 'Inti diżunur għal din il-familja. Minn issa, mhux se nqisek aktar bħala binti.'

~you are a disgrace to this family. From now on, you are no longer my daughter.

My mother refused to speak. I longed to hear her voice.

With my father's Maltese words, something inside of me broke loose, not my heart, something else. I began to crumble. My sense of being, of worth, of belonging, of identity began to flake from me. And Matt tried to hold me, to stick me back together.

I married Matt when Christopher was eight months old.

I betrayed my Maltese name.

Erbgħa

~four

> ❛ And here we have Liverpool Metropolitan Cathedral of Christ the King, known to the Merseyside locals as Paddy's Wigwam. This is said to be linked to the large Irish Catholic congregation and the building's architectural design, which draws on that of a Native North American wigwam... ❜

I first met Jesus in Liverpool.

There are two cathedrals in Liverpool. The Metropolitan Cathedral stands proud; it lives in harmony with Liverpool Cathedral. The two majestic beings face each other along a street that is called Hope.

When I first arrived, that street, that view, the two churches, made me feel safe. In Malta domes and steeples take over the skyline. On the corner of Hope, I felt closer to my island, to Malta, somehow.

When I first arrived here, I was living in student halls just off Hope Street. I could see Catholic faith from my window. I could attend mass, be thankful, continue to grow.

When I broke my promise, my mother's heart, I refused to walk along that street called Hope, again. There were other routes, longer routes and I took them. I felt that to walk that street would be to play with my Lord, to tease, to laugh. I did not deserve to feel protected, safe, any more. It was my belief that in the insulting of my parents, my island, that I must also refuse that link with my Lord that connected my people.

I did not realise, then, that my Lord was vengeful.

At the end of Hope, tourists, visitors, students stand on grey pavement. They look up the stone steps to the concrete construction formed into a giant tepee of a Catholic cathedral. Tent poles stick out from the top, catching my Lord's sunlight and my Lord's tears.

When I first arrived, I approved of the cathedral, the construction. A giant tent, connecting, sheltering and yet crafted into a fine-looking thing. There was something about the vast space, the structure, the contrasts: uniqueness.

⊚

Three days ago I missed, I longed for my mother.

I thought of the tepee of the cathedral.

I did not understand the link.

⊚

Three days ago, before this journey began, I found myself on the corner of Hope Street, Liverpool. My Lord was weeping, again. It was raining, I had no umbrella, my hair was curling, frizzing into a nest.

I felt cold in my bones, shiver shiver, shiver shiver.

'Welcome to Paddy's Wigwam,' I whispered.

⊚

Three days ago, I stepped out into the road, not checking for cars.

I thought of my Lord. I thought that if He was there, watching, listening, wanting, then He would do as He wished.

Three days ago, I did not care.

I had nothing.

⊚

    I walked a.

$$\sim z - ig.$$

    a.

$\sim z - ag.$

    across the road.

Cars stopped, waited, beeped. Drivers moved their lips, cursing. I could not hear their words. Tourists gathered at the bottom of the grey steps. Some spilled from the shop, some stood very still, eyes fixed on the cathedral, mesmerised; others listened to a guide who spoke of architecture and history. I pushed through, I divided a tour of day-trippers, huddled under huge yellow umbrellas. I climbed the steps leading up to, down from, the overwhelming cathedral.

◎

The doors opened, automatically, dramatically, sensing my movements on the welcoming mat. I walked in, demanding, needing.

◎

I had been sitting, staring, searching the inside of the cathedral for some time. Father Sam knew me, he knew my grief, my rejection. He came to me, sat next to me, cupped my hands in his.

'I'm being punished.' I spoke in a hush, a respectful hush.

'It doesn't work like that.' Father Sam spoke softly, carefully, his hands joined over mine. I remember seeing a blue ray reflecting over our hands. For a moment I dwelled on the light, on my Lord's breath, on union.

'I don't trust your faith.'

'Why Nina? Tell me,' he asked.

'I failed to keep a promise. I broke a promise to my parents, to my island.'

And then, suddenly, I was sobbing and as I started, it grew, increased, my weeping was uncontrollable.

the tears fell, my shoulders shuddered.

~shud – der.

~*shud – der.*

~*shud – der.*

I was beyond restraint.

'Tell me, Nina,' he said.

'I thought that I couldn't cry any more, that I'd forgotten how,' and with those hushed words all of the tears that had failed to be shed were released.

My tears formed into a puddle.

'We have choices in life, Nina. You are clearly distressed. You are living in a hell of your own making.'

'My son, Christopher, has gone,' I sobbed.

'I know.' Father Sam lowered his head and began reciting a prayer.

'Please don't.' I began to rise. 'I'm sorry. I can't be here.'

'You need to find your way, Nina. You need to allow God into your heart.'

'I have nothing.' I stood, I turned, my knees shook as I staggered towards the exit.

'You have a husband, a daughter. Think of how you are affecting them, of the punishment that you are binding onto them.'

I kept walking, ignoring his words, lurching towards the exit. I heard him, fast, catching up to me. I felt his palm, heavy on my shoulder. I stopped.

'Go to Malta. Speak to your family and tell them that God sent you,' he whispered into my ear.

I carried on, forward. I did not look back. I could not turn. I could not articulate.

◎

I stopped when I reached the top of the steps leading up to, down from Paddy's Wigwam. I tried to breathe in and out, in and out. I thought of my life, of my inability to love since Christopher passed.

It had been six short years and in those six years I had never considered that I was affecting Molly and Matt. I had never considered the burden, the punishment that I was tying to them.

I had thought that I was protecting them. I had thought that if I loved my husband, my daughter, that if I devoted myself to them, then my Lord would come, that He would punish me, that He would pick them away from me, one by one.

◎

Father Sam had told me that I was living in hell, perhaps,

perhaps not.

◎

Three days ago, I stood on the steps leading up to, down from Liverpool's Catholic cathedral and I thought about my view, my vision of hell. My hell was burning damnation, with a devil, with chained slaves stoking eternal fires. My hell would not contain an innocent child. I felt confused. Father Sam's words were shooting in, out, through me. He did not make sense to me.

◎

Three days ago, I thought of my daily life. I still had Christopher. I felt him, I heard his voice, I saw him. He was still there. I thought of how his coming back to me had been unexpected. At first I had thought that it was my mind playing tricks with my grief, that I was imagining his presence. But I was not, I am not. He has been back with me for two years.

◎

It is simple. I can see my dead son and his spirit brings me peace.

◎

Three days ago, I began to walk down the steps.

I heard my name.

Voice: Nina.

I stopped, I turned.

Voice: I am Jesus.

I expected to see, something, someone. I felt a chill sweep through me then the smell of stale alcohol covered me, enveloped me. I carried on walking, slowly. The smell travelled with me. I heard the voice, again, my name, his name.

Jesus: Nina, I am Jesus.

The voice was gravel filled, harsh, guttural. I turned, I spun. He was not there. I was standing, alone, my Lord's tears falling onto me.

I began to descend the steps, again. The same chill swept through me, quickly, the same smell of stale alcohol covered me, stilted me. I was stunned. I stopped. The rasping voice had a familiarity, it connected, it stuck into me.

Jesus: Nina, I am Jesus.

The voice existed, without a body, there was no physical presence.

I did not move.

He spoke, again, with the same gravel-filled harshness.

Jesus: Nina, I am Jesus.

'Stop it. Stop it,' I shouted the words.

I held my hands to cover my ears. His voice, inside of my head, stayed at the same volume, constant, continuous, on a loop. We were talking through tin cans, connected by nothing.

> **Jesus:** Nina, I am Jesus. You blame your Lord.

'Stop it. Stop it. Stop it.'

> **Jesus:** Nina, I am Jesus. I sent him back to help you. I thought he could help you.

'Shut up!'

My knees crumbled, I fell to the steps. With my palms clutching my ears, I bowed, forwards, backwards, rocking, sobbing.

The voice was silent, minutes passed by, silence, more silence.

I waited, I lowered my hands to the step; I steadied myself as I stood.

> **Jesus:** Go to Malta, my Nina. I am Jesus. Bring Cadbury's chocolate with you.

◎

Matt,

I dreamed of you last night, the 'of you' was in a feeling, in the sensation that it evoked.

50

In my dream, I was sitting at Manchester airport. I was sitting on the floor, next to that backpack of yours that you loved so much, when we were students. A shabbily dressed lady staggered over to me. She was carrying a basket of handmade lace.

She spoke to me, 'x'temp hazin. x'temp hazin.'

I couldn't understand her words. She spoke in my tongue. She thought that I would understand. She thought that something within me would make me understand. I tried. I tried to pick out the words, but I could not.

She spoke again, in English. 'What awful weather! What awful weather!' I smiled at her. She laid her sun-blessed finger onto my head. She spoke in whispered tones, 'Gara incident. There's been an accident. Gara incident.'

I woke from my dream sobbing. You do not come to me in the night, instead you send me old women with tongues that, with darkness, I can no longer understand. They speak words that I have, that I know, that I knew, once. And all the time I am longing. I am aching. I feel that I am dying inside to out. There is no life. There is no breath. There is nothing without you in my life.

I wish that I could tell you, that I could send this, leave this, that you would begin to understand. My love for you grows, it is deep rooted within me and even if I try to deny it, if I ignore or block it, it still grows. My love matures, stronger with each neglectful day. I am truly lovesick.

But Matt, I am leaving you; tomorrow I am flying home to Malta.

Nina x

Ħamsa

~five

Christopher Robinson, born 20 December 1991.
Christopher Robinson, killed 5 February 2002.
Ten years old.

The plane is taxiing, gradually, searching to meet the metal stairs.

'You look sad, Mama.'

Christopher breaks my thoughts.

'I'm just thinking, Ciccio,' I say.

'About when I passed over?'

'Yes, about when you died.' I whisper the words.

'I can hear you, even when you don't speak.'

He tells me.

◎

Speaking to my dead son helps me, to remember.

◎

The fifth of February. It was an insignificant day, the date meant nothing. I dwell on this, sometimes. I think about how life can change, can fall, crumble with ease.

I made the wrong decision, a mistake, a split second error in judgement.

The weight of consequence is beyond measure.

◎

I do not work, I never have. I like it that way. I love to be at home, making a home. I cook, I clean, I wait for the end of the school day.

It was the same then.

I would wait for the end of the school day, for my Ciccio. It was how I wanted it to be. I was happy, deeply happy, pretending to be happy. We had enough money; Matt was working his way up the company. He was clever, a genius.

He still is.

Christopher was ten; he was keen to be independent, to help. He loved food, the combining of ingredients. He would watch me cook, his questions were intelligent. I would describe food, cuisine, Maltese traditions to him. He would eat up my words, my snippets of language, my customs.

I would tell him about my special place in Malta. I would tell Christopher how I used to go to a café with my mother, after school. I would describe how my mother and I would sit near to the window, how we would talk and look down onto the bay of Mellieħa. I would tell Christopher about the food that we would eat, always the same food. I would talk to Christopher about that time, I would try to describe ftira biż-żejt.

~Maltese flat bread seasoned with salt, with
peppers, with tomatoes, with capers, with
olives, with olive oil.

His eyes would light, his taste buds tang. I longed for him to savour. He never did.

I gave him words without flavour, without texture.

Sometimes, in life, we put off, we think that there will be a tomorrow.

We are told that we will blossom and then wither.

I guess that I gave my son the skeleton, the remains of a culture. I spoke an outline of a country that he was drawn to, that he needed to understand. I offered him words without images that he could attach to. I lacked commitment; I feared the joining of him to his roots, my roots. I barely spoke with my mother tongue, not until after Christopher's death, not really.

We lived close to the primary school. Christopher pestered to walk home with a friend. He would have to cross one main road, but they knew where to look, how to look left and then right and then left again. They were sensible boys, I gave in. They had managed the walk home for six, maybe even seven weeks.

School finished at 3.20 p.m.

On 5 February 2002, Christopher's friend James was ill. His mother had called in the afternoon, just to let me know that Christopher would be making the walk home, alone.

I began to worry.

I decided that I would wait for him, on the home side of the main road; that I would almost pretend to be shocked to see him.

It was a simple plan.

I got to the main road at 3:20 p.m. I stood down slightly, out of sight, almost, as if I had come up from the village and was making my way home. Christopher had not seen me. He was standing at the opposite side of the main road, waiting to cross.

I called his name, shouted out Ciccio.

He looked at me, a huge grin on his face.

And, then, he stepped out onto the main road.

◎

He was killed on impact.

◎

There was nothing that I could do.

◎

But that is not the complete story of our relationship, not really. Christopher knows that my recall lacks context, depth, texture. That is the story that I have formed, developed to convince people to offer sympathy, to empathise. There is a truth, blocked, hidden where only the spirits can see. There was another side to our mother and son relationship.

Sitta

`~six`

Malta's top 5: *About Valletta*

✳ 1. The Knights of St John

Valletta is indebted to the Order of the Knights of St John, who originally designed the city as a sanctuary to tend to wounded soldiers during the defence of Malta against the Ottoman Empire in the sixteenth century. Before this, the order was situated in a little watchtower, named St Elmo, the only construction on Mount Sceberras, which lies between two harbours. The valiant conqueror of the Great Siege, Grand Master La Valette, understood that for his order to uphold its grip on Malta they would have to build sufficient fortifications. A plan was devised for the fortified city which was given the name Valletta, in honour of La Valette.

The air steward's voice is monotone, floating over the bustle of the tourists.

'Please stay seated until the aircraft is stationary.'

They do not, of course.

> within the minute the click.

> *~cl – ick.*

> *~cl – ick.*

> *~cl – ick – ing.*

> of metal is heard.

People stand, push into the aisle, pull coats and bags down from the overhead lockers.

The stairs are being attached. The door opens.

I squeeze into the queue in the aisle, clutching my handbag and my shawl to my chest. Christopher follows, pinching in behind me, invading my personal space, again. We do not move.

I am impatient.

I want to be off the plane, I need to be in the open space, breathing in the dust of Malta. I want to scream. I want to tell the tourists to move out of my way.

We begin to move.

We take small steps, we shuffle; I do not let other passengers step in front of me. I avoid eye contact. I ignore the pregnant woman, I ignore the goodbye from the air steward; I walk down the metal steps.

the heels of my boots clip clap.

~cl – ip.

~cl – ap.

~cl – ip.

~cl – ap.

but there is no blast of heat, no warmth from my Lord's smile, not today.

the heavens are spitting, spatting.

~sp – it.

~sp – at.

~sp – it.

~sp – at.

I lift my face up to creation. The sky is grey, sullen, moody.

His rain falls onto me. He spits on my face.

My Lord blesses my soul.

Merħba.

~welcome.

I walk in my Lord's spit, following the trail of people, staying in between the yellow guide lines that direct into arrivals. We are close to the terminal, no bus is needed.

I hear the engines thrusting their whirs.

>they whirl.
>
>*~wh – irrrr.*
>
>*~wh – irrrr.*
>
>*~wh – irrrr – llll.*

The airport is calm, quiet. I wait for my suitcase to churn around on a conveyor.

I feel a chill. I shiver shiver, shiver shiver.

My bones are cold.

The airport smells of popcorn.

I am hungry; the sweet airport air has increased my need. I cannot remember when I last ate. My stomach churns. I am famished in Malta.

I lug, I wheel my suitcase. I do not collect a metal trolley.

I walk through customs, nothing to declare, I step onto the escalator. I travel down, slowly. I look onto the crowd that stands waiting for people to arrive. My eyes search, in vain.

I walk, I stagger through the crowd and out, into His rain.

I queue for a taxi.

Christopher follows, several steps behind me. He does not speak.

We are in a taxi, going to Valletta, my suitcase is in the boot. It will take twenty-five minutes, I think. We are going to my mother's house, home. I dwell on the word home.

I long for a home.

I watch through the taxi window; the island rushes, blurs past my eyes with colours, with whites, with greens. The sandstone constructions are greying through the drizzle, they look weary, lost. I watch cars slip and slide past us, some are shiny, promising wealth and importance; they dance in the rain. We travel along a new road, an unknown journey. I search for familiarity, I need familiarity. I could be anywhere, any Mediterranean country, any foreign soil.

I seek acquaintance, for something to connect me to my roots. My eyes rest on golden arches, McDonald's.

Time has altered my island.

◎

'John Lennon lives in Malta.'

My son says. I laugh, ha ha ha.

'Oh Christopher! Who told you that?' I say.

'Jesus did.'

My son tells me.

'I'm hoping to meet with Jesus,' I say.

The taxi driver looks in his rear-view mirror, his dark eyes meet with mine. I smile at him, I raise one eyebrow. He looks away, quickly, back to the road.

'Geordie shares Cisk with him in Larry's bar.'

~Cisk lager was first available in Malta in 1928. It has an alcohol content of 4.2 per cent.

'Geordie?' I ask.

'Elena's husband.'

'Elena?' I ask.

'Geordie's a spirtu, a spirit, like me. He's waiting for

Elena to pass over. She's your mother's aunt, lives in Newcastle.'

Christopher is right. I recall, the words connect, ignite.

I have heard the stories of Elena, the family shame, the ostracism. She met Geordie, an English soldier in Malta, during the war. The family rejected her union. I do not know the full story. I know only fragments.

'Geordie told me Jesus sent me back to help with your grief.'

My son breaks my thoughts.

'Well his plan backfired, didn't it?' I say. 'And I'll tell him so when I see him.'

The taxi driver tuts.

Christopher does not speak for the rest of the journey. We travel in silence. The taxi driver switches on the radio; it crackles, interference. I hear a voice, loud, clear, through the rustles, through the static.

Jesus: Welcome home, my Nina.

The taxi driver does not speak.

◎

I am unsure if my mother knows of my arrival. I suspect that Christopher may have told her. He tells me that he visits her, often.

He tells me that he can do that.

He says that he can be with different people, in different places, at the same time.

He tells me that he is like God, but very different. He tells me that he is like God because God can also be in so many different places at the same time.

I believe in Christopher more than I believe in my Lord.

The taxi drops us outside of the walls of Valletta. The driver keeps his eyes down as he speaks of the money that I must pay.

I fumble with my purse, with my euros.

The taxi driver does not move from his seat. He presses, something, inside of the car. There is a click. The boot springs open, slightly. The taxi driver waits, in his seat. I struggle with the boot of his car and then with my suitcase.

Christopher has not the strength to help me.

I wobble with my suitcase.

~cl – ip.

~cl – op.

across the bumpy pavements.

I am clumsy, I walk.

◎

I walk through the City Gate and into Valletta, il-Belt.

`~the City.`

My heeled knee-length boots feel awkward, clumpy.

The roads and the pathways of my Capital, of Valletta, are uneven. I wobble over them; I am cautious, fearful of falling. Malta could never be smooth, perfect without blemish, there is too much history, there are too many marks, injuries, scars. Today, I am fearful of the cracks swallowing me.

I walk, gracelessly, slowly, as the Renaissance streets open up before me.

I.

~cl – ip.

~cl – op.

along the side of the road, pulling my suitcase behind me, watching my son lead the way.

◎

67

Last time I walked these cobbles I was with Matt and with my five-year-old Christopher. The memory stings. I remember our walking through the City Gate and into Valletta. I remember the blistering warmth. I remember that Christopher was tired, the early morning journey and the high temperature were taking their toll. I remember Christopher was dragging behind us, no hand to hold, no comfort to be found. I remember Christopher asking me why the Opera House was broken. I remember ignoring his question, walking up again, then down again. I remember that it was busy, packed with tourists wearing as few clothes as possible, yet still dripping in sweat. I remember that Christopher moaned with each step. He wanted to go home. I remember that Matt did not complain, that Matt never complained.

I look up, I feel His spit on my skin. I look to the buildings. They embrace the past, leaning to me, crumbling, neglected. The details speak of disregard, of bombardment.

I turn right, I.

~cl – ip.

~cl – op.

past the broken down Opera House, up again.

'It was bombed,' I tell Christopher.

'I know, Nanna told me.'

He says.

I turn, left, down again. The course is familiar, instinctive, unchanged. I have walked this route before, alone, with others, with my sisters, with my mother, with my father, with cousins, with Matt, with Christopher.

All streets slope down to the harbour.

It is morning, spitting, cold and busy. Tourists still visit in February.

I bump my suitcase down each of the stone steps, making my way down the slant of the steep street. The roads are narrow, the buildings tower, built to provide shelter from the overpowering heat of the summer. Today they would say that it rains lightly, I would say that my Lord spits, but the narrow streets of my home offer protection, of sorts.

I am wet, cold in my bones, shiver shiver, shiver shiver.

I reach my mother's green front door.

Sebgħa

~seven

Malta's top 5: *About Malta*

✱ 2. Language
Spoken by over 360,000 people on and off the
Mediterranean islands of Malta and Gozo. Malti is
the national language. It is a Semitic language, filled
with borrowings from Italian, Arabic and English,
written with a Latin script. The co-official languages
of the islands are English and Maltese, making
Malta an ideal holiday destination for English-
speaking tourists.

I stand on the bumpy pavement facing my mother's front door. I am very still, I am a statue, I think about holding my breath. I think of a childhood that was filled with laughter, with noise, with warmth.

I listen, the sounds are unfamiliar. Doors slamming, footsteps, muffled radio, rain.

I think of my sisters, Maria and Sandra, and of how we would play il-passju.

~hopscotch.

We would draw onto the pavement and curse the slope. The slope would ruin, make the game almost impossible, but still we would play. I look to the pavement, searching for chalk lines, for remnants of my past.

I think of noli.

~hide and seek.

I think of boċċi.

~marbles.

I long for this home, for my mother's house, behind a green front door in Valletta.

◎

I knock.

~kn – o – ck.

~kn – o – ck.

on the green front door.

I long to see marble, rich embellishments, beautiful paintings, elaborate chandeliers. I know what I expect to see.

No one answers.

I knock.

~kn – o – ck.

~kn – o – ck.

again, louder.

No one answers.

My eyes begin to focus, to notice. I look up to the balconies, there are two. The house towers, leans forward, slightly. The wooden balconies look as though they will crumble with a gust of wind. I look to the façade, discoloured, flaking plaster, cracks. I look to the green front door, weathered, drained of colour. There is a rusted padlock, a tarnished chain, to keep those in.

I need to be inside.

It is Christopher's idea.

Of course he has been near to me the whole time. I was not really focusing on him; he was probably behind me, in front of me, over me. I do not really know.

'Don't worry, Mama, I know how to get in.'

He tells me.

'You do?' I ask.

'Of course, through a cracked window in the basement. Nanna told me. Tilly broke the window.'

He says.

'Tilly?' I ask.

'The Fares.'

~ghost, usually the protector of a house but may become resentful.

And so, Christopher slips through the crack and into my mother's house.

I hear a key turning.

and a.

~*cl – unk.*

as the barrel revolves.

The chain and padlock come undone.

I hear the chain clunk.

~*cl – unk.*

74

~cl – unk.

to the floor.

And then it is gone.

I cannot explain where it has gone; only that it no longer keeps those in, those out.

⊚

I walk into my mother's house, dragging my suitcase over debris. My eyes begin to adjust. I see through the dust and the rubble and the rubbish. The smell hits me, decaying, riddled.

I stop. I begin to hold my breath, to count, in Maltese.

I close my eyes.

Wieħed, tnejn, tlieta, erbgħa, ħamsa.

~one, two, three, four, five.

I open my eyes.

My eyes transform the tumbled ceilings, the broken banisters and within moments I am standing in my mother's hallway. A grand sweeping staircase is on my right. A wooden coat stand, garnished with elaborate carvings, is to my left. I take off my shawl. I drape it onto the stand, next to my mother's lace shawl. I release the grip of my suitcase, resting it near to the wall.

I shiver. It is cold in Malta. I feel cold in my bones, shiver shiver, shiver shiver.

And then, my mother walks in from the kitchen.

She is ahead of me, rubbing her hands over her hair, shaping her black backcombed locks into a ball. She looks young, fresh, alive. She looks my age, mid thirties, I see my shape in her curved figure. Her lips are covered in red lipstick; she is wearing her house clothes, covered with an apron. She has been cooking, I smell, I am hungry.

'Nina, qalbi! Ġejt lura d-dar, għalija!'

~Nina, my heart! You came back home for me.

She holds out her arms, wide, and as I move towards her I become enveloped in her scent.

'Jien qiegħda d-dar,' I whisper.

~I am home.

◎

The embrace is broken.

'Christopher, where is he?' I ask.

My eyes search, I panic.

'He will be with Geordie, Aunt Elena's Englishman, don't worry. Ikunu qed jaqsmu l-birra ma' Ġesú.'

~they will be sharing beer with Jesus.

My mother is smiling.

'Ciċċio says that Jesus lives in Malta.'

'He does, you'll meet him.'

My mother says.

'Why are there so many dead people here?' I ask.

'All troubled souls come to Malta, qalbi.'

~my heart.

'But why, Mama?' I ask.

'You don't remember, qalbi? To heal, the good come here to heal.'

My mother says.

◎

We are in the kitchen.

My mother stands near to her cooker; two plates, a bowl, two forks and a large silver spoon are laid out, ready. I lean my bottom onto one of the wooden chairs; there are six surrounding the kitchen table. In the centre of the table, a glistening crystal bowl contains one single orange.

'Ciċċio told me that you were coming.'

She says, spooning out arancini.

~baked rice balls filled with cheese, meat
sauce, peas, rice. The outside is covered in
breadcrumbs.

I watch my mother.

I look as the perfect rice balls are transferred from bowl, to spoon, to plate, with ease. It was my favourite dish as a child, my mother has remembered, she has cooked them to welcome, without words. Her rice balls are filled with mozzarella, the taste used to linger, melt. The taste was unique to my mother's recipe, different, special.

I smile.

I cross my arms over my chest, my hands rubbing to warm the tops of my arms. My mouth is filled with anticipation, juices.

'Are you cold, qalbi?'

~my heart.

'I am cold in my bones,' I say.

'You will find warmth, come, eat.'

She hands me a plate and a fork, the arancini roll, slightly. I uncross my arms, pull out a wooden chair and place my plate onto the table.

I think to how Christopher and I would attempt to replicate, to make arancini and how frustrated I would become. I used to think that I was cursed, that my inability to perfect arancini was my punishment for breaking my word, my promise. I was naïve. My Lord does not punish people with an inability to make rice balls. My Lord punishes with the death of a child.

I shiver.

I think of Molly. I have never cooked with Molly. Her daddy has, I cannot.

I shiver.

My mother sits next to me.

'You cooked my favourite, thank you.'

I want to talk, to spill, to tell my mother all in the hope that she will help me, that she will make me better. I cannot find the words, not yet. My mother reads my thoughts.

'Listen. Eat, relax and then we will talk, but not of our past, qalbi. You came home, I forgive you, qalbi.'

~my heart.

She says and then brushes her cold hand over mine.

◎

I eat.

And when I have finished my mother peels me the last of the oranges that have fallen from a neighbour's garden, into her backyard.

'Listen, I have had too many this year, that neighbour should trim his tree. You remember that I hate waste, qalbi.'

~my heart.

She tells me.

'But you like oranges so,' I say.

'There are many wasted this year. They have been rotting on my floor. Listen, there are too many spiders in the backyard and you know that I have such fear of creepy crawlies, qalbi.'

~my heart.

She tells me.

I think to my mother and remember her screams each time a spider, a cockroach, any insect and sometimes a simple house fly would enter into our home. My mother's screams would be heard all the way down the slope and from boats within the harbour. I lift the orange segments, smiling.

The orange taste tangs, bitter sweet. I lift my fingers to my nose, I inhale. My fingers are covered in the smell of home.

'Għandek swaba ta' pjanist.'

~you have the fingers of a pianist.

My mother says and then laughs, ha ha ha.

'I never had the patience to learn, my feet liked to patter too much,' I say.

There is a silence, slightly too long.

'Go into the parlour, qalbi, you look so tired, rest in my chair, use my blanket.'

~my heart.

She speaks softly, clearing the dishes from the table, placing them into the plastic bowl in her sink. My mother has her back to me.

'Your bedroom is the same as when you left. You will feel safe in there, qalbi. It will help you to remember.'

~my heart.

I move into the parlour, I curl onto the chair.

I turn my knees, my body, so that I fit. I drift into sleep in my mother's chair, with my mother's crocheted blanket wrapped around me, warming my cold bones, but still I shiver shiver, shiver shiver.

◎

Matt,

    I dreamed of you last night.

I was sitting on the steps outside of the Rotunda of St Marya Assunta. The midday sun was beating down onto my shaven legs. They were itching; I had nipped the skin around my ankle, the itch was forming a scab. I was beginning to heal. I had hitched up my white cotton dress and enveloped the skirt to under my thighs. I had forgotten my sunglasses. My right hand shielded my eyes from the white glow. I was squinting. I was waiting, for you. I will always wait, for you.

In my dream, I tag on to the flowing skirt of a passer-by. She is Maltese. Her skirt is harsh between my fingertips. In my dream, I open my mouth, poised to ask her the time. But the Maltese words will not flow from me. I have forgotten my words. I have forgotten the words that I was born knowing, that are woven through my lives. In my dream the words escape me. They do not grip to my tongue. 'Skużi. Tista' tgħidli x'ħin hu?' (Excuse me. Can you tell me the time?) In my dream I long to speak these words. I long to find words that are beyond me.

I said that I dreamed of you. I did not tell you that you were not present in my dream. Instead, I was covered with a feeling and that feeling has become you. A covering that is longing.

You are the tongue that I long for. I ache with lovesickness,

Nina x

Tmienja

~eight

✳ 4. Transport

For those who do not wish to risk hiring a car and driving around Malta, the buses on the island are easily recognised by their bright yellow bodies and orange stripe. They are a cheap and convenient mode of transport, offering a slow but scenic ride. Most journeys begin at the bus terminal in the capital city Valletta.

I have been back in Malta for one day, I think. It feels longer. Already time has little importance, is being blurred, lost.

I am sitting at my mother's kitchen table. My mother has opened her cupboards and is balancing on her tiptoes, stretching in, moving around tins, jars, pasta, vegetables, flour. She has her back to me. Her dress has risen to the fold in the back of her knee. I look to see the perfectly formed muscles on her stretched calves. She always loved dancing with my father. My mother talks into the wood of the cupboards, ignoring my responses to her food-related questions.

She wants me to eat more, she wants to prepare something additional, extra, indulgent for me, but I am full to my throat. I refuse, over and over. She does not listen.

My fingers are trailing the rim of the empty crystal fruit bowl.

'L-aqwa li ġejt lura id-dar, dak biss li jgħodd.'

~you came back home, that is all that matters.

My mother breaks my thoughts.

'I'm too late,' I reply.

'Listen, when you left I told you naqta' qalbi.'

~I cut my heart, I lost hope.

'I remember,' I say.

'But you came home to Malta and now again I have hope.'

'I have no hope. I'm lost Mama.'

I sob.

'No, qalbi, no. There is always hope.'

~my heart.

'I'm here; I've abandoned my husband, my daughter. I don't know what to do next. Please will you help me?' I ask.

'Search the island Nina, find yourself. And then we will talk.'

My mother tells me.

'Come with me, guide me, please,' I say.

'I cannot. I will only leave this home one more time.'

'I don't understand,' I say.

'You will.'

She speaks the words softly and then moves to me. My mother places her cold hands onto my shoulders and looks into my eyes, then over my face.

I shiver.

'U qalbi.'

~and my heart.

She says.

' Inti għarwiena mingħajr lipstick.'

~you are naked without lipstick.

She tells me and then pulls me into her scent.

'Have you seen your bedroom?'

My mother asks.

'Not yet,' I say, into the material of her house clothes.

The wooden banister is smooth under my fingers. My great-grandfather had carved it, a wedding present for my grandfather, my mother's father. My mother and I would polish it every day. It shone, it gleamed, it was proud and glorious. My fingertips tease the surface as I walk the marble steps of my mother's grand sweeping staircase.

My bedroom door is open, welcoming; the morning light, my Lord's smile, shines in through the window's net covering. I stand in the doorway and my eyes flick around the room, as I hold my breath from fear that I will exhale and puff the image away. It all feels so fragile, delicate, temporary.

Everything is as it had once been. My summer clothes

hang in the open wardrobe, all pressed and blemish free. My bookcases are crowded with childhood books, Enid Blyton, Roald Dahl, with bootleg cassettes bought from Valletta's Sunday morning market, with frilly favours from family weddings and baptisms, with statues of Cinderella, so many statues of Cinderella. I dare not step into my room. Instead, I look at my walls, at the framed photographs of my cousins, my sisters, my grandparents, of me. And then I look at my bed, my Rosary lies across my pillow, a crucifix is nailed to the wall above; a photograph of my parents is framed, is perched on my bedside cabinet, is making my stomach churn.

I step back, I close my bedroom door, I walk down the marble steps and I drag my suitcase from the wall near to the wooden coat stand and into my mother's parlour.

I am dressing, clothes spilling from my open suitcase and onto the floor, next to my mother's chair.

I hear banging, glass smashing. I run half-dressed, my white cotton dress unbuttoned, into my mother's kitchen. I am full of fear.

My mother is at the sink, safe, facing the doorway, water is dripping from her hands and to her sandalled feet.

      there appears to be a swirling.

~s – wir.

~s – wir.

whirling see-through ghost swishing around the room. She is grey, rotating the kitchen at top speed.

'Mama?' I shriek.

My mother smiles, calm, then raises her eyebrows, a frown.

'It is just Tilly. She is our resent-filled ħares.'

`~ghost, usually the protector of a house but`
`may become bitter.`

My mother says the words in a loud, a stern voice.

'Mama, why is she here?' I ask.

'She is healing.'

My mother says.

Tilly stops spinning, flipping on the spot, instead.

'You're a lucky cow.'

She says to me; then she drifts, floats, spins out the kitchen, out through me.

'Mama?' My voice is high pitched.

'It is just Tilly. You will get used to her, qalbi.'

~my heart.

⊚

I return to my mother's parlour, buttoning my dress with trembling fingers.

Today I wear layers, a white cotton dress, a shawl, a cardigan, to unpeel. I am an onion. I discard my knee-length boots. I find flip-flops next to my mother's chair, perhaps they once belonged to one of my sisters. My mother has told me that it is hot outside, unexpectedly for February; my mother tells me that my Lord is happy.

I frown.

'Will you move your suitcase to your bedroom, qalbi?'

~my heart.

My mother asks.

'Maybe later,' I say, I lie.

Christopher walks in from the kitchen.

'Will you come with me today?' I ask my son.

'No, I can't. Go find yourself, Mama.'

He tells me.

I know that he has been talking to my mother.

'But what will you do?' I ask.

'I'm meeting Geordie.'

He tells me.

'Why is he in Malta?' I ask.

'He's waiting, like me.'

He tells me.

'What will you do today?' I ask.

'We will share beer with Jesus, of course.'

Christopher says and then laughs, ha ha ha.

I think, you are too young to be drinking beer. I think, Jesus should know better.

Christopher runs out through the door, laughing and shouting over his shoulder.

'Mama you worry too much. Age does not matter in my world.'

I smile.

◎

I am leaving my mother's house.

I open the green front door and stand on the step.

The door closes behind me, I hear a key turning.

　　　　and a.

~cl – unk.

as the barrel revolves.

I am forced out onto the cobbles.

I look, the chain and padlock are connected, have reappeared.

◎

I flip, I flop up the slope.

~fl – ip.

~fl – op.

~fl – ip.

~fl – op.

hurrying to catch a yellow Maltese bus.

The sun beats down. I walk in shadows, in shade. I look to the floor and I concentrate on the sounds that flip and flop behind me. My feet offer rhythm. I smile. I focus on my musical feet and alter my flip-flopping to create patterns that are flowing, melodic, light. I offer small leaps; I twirl as I flip, as I flop.

I must look ridiculous, but in this moment I do not care. I feel different, already, today. I do not know if this is good or if this is bad.

I feel lighter. I feel that I could float, or fly, or hover.

◎

I want to fly.

◎

I leave the protection of the city walls and the buildings that lean inwards, that shelter. I walk out through the City Gate. The sun beats down, bubbling my blood. I sweat.

I am at the bus terminal. The pavement is curved with kiosks in varied sizes, in different colours, each selling drinks, snacks, newspapers, cigarettes, magazines, souvenirs. The kiosks mark a line, a curved line, for where the buses will stop, where people must wait, must buy.

I pick up a bottle of water from the smallest blue kiosk. A little girl stands on an overturned plastic crate, behind the counter. The kiosk smells of stale alcohol, the girl is alone. She looks to be the same age as Molly, small, innocent, unaccompanied. I look around for an adult, for her parent.

'Fejn hu il-ġenitur tiegħek?' I ask.

~where is your parent?

The child does not speak. She holds out her palm, with her almost black eyes drilling into my face. I stare at her palm. There are no lines marking the skin, it is smooth, clean.

I fumble, I place a single euro into her hand. The child does not speak, she does not smile, she does not retract her hand, she does not remove her eyes from my face. I turn, I walk. I feel her stare following me as I flip-flop away, to the bus.

I climb the metal steps, one, two, three, of the first bus that I reach.

The white roof, the yellow paint, the orange stripe, they comfort.

As the bus pulls out onto the road, I look to the kiosk. The child has gone. A bearded man wears a pink sun visor. He tips the pink plastic peak to me and then, inside my head, I hear his gravelly laugh, ha ha ha.

The bus is not busy. I am glad.

I rest the side of my head onto the cool window and I move with the bus. We bounce, we swerve, we dip, we jolt. I press my face, harder, onto the glass. It cools me.

I think, I am invisible.

I close my eyes and I breathe the dust, in and out, in and out.

I listen to the quiet prayers that the bus driver mutters.

He is blessing my soul.

I wonder if he is too late.

◎

The creaky bus is fast.

I watch from the window.

The bus takes me through Birkirkara, slowing to a crawl past the house where my grandmother was born. I look to the balcony, to the room where she entered the world. I see her. She waves.

The bus picks up speed.

The bus hurries past familiar houses, past shops, past families walking the crooked pavements. They are blurred. The buildings vary in size, in purpose; they are known, almost untouched, unaltered during the missed years.

I smile.

◎

The bus stops. Its final destination.

Disgħa

~nine

Malta's top 5: *Churches and Cathedrals*

* 5. The Rotunda of St Marija Assunta, Mosta
The magnificent dome is said to be third largest in Europe and was targeted during World War II. While a congregation prayed, a bomb penetrated the dome and fell to the ground, yet no one was harmed. The bomb is displayed within the church.

I walk to the stone steps, those in front of the church of Mosta whose dome dominates the beautiful skyline of my island. The steps are insignificant, lost beneath the mighty church. The Rotunda of St Marija Assunta, Mosta marks the heart, the soul, the essence of the island.

I sit down.

I am on the top step.

>my feet are moving.

>*~p – it – ter.*

>*~p – it – ter.*

>pattering, restless.

I am looking at my ruby red toenails, at the cracks in the layers, the imperfections. I always do that; I know that Matt would agree. I see negatives in myself, beauty in others. I wish that I had thought to remove the nail varnish, to repaint my toenails and then I laugh, ha ha ha. I had not planned this journey, I had not thought.

My toes are covered in a fine layer of white dust, Maltese dust, the leftovers of lives. A fine layer of white dust has already settled onto the smooth steps; I wonder which fragments of lives, of memories exist beside me, covering me. Some of the remnants will be lost within the white cotton of my dress. I think, I will not wash my dress.

I rub my hands down the cotton material. I turn my palms to look, to see. A fine layer of white dust coats my skin. I smile. The dust should sink into me, become me. I hunch over, leaning forward, my breasts point down towards my lap. I stroke my dusty palms over my calves, the hairs are soft, relaxed. I rarely shave in the winter. I should have thought, I laugh again, ha ha ha. I can see the hairs, dark on pale skin, others will too.

I can no longer pretend to be perfect.

I smile.

◎

I sweep my hair around to my left shoulder, twist it smaller, tighter, twirling down the hair until it pulls at my roots. My hair is thick, too thick, neither straight nor curly, just thick. My hair has character, I am told. As I grip the twist in my hair, my neck is exposed, hoping for a breeze to swirl over. I long for a cool gush of breath, the blowing of my Lord's breath onto, into my being.

The midday sun is peaking, uncharacteristically hot for February. I wonder if my Lord is happy with me. I wonder if this is another test, endurance of sorts. Sweat trickles from beneath my thick hair, down my neck, slowly, down my spine.

◎

I refuse to move from the step. I stay. I take His torture.

My eyes are searching, for Christopher, for Matt, for Molly.

I am an adult, I remind myself.

I need to gain control, I remind myself.

My right hand attempts to shade my eyes from the burning sun. I am scanning the beeping cars, the hustle, the queues of traffic, the lines of buses. I am searching faces. I am squinting into eyes. I am searching for people who are no longer there, here, not really. I do not want to go into the church, alone.

I wonder if Christopher can hear me.

I shout to him, inside my head.

I shout to Jesus too.

◎

Christopher does not appear.

Jesus does not appear.

◎

The dust is rising, circulating.

I am lost within the moment. My Lord's emotions are

controlling me, His blood is the bubbling sun, the dust is in His swirling breath.

I have no choice.

Life is not full of choices, not in the way that we are taught, that we believe. We are being controlled, guided, influenced. There is no free will.

I grab my shawl; my cardigan is shoved between the straps of my handbag. I snatch my almost empty bottle of water. I stand, push my toes until they rub into the bar of the flip-flops. They are pink flip-flops. I think of Molly. I sweep the shawl round to cover my naked shoulders, a church entry requirement.

I turn, I flip-flop.

~fl – ip.

~fl – op.

~fl – ip.

~fl – op.

up to the Rotunda.

I stop, in the doorway, in the shaded, the cool. I look into the vast, the beautiful space within the church. Rays of sunlight shine down through the dome, into the centre, bringing illumination, bringing focus. I look to the empty wooden chairs that are lined, facing the intricate altar. I think to the congregation.

◎

The Rotunda of St Marija Assunta in Mosta stands tall and proud. It is a church where an incontestable miracle occurred. The ninth of April 1942 is a date etched within Maltese roots. It is a date that has been passed down through generations. The air bombardments of World War II were destroying the island of Malta. My people feared for their lives, yet as a nation they did not wait helplessly for death. The people of Malta pulled together, united in prayer; they trusted in their God.

On that very day in April, it is said that around three hundred of my people were praying in the Rotunda of St Marija Assunta, Mosta, as a German bomb penetrated through the huge dome, falling into the heart of the congregation.

It is believed that a miracle happened. They say that the impossible occurred.

It is said that that Axis bomb bounced to the floor and failed to explode, that no one was injured.

When I was a child, my mother would tell me that the bomb

not exploding was God's answer to our people's prayers for protection. She told me that God had rewarded their united faith. She told me that the bomb not exploding was evidence of God's existence and that belief in His being was beyond doubt, beyond question. The bomb was faith.

I think that a renewed conviction connected those people, those who had seen that miracle, who had had their prayers answered. Their world, their island was crumbling to ruin, but their God had shown them that He was trying, that He was there and that they would be rewarded, eventually. There could be no questioning of faith, of God, not after the bomb that failed to explode.

I understand that.

Their reward, I guess, came in the renewed sense of community, of belonging, from a faith that was beyond question.

◎

I do not have that faith. I do not have a miracle to pass through generations.

◎

I am standing in the doorway, away from the sun that bubbles my blood.

'I doubt you,' I say.

'Are you listening?' I ask.

'I don't believe, I doubt,' I say.

Then I hear that voice.

> **Jesus:** Then answer this. Who do you talk to, my Nina?

He says and I hear, but I do not speak.

> instead, I flip-flop forward.

> *~fl – ip.*

> *~fl – op.*

> *~fl – ip.*

> *~fl – op.*

☺

As people enter the great domed church in Mosta, the Rotunda, they can be heard to gasp. There is beauty, there is magnitude, there is scale, there is decadence.

Within the Rotunda of St Marija Assunta there are blue walls, frescos, statues, gold, ornate exhibits of worship, of united faith. The church speaks of wealth, of generous donations made to please, to compete with other villages. All is lavish, a magnitude of curves, with intricate details into each arch, into every nook.

I enter the Rotunda and stop.

I make no gasp.

◎

'Support the church, support our cause.'

He rattles a wooden box. His accent is broken, clearly spoken English with a Maltese twang. The <th> sound is more of a <t>. I smile, I have the same. I have tried so hard to pronounce the digraph <th>. I think of Matt, of how he would tease me and giggle as I tried to sound English, to act English.

I never could, not really, of course, because I am not, I am not English.

I turn to face him, the man rattling the wooden box.

'Jiena Maltija,' I say.

~I am Maltese.

The man with the box does not respond.

He is not too close, arm's length perhaps, but I can still smell stale beer. The smell is strong, covering him. I think that it is pouring from him, with his sweat.

I fumble in my handbag, in my purse for a euro.

I miss the Maltese Lira. The euro puzzles me.

I place a euro into the slot on the top of the wooden box. I hear it drop onto the other coins. The man does not thank me. Instead, he rattles his wooden box and he chants his mantra.

'Support the church, support our cause.'

Minutes have passed, I have not moved. I am still standing at the mouth of the church. I am clutching my handbag tight to my chest.

I have been here before, of course, but today I am a tourist. I have lost what it is to be Maltese.

My eyes they flick, they flack, left, right, forward, upward, downward.

> my eyes, they.
>
> *~fl – ick.*
>
> *~fl – ack.*
>
> *~fl – ick.*
>
> *~fl – ack.*
>
> rapidly, until they find a point of focus.

There is a highly decorative marble baptism font, close

to the door, on my left. The font is covered now, no longer used. That font reeks of death, not of birth, not of celebration. Infant mortality was high; baptisms were made within a few hours of birth, once upon a time. The death of a child was almost expected.

My eyes rest on the covered font, a sign of progression.

I think of Christopher, of his body, broken and bloody, in the road.

◎

My bones feel weak, they will buckle and bend; I need to sit.

There are wooden chairs, in front of me. They form rows for the congregation, for those who have faith. The hard-backed, not cushioned, chairs face the intricate altar. They are not there for comfort, or to offer rest, they are for those who believe, for those who have no doubt.

I cannot allow myself to sit there, not on the congregation chairs, not there.

My eyes search for a place to rest.

I want to see the bomb, but my legs will not work, they are crumpling.

◎

I.

~sp – in,

~sp – in,

~sp – in.

slowly, spiralling on the spot.

I go around and around and around, searching for a place to sit.

I drop my handbag, it makes no sound.

I fall to my knees, to the marble floor.

People are walking into the Rotunda; I know that they will be staring.

Għaxra
~ten

Malta's top 5: *Festivals and Other Events*

✳ 1. A Festa

The Maltese festa, or village feast, is a much anticipated event within each parish's calendar. It is a celebration in honour of a patron saint. Days of preparations lead up to the event. Floors are polished, windows are cleaned, shutters painted, doors opened, banners are hung, flags are raised, lights are strung. The night air is filled with excitement, street vendors appear selling nougat and pastizzi, pastries, as people travel from all over the island to celebrate. The highlight of the festa is marked by the procession with the holy statue of the village's patron saint, closely followed by the loud village band, a convoy of Maltese people, strips of paper becoming confetti and then a firework display.

I am kneeling on the floor, still at the mouth of the Rotunda of St Marija Assunta. My body bends forward, bowing to the altar, my shawl falls from me, exposing flesh to my Lord.

I stay very still. I do not recover my shawl.

'Move, English girl, move.'

The man with his rattling box kicks my lower back with the ball of his bare foot. A stab of pain enters me.

I look up to the ceiling, to the light in the centre of the dome. I look to see the blemish. There is a flaw, a perfect flaw, signalling where the miracle had entered. I wonder why it was never put back to its perfect state, but I know the answer.

Malta is an island that rose from rubble; the reminders give faith, show survival.

I need to see the bomb.

The man kicks me again, harder.

'Move, English girl, move.'

His breath pours over me, covering me in the stink of stale beer.

He kicks again, the pain stabs, again, then he walks away. I hear his box rattling.

◎

I am on the floor, still. I lift my shawl and sweep it to cover my exposed flesh.

People walk around me, I know that they will be glancing down; I hear their footsteps slowing, slightly.

And then, I hear his voice, gravel filled, harsh, guttural.

> **Jesus:** You are searching with your eyes closed, my Nina.

I look behind me, but he is not there. A wooden chair is vacant, near to the door.

◎

I am ridiculous.

◎

I make my legs work; I stand up, still, in the mouth of the church.

The kicking man, with his rattling box, is back. He is circling me, chanting at a whisper. I clutch my handbag to my chest. I try to ignore him and look to the marble floor. The man is padding in bare feet, his toenails are painted ruby red. I ignore him, pretend he is not there.

I remember there being a small museum, of sorts, in the Rotunda. It was through a door, up a couple of stairs,

I think. In the summer there would be a pilgrimage of tourists, finding their way. There were things to buy.

As the kicking man walks his circle behind me, I pace forward.

Something guides me left, around the wooden chairs, to the far left, to a door, to the room.

I enter.

◎

The bomb is housed for all to see. It is a replica, of course, but not everyone realises. For some, that bomb is sacred. I could be convinced, I think. I could touch the mock-up of a moment never forgotten and then my faith could be restored, instantly.

◎

The murky room is quiet from tourists.

The door closes behind me; I hear a key turning in the lock.

I hear a.

~cl – unk.

as the barrel revolves, locked.

I am not scared.

My eyes scan the room that is dark, dusty; a single window hosts a half-open shutter, allowing fragments of my Lord's light to enter. I walk to the window, I push the heavy shutter back, letting brightness fall into the small square room.

◎

The room smells of the kicking man. There is stale beer and sweat trapped in the air. My eyes search. I see il-vari.

~the statues used in the holy processions.

My eyes rest on il-vara il-kbira.

~one of the statues used in the holy
processions of Good Friday. It is the one
with the crucified Christ with St John, Mary
Magdalene and His mother, Mary, looking on,
distraught.

The statues are beautiful, heavy, used in il-purċissjoni tal-Ġimgħa il-Kbira

~the procession on Good Friday.

and for the festa in August.

My mother's brother, my Uncle Mario, was once given the honour of being one of those carrying il-vara il-gbira. There was a family party in the backyard of my mother and father's house, to celebrate.

I feel an overwhelming need to speak to my cousin, to talk of the time, the day after the party, when my Uncle Mario took us on a boat. He had asked for only me to go and I remember how angry Sandra became, I remember her jumping on the spot, full of rage, of frustration, but still we went without her. I remember how my Uncle Mario had tried to climb from the boat, of how he had told us children to take care, to follow him. I remember how he fell into the water in his clothes. We laughed so much, we laughed and laughed. I remember and I laugh, ha ha ha, ha ha ha. My amusement bounces around the small room.

◎

I walk around the room. There is no stall, no shop selling souvenirs, relics. There are no tourists, today.

There are photographs of the hole in the dome. They are framed, decorating the wall, documenting the fixing of the dome to a not quite perfect state. The photographs are smaller than I remember, framed, fading.

And then, I see it, the bomb.

◎

I walk to it, standing just in front. My eyes take in detail, searching up and down. That replica bomb is filled with hope. That replica bomb speaks of an event, of an occurrence that was filled with hope. A bomb, not that bomb, had fallen from the heavens, had fallen to the ground with a bounce. A bomb, not quite that bomb, had not quite exploded; the faith of the congregation had been deep-seated.

And then, just before I move my hands onto the replica, I pray for that intensity of belief. I think the words, they form into a prayer and I offer them into the heavens. And the longer that I am standing in the room and the longer that I am breathing the dust within the Rotunda, the stronger my needs are becoming.

I need to worship, something.

I study the photographs, the information framed and hanging on the wall, above the replica bomb. I learn that the Rotunda had been built over another church. That it was doubled in religious standing, but that the smaller or the weaker had been demolished.

◎

Within the Rotunda my sense of self is layered and full of depth.

◎

And then, I place my two palms onto the replica bomb and I speak.

'I could return to you one day, replica bomb,' I say.

'But I would need a miracle,' I say.

'And with that miracle I could have faith. You could become my new Lord.'

I stroke my two palms down the replica bomb's rough, rusted exterior. I am not overwhelmed, I am not covered in a renewed sense of faith. I lift my palms to cover my face.

I smell stale beer.

⊚

I walk to the door.

    I hear a.

    ~cl – unk.

    as the key turns.

The door opens. There is no one there. I flip-flop out from the room, round the wooden congregation chairs and to the doorway.

I look for the kicking man with his rattling box. He is not there, his wooden chair is empty.

⊚

As I leave the Rotunda of St Marija Assunta, the heavens open.

He cries, it rains, again. I have layers. I pull my cardigan from in between the straps of my handbag; I wrap the shawl over my hair and shoulders. My Lord weeps onto my toes, the fine layer of dust will not wash from them.

I do not understand what this means.

I flip-flop.

~fl – ip.

~fl – op.

~fl – ip.

~fl – op.

through His tears, away from the Rotunda, confused.

◎

Matt,

I dreamed of you again last night.

I was sitting on the steps outside of the Rotunda of St Marija Assunta, Mosta, again. A woman came to me, she was you, the feeling that she evoked was you, Matt. I could not make her face real, she blurred at the edges. I fear that I am going insane. She yanked at my hair, pulling my head back to look up at her. Then she shouted down onto my face. I remember feeling a splattering of spit covering me.

'Hawn xi ħadd hawn li jaf bl-Ingliż?' she shouted. I did not understand her words.

I told her, 'I'm sorry, I don't speak your language.'

She shouted, 'Hawn xi ħadd hawn li jaf bl-Ingliż?' She shouted over and over again, 'Hawn xi ħadd hawn li jaf bl-Ingliż? Hawn xi ħadd hawn li jaf bl-Ingliż?'

Then she stopped. She looked straight at me, she released the grip on my hair and she spoke, 'Is there anyone here who speaks English?'

I could not answer her. The words would no longer roll. My tongue could not work. I woke. My eyes wide, searching my mother's dark parlour, feeling truly alone. I longed for your arms, for your comfort.

You are the breath that I need. I am sick, with love, for you,

Nina x

Ħdax

~eleven

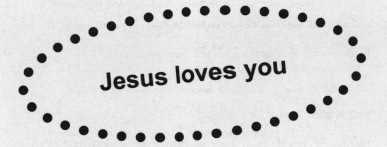

I have been in Malta four days now, I think, perhaps. Time is not as it once was. I have been sleeping, curled on the chair in my mother's parlour. I think that I have slept for a day or possibly for longer. I do not, in all honesty, know.

Christopher woke me a few hours ago.

'Jesus wants to share a glass of beer with you.'

He told me.

'You what?' I said.

'Get ready, brush your hair, put on your make-up. I'm to take you to him.'

He told me. His face very serious.

I uncurled from the chair. I did as my son told me to do. My mascara flaked and clogged as I attempted to curl my eyelashes; my lipstick did not suit my too thin lips, my too pale skin.

◎

'Are you ready?'

My son asks, impatient.

'OK. OK.' I hurry, pushing my feet into the pink flip-flops.

Christopher walks through the door, laughing, ha ha ha.

I open the green front door and stand on the step. My son runs down the slope, backwards. He waves to me, beckoning me to run with him.

I move off the step. The door closes behind me; I hear a key turning.

and a.

~*cl – unk.*

as the barrel revolves.

I look, the chain and padlock have connected, have reappeared.

I look up to the balcony. I see Tilly close to the window. I wave, she disappears.

I take my feet out of the pink flip-flops. I bend to the floor, scoop up the shoes. I push them into my opened handbag.

I pull the zipper across.

it snags on the material that has strayed onto the zip.

~*z – z – z – z – ip.*

and then I run down the slope.

~*sc – ream.*

~sc – ream.

screaming, my arms flapping, free.

◎

I stop running when I reach Christopher. He's at the bottom of the slope, bent double laughing, ha ha ha. His eyes are tearful, they sparkle.

'You run like a penguin.'

He says.

'I do not,' I say, I laugh, ha ha ha.

'Did you remember his chocolate?'

He asks.

'Of course,' I say, I smile.

◎

Let me set the scene.

I am sitting in Larry's bar, on Strait Street, in Valletta. The sign outside hangs off the wall and quivers down towards the cobbles. The plastic cover is smashed in parts, the light strips behind exposed, the letters that make up the name have been worn, shattered. Only the "arry" can be read and even that is fragile, loose.

We should not be here, in Larry's bar, not really. The bar

closed down years ago. Christopher told me that there had been talk of police corruption, of improper business, of Larry selling women to his customers. Apparently, now, Jesus likes to treat this place as his office.

I have not had a drink of beer, yet. The empty glasses on the table are still cool. I am running my finger around the rim of the closest one and smiling. Jesus is at the bar, head close to Larry, whispering, laughing, smiling.

I think that Jesus has been drinking all day. I have counted twenty-six empty pint glasses on the table. The air smells stale, a linger of beer that has long been consumed.

Jesus walks. His movements are slow, his feet bare and his toenails painted ruby red. I smile. He comes to the table; he places two pints of Cisk in among the empty glasses. He pulls out the wooden chair, twists it so that the back faces the table, then straddles the seat. He reaches for one of the pints of Cisk. I see that his fingers are thin and long, stretching around the glass.

~Cisk lager was first available in Malta in 1928. It has an alcohol content of 4.2 per cent.

Jesus: You shall remember His words, 'I am the

Lord your God: you shall not have strange Gods before me.'

he lifts the pint glass of Cisk to his mouth and gulps.

~gul – p.

~gul – p.

~gul – p – s.

down half of the liquid.

His gulps are loud, open throated. I watch as he places the glass next to the other, the still full pint.

'Sorry? I'm confused,' I say.

Jesus: I watched you the other day, making a pact of devotion with the replica bomb.

'I was having a private conversation. Did you follow me?' I ask.

He does not answer, straight away. Instead, he picks up the other full pint, and gulps the liquid loudly, three times. Then, he replaces the glass on the table.

Jesus: Yes your only Lord asked me to. I was the old man rattling the wooden box.

'The one who kicked me, twice, when I was on the floor?' I ask. I am angry.

Jesus: Yes. You were making such a show of yourself. Why do you search for a miracle my Nina?

'It's all that I have left, to cling to,' I say. I want to sulk. I hate that he has judged me.

Jesus: I sent Christopher back to you, to ease your grief, to help you. He was your miracle, yet still you seek the impossible, my Nina.

'You gave me the impossible,' I say. 'But your plan backfired, didn't it? I want to be with my son. I need a different miracle.'

He looks to me, then he winks. Then, he takes both glasses of Cisk. He holds one in each hand. To begin with he drinks the one in the left hand.

he gulps continuously.

~*gul* – *p*.

~*gul* – *p*.

~*gul* – *p* – *s*.

until the liquid is consumed.

His right hand remains perfectly still, no quivers, no shakes. Jesus lowers the empty glass from his lips, but does not replace the glass onto the table. Instead, he lifts the glass in his right hand to his mouth.

then, he gulps the liquid.

~gul – p.

~gul – p.

~gul – p – s.

until the glass is also empty.

Then, he places the two glasses next to the other twenty-six empty ones.

Jesus: And you would sell your soul for a miracle?

'I don't understand,' I speak, a whisper. I must admit, I am confused.

Jesus: Think carefully on your pacts, my Nina. Seek your miracle in the here, the now; let me guide you.

'And where will you guide me to?' I ask.

Jesus: Later my Nina, later. Now let us share more beer and let me look at the Cadbury's chocolate that you brought for me.

'How did you know that I would?' I ask.

Jesus: Because you believe, my Nina. You try to fight your belief, but I see into you.

'Sorry?' I ask.

Jesus: Oh my Nina, you really are disconnected.

'I'm sorry.' I unzip my handbag and pull out a plastic bag. 'Here,' I say.

Jesus takes the plastic bag and looks inside, in silence.

'I've brought you a selection. The Cadbury's Caramel is my favourite,' I say.

He removes the single bars of chocolate, one by one. There are seven. He lines them onto the wooden table, he moves the bars, alters the order until they fit, until they make a perfect arrangement that only Jesus understands.

> **Jesus:** Your kindness will not be forgotten. Thank you, my Nina.

He looks into my eyes, he smiles, he winks. I feel my cheeks flush.

> **Jesus:** Would you like to share another beer with me?

◎

Matt,

I dreamed of you last night, again.

My palms were touching the replica bomb within the Rotunda of St Marija Assunta. I do not know how long I had been standing with my palms stuck to the bomb. My hands were cold. I felt stiff in my bones, unable to remove myself, not wanting to step away from hope. And then I felt a shiver as a finger tapped my right shoulder.

I turned to see an old lady; she was you, that evoked feeling, again. Her face was etched in grooves. Her face told of her life and of her pain. She was smiling. Her eyes, her face, her smile, were all so tender. She removed her blue headscarf. She handed it to me. I moved my hand from the replica bomb, I reached out my palm and she closed my fingers around the headscarf in my hand. Her warm fingers enveloped mine into a clench. I felt a wave of heat rush through me.

'Qalbu maqsuma,' she whispered in a voice that sang. 'Qalbu maqsuma.'

'Ma nitkellimx bil-Malti,' I responded. 'I don't speak Maltese.'

'His heart is broken,' she whispered in a voice that sang. 'His heart is broken.'

In my dream I brought her blue headscarf to my cheek. The fabric was cheap, rough and covered with starch. She watched me, her eyes seeping tears. I closed my eyes. I moved her blue headscarf to cover my nose and my mouth. I inhaled. I inhaled her scent, your scent. As I opened my eyes, the old lady with the story etched into her face had gone.

I awoke in my mother's parlour, seeping tears into my mother's crocheted blanket. I ache for you,

Nina x

Tnax

~twelve

Geordie Smith
birth: 07.06.1921; death: 30.09.1996
service number: 935129.

Another day passes, I think. Darkness and then light, I think. I cannot focus. My mother's house is rattling.

Tilly is.

~b – ish.

~b – ash.

~b – ish.

~b – ash.

banging around and around upstairs.

She is shouting, screaming, full of anger.

I can stand it no longer. Her movements are full of fury, resentment, disbelief that she has passed. She irritates, she disturbs my peace.

'Iskot!' I yell.

`~shut up!`

She does not understand my language, she does not care and so she continues with her banging and screaming. She makes the house rattle.

I feel that the walls are falling; I need to step outside.

◎

I open my mother's green front door. I do not want to leave, to travel, not today. It is only Tilly's incessant banging that unnerves me. I stand on the step.

The green front door closes behind me. I hear a key turning.

> and a.
>
> ~*cl – unk.*
>
> as the barrel revolves.

I am forced out onto the cobbles.

I look, the chain and padlock are connected, have reappeared. I bang on the door, I want to be inside. No one hears my need.

I am tired, feeling fragile, low, empty. My only Lord is weeping, again. The doorway offers little shelter.

I feel cold in my bones, shiver shiver, shiver shiver.

I sit down on the wet stone step, my back resting against my mother's front door.

◎

I see my son.

◎

'Where are you going?' I shout down the slope.

Christopher is walking with a man in uniform. I can see that they are laughing. I can see their backs, their sides, their laughing profiles. They turn, face me, see me, wave and make their way back up the slope to my mother's house.

'Mama, this is Geordie.'

Christopher flops his arm around the man next to him. I look to the young man, tall, early twenties, dressed in uniform, attractive. His blue eyes pierce. His uniform is perfect, no blemishes, no creases.

'Pleased to meet you.' I hold out my hand.

Geordie replicates my gesture, a firm cold handshake.

'Where are you going?' I repeat.

'To share Cisk, in Larry's bar, with Jesus.'

~Cisk lager was first available in Malta in 1928. It has an alcohol content of 4.2 per cent.

Christopher smiles.

I laugh, ha ha ha. Geordie smiles.

'Jesus drinks too much,' I say.

'He can't get drunk, Mama.'

Christopher laughs, again, ha ha ha.

'I don't understand,' I say.

'Jesus drinks beer but he can't get drunk. We can't figure out why, so Jesus is trying to see if it's possible. His record is twenty-nine pints and still nothing.'

Christopher says.

I am lost for words.

'We're gunna celebrate.'

Geordie breaks my silence.

'Celebrate?' I ask.

'Me Elena's passed. Sheh's comin' te Malta.'

Geordie says.

'Come with us, Mama.'

Christopher says.

I shake my head.

And something inside of me twangs and tweaks.

I long for Matt.

Geordie and Christopher turn and walk, they go to share beer with Jesus. I sit on the stone step outside of my mother's house. I watch them walk away.

My eyes follow their footsteps until they turn the corner, are out of sight.

I do not move from the step, instead I sob.

~s – *ob*.

~s – *ob*.

~s – *ob*.

A tourist takes a photograph of me.

'Do not cry, Nina.'

She says.

I look up, to her, from the stone step outside of my mother's house. I am staring at a woman, a grandmother perhaps, in age. Her hair is jet black, dyed, and backcombed from small curlers. She is wearing glasses, her teeth false and white, in a perfect smile. I look down to her brown sandalled feet and up her American tan tights, to her slightly pleated navy skirt, back to her perfectly straight smile.

I do not know her.

'Do I know you? How do you know my name?' I ask.

'I am Elena, I am your mother's aunt.'

She says.

I stare at her, rudely. I think of Geordie and of how young he looks, in comparison. I wonder if he will be disappointed.

'I will grow younger.'

She says.

My cheeks flush, embarrassed.

'I am accepting of my death and I am already growing younger. Can I stay with you a while?'

Elena asks.

I move slightly, bobbing over on the step, onto the wet, the damp. Elena bends down next to me.

I look at her face, closely. Her skin is smooth, vibrant. She is beautiful.

My only Lord stops His weeping. Elena and I begin to talk.

◎

'Are you truly dead?' I ask.

'Of course.'

She says.

'Have you seen Geordie? He's with Jesus,' I ask, I tell.

'I know, I will soon. I thought I'd be your company for a little while.'

She answers.

'I miss Matt,' I say.

'I know.'

She says as she puts her cold arm around me

and I cry onto her shoulder –

Elena

Of course I knew that she was Nina Aquilina from the moment that my eyes fixed upon her. Her hair was dark and thick and her eyes were the Aquilina family hazel.

On the step, Nina wept. I had been waiting for some time for her to emerge from her mother's house. Jesus had instructed the ħares to drive Nina out. I had been guided here by him and I watched him taking a photograph of Nina prior to leaving me to my task.

~ghost, usually the protector of a house but may become resentful.

I waited after Jesus left, watching Nina for the smallest amount of time and knowing that I had to find a way of proffering comfort upon her.

This Nina, the one that I viewed from a short distance, she was shrouded in grief and I could see that she was broken.

'Do not cry, Nina,' I said to her.

She looked me up and down and as she did her eyes told me that she did not know of me.

'Do I know you? How do you know my name?' she asked.

'I am Elena, I am your mother's aunt,' I told her.

I observed as her mind flashed full of images of my young Geordie in his uniform. There was much that Nina was yet to learn about the spirit world. She failed to acknowledge that I could read her thoughts and that I could hear that she was thinking that Geordie may be disappointed when he meets me in my spirit form. Nina should have known better than to think that my appearance would somehow alter Geordie's love for me. Her fleeting thought had annoyed me but I knew that I could not dwell on it and that Nina's ignorance would be cured with time.

'I will grow younger,' I told her. I let her know that I could see into her mind and that I could hear her thoughts. I believed that was the correct thing to do. She smiled at me and I heard her apologising, but I knew that she was still confused.

'I am accepting of my death and I am already growing younger,' I explained.

Nina nodded.

'Can I stay with you a while?' I asked her.

She shuffled along slightly and offered me a dry space next to her on the wet step. As I bent down close to her, she looked into my face and I read her thoughts. I smiled and we began to talk.

〜 〜 〜 〜 〜

'Are you truly dead?' she asked me.

'Of course,' I told her and I smiled. My mouth felt strange as the words formed. I flicked my tongue over and behind my false teeth. I was distracted. My body was already changing and I could feel my own teeth pushing out the false veneers. I was full of desire to remove the false teeth from my crowded mouth.

'Have you seen Geordie? He's with Jesus,' Nina asked me.

'I know, I will soon. I thought I'd be your company for a little while,' I said.

I could not tell her that I have for ever or that I could talk to my Geordie over time and space. I had been warned by Jesus that I must be careful not to tempt Nina into death and for her to think that death was the answer to her problems. I felt that a weight of responsibility was upon me.

I looked into Nina and I felt her fear. I could see that her mind was fragile and that she was losing herself within the spirit world. It was clear that Nina no longer saw the beauty and the gift that were life.

ᨆ ᨆ ᨆ ᨆ ᨆ

'I miss Matt,' she told me and I saw flicking images of Matt within her head.

'I know,' I told her. I placed my arm around her shoulder and I welcomed her tears into me.

ᨆ ᨆ ᨆ ᨆ ᨆ

I knew that I had time for Nina and I knew that I was one of the few who could understand her lack of roots and her loss of culture. I had been sent to Nina to help her and to guide her in my small way. I knew that my Geordie would come to me soon and that he was both listening and waiting for me. He was with Jesus and with Christopher. They were all examining my progress and hoping that I could guide Nina. I felt such pressure and I worried that I would fail them all. This was my new role in life, my purpose.

ᨆ ᨆ ᨆ ᨆ ᨆ

I began to talk to Nina.

138

I told her.

'The island is much changed in my absence,' I said.

'Too much,' Nina said. 'They are still rebuilding.'

'Were you away from here for a long time?' I asked.

'Yes. I had a new life,' Nina said.

'What have you left behind? A new family? A job?'

'My husband and my daughter. I never found work.'
Nina spoke the words and then looked down the
sloping street. Her thoughts flicked to her family
home in Liverpool.

'There was a time when I wanted to be a teacher,' I
interrupted her thoughts.

Nina shifted her position, turning slightly. I waited for
her to settle.

'Then the war broke out and priorities altered.
Everything altered. It was how it had to be, we had no
choice. I applied for a job at Lascaris, the war rooms,
do you know them? I think you can pay to go in. But
perhaps not in the winter. Everything closes in the
winter. No tourists, you see,' I told her.

Nina nodded at me. She had no words, so I continued.

139

'Being Maltese, I did not think that I would get the work, but my English was good. I had had a superior schooling. My father was working in Alexandria at the time and so I was fortunate to not have to ask his permission to work. He would have denied me. Of course he would have, you see he preferred for me to be safe and protected.' I paused. 'He was a good man, a strict father, but of a good heart. And so, with my father working away and my mother trying to maintain a home, I was interviewed and successful. I was trained to plot aircraft and convoys coming into Malta. Do you understand what that means?'

'Nifhmek.'

~I understand.

Nina said, nodded and shifted slightly on the step outside of her mother's house. Her Maltese impressed me. I wondered if she used those words in her own home. I wished that I could have talked to her about the trivial, of other matters. I looked at Nina and I felt that she was like me, that in another life we might have been friends.

~ ~ ~ ~ ~

I heard Jesus. He told me to focus my thoughts. I suppressed my desire to laugh out loud.

࿔ ࿔ ࿔ ࿔ ࿔

'Buses had stopped, due to a petrol shortage,'
I continued. 'Some days I would have to walk
seven miles to work, or I would cycle. We lived in
Birkirkara, in my father's house; it has been passed to
my brother's son now. My daughter was born there
too. What relation would she be to you?'

'I was thinking just that, a few days ago,' replied
Nina. 'Christopher mentioned you to me. I think that
your daughter would have been my mother's cousin.
Kif tgħidha bil-Malti? My sekonda kuġina, naħseb.'

~what is that in Maltese? My second cousin,
I think.

'Yes, that's right, they are the correct words. Your
Maltese is better than mine these days. I have lost
so much of my ilsien pajjiżi, of my mother tongue. I
think you call it that?'

'Yes, please continue.' Nina opened her palms to me,
as if giving me the space, the floor to continue with
my tale.

'The war, my work, it covered day and night duty.
At night, an air force lorry took me to work and we
were often attacked as the aircraft came down low. I
frequently think about how close we came to being

killed, we were lucky to arrive safely. Our united faith was strong, the people of Malta can be very determined.'

'Iva, I know,' Nina said and smiled with my words.

~yes.

'Life was difficult for everyone on the island, we had no food and the air raids were bombing to rubble. We were soon a near starving population, in ruins.' I paused, knowing that I needed to stay purposeful and strong. 'Our nation was wounded, homes destroyed, isolated. You'll have heard descriptions. Our island was covered in a dust of death and destruction. Do you understand? But still our people did not fall to the ground and surrender. That isn't what we Maltese do, is it?'

'Iva... I know,' Nina said and then began to cry. I thought that she was beginning to understand my message.

~yes.

'We converted underground catacombs, dug into the rock, formed elaborate tunnels and rooms. We were protected and joined. We did everything that we could to survive. We did not wait for death to take us. As the air raid sirens began to woo hoo woo, people scurried underground. We crammed into white walled caves, worrying about light and oxygen. We had real worries, we did not dwell. '

⁂

I looked at Nina, tears were staining her cheeks. I knew that I must continue with my story, but I seemed to be upsetting her so. My words were sharp and they were hurting into her. I heard Jesus, he was telling me that I was doing well and so I nodded and spoke.

'My grandfather had paid for his own room, our own shelter,' I continued. 'We would cram in together, my mother, my brother, my sisters, my grandparents, aunts, uncles, cousins. Together, we would offer prayer.'

I paused. I looked to the heavens. I heard Jesus telling me to continue. His voice was gentle and warming.

⁂

'When I applied and so when I signed up to work, I was taking myself away from the shelter and into the minds of the destruction. My ears were filled with sounds that had been dulled, lessened from within the shelter. Your mother is too young to remember. How is your mother?'

'Tinsab tajba, grazzi,' Nina said, quietly, but I still heard her.

~she is fine, thank you.

'I look forward to meeting her. I will see her later, with Geordie, I hope,' I said. 'I still hear the sounds, you know. The boom of guns, the screaming whistle of the Stuka dive bombers, the endless procession of planes and bombs. I have seen and I have heard perhaps too much. I think that many of us try to block it and to pretend that the sights and sounds were not as they were. But some sounds and sights stay with you for ever and you grow with them.'

Nina thought of Christopher. The image of his bloody body flashed into my mind. I wanted to shake and I wanted to cry, but I did not. I did not rush her. She was connecting our memories and fitting together fragments.

❧ ❧ ❧ ❧ ❧

'Inti tlaqt dan il-pajjiż, bħali?' Nina said; she looked directly at me.

~you left this country, like me?

Her eyes were filled with tears, waiting.

'I may have moved to another country, Nina, but the

144

sounds, the smells and the dust all went with me. My house was always dusty. Geordie used to say that I imagined the dust, but I really do not think that I did. It covered my collection of bells and managed to climb into the glass cabinet and form a layer. I could not get my house clean. Geordie would say that I was obsessed with cleaning and that I needed everything to be perfect, but I was not and I did not. It was the dust. I hated to see the dust, it made me remember.'

'Tell me more about the island then, my island, please,' Nina said; she had a pleading twang added to her 'please'. I did not understand why. I paused to try to formulate it all. I wished that I could stop, but I was urged to continue. Jesus was guiding me. He is a very driven man.

◦✳◦ ◦✳◦ ◦✳◦ ◦✳◦ ◦✳◦

'You know that the raids were documented, that they were chalked and tallied? The damage and the loss were seen by all. This island was brought to rubble. Our customs, our ease of life were disrupted. But we learned to adapt with each new day, through the three thousand, three hundred and forty air raids that were forced upon us,' I explained.

Nina nodded.

'We had communal food kitchens, we ate minestra, later we went on to eating dog. We survived on harruba, perhaps it is called carob? Do you remember the harruba? It is a tree; I think a fruit of sorts. As the green turned to brown, we sought and we chewed. We were near starving, but we survived.'

~minestra is a vegetable soup containing local or seasonal vegetables, potatoes, noodles.

'I never tried it; Christopher jixtieq iduq il-ħarruba. I think Geordie talks of it,' Nina said, she smiled again, but her eyes were still glistening.

~Christopher longs to try carob.

'People survived. We are a country of survivors,' I spoke slowly and clearly.

Nina nodded.

'And then, covered in dust, I found Geordie.'

'Yes, you found love. Jekk jogħġbok għidli,' Nina said.

~tell me, please.

ﷺ ﷺ ﷺ ﷺ ﷺ

'Besides being a plotter, I was a radio-operator. I would receive calls and redirect them to the persons concerned, by handling the old-fashioned communication board. I guess that you will have seen photos. There is a museum on the island, not Lascaris, another. Have you been?'

'No, jiddispjaċini,' Nina said.

~I'm sorry.

'One night, while on duty, a call arrived. I remember it being a quiet night, one with no air raids and I was alone on switchboard duty. The others were asleep, but I could never sleep on night duty as I was far too terrified of creepy crawlies. I think that your mother is too; it's a family thing, I think. The telephone rang, but the caller was not asking for an officer. He just wanted to talk. He asked if I would talk with him as he was very heavy-eyed and did not want to fall asleep on his shift. He did not want to get into trouble with his superiors.'

I heard Geordie inside my head. He was saying those first words that he said to me. I smiled. The sound of his voice covered me in love, filled me with anticipation, but then Jesus told us both to concentrate on the task.

༺ ༺ ༺ ༺ ༺

'Of course I accepted. We talked and talked. And those phone calls with the mystery soldier became frequent. Over a few days I realised that I had fallen in love with this gentleman, even though I had never seen him in person,' I explained.

'Geordie?' Nina asked, her eyes were locked onto my face and I felt her searching for something, I did not know what.

'Wait and see, my dear,' I laughed.

Nina smiled but she did not laugh.

'And so one day I was busy working when I felt that someone was standing behind me. I turned back and even before the young gentleman could introduce himself, my heart leapt. I knew immediately that the uniformed man standing in front of me would be the man that I married.'

'Geordie? Jekk jogħġbok għidli,' Nina said; she was smiling weakly.

~tell me, please.

'He introduced himself as Geordie Smith, my mystery caller. I could not even speak, my heart was beating so quickly. I noticed his blue eyes and now when I think back I can see him holding a cucumber sandwich, but I know that this is not really true. It cannot be true.' I laughed again. I heard Geordie laughing too.

'Ħjara ħjara?' Nina said, and then she laughed.

~a cucumber?

Her laughter warmed me. I heard Jesus releasing a guttural laugh and Christopher chuckled too. My head was filled with sounds that connected us all.

❦ ❦ ❦ ❦ ❦

'Geordie wanted to start dating but I knew that my father would never allow it,' I continued. 'So, we timed our work breaks together, perhaps taking a little longer than we should. Those brief moments were soon not enough for us and so we agreed to meet secretively in church. Geordie would walk all the way from Valletta, every day, just to sit next to me in church for twenty minutes. Can you imagine walking from Valletta to Birkirkara each day?'

'Għall-imħabba... kollox,' Nina almost whispered the words.

~all for love.

I stopped talking. I felt full and I needed to see my Geordie. Again I heard Jesus. He told me that I was doing so well but that I needed to stay focused.

❦ ❦ ❦ ❦ ❦

'My sisters, my brother and even my auntie did not say anything to my parents. They did not want to put

149

me into trouble. Everyone could see that I had fallen
for the Englishman. But, this spell of tranquillity was
short-lived. We wanted more.'

I paused.

As I spoke, I felt my life was flashing out in words. I
felt that I should have been displaying emotion and
that it should have been etched into my face, but I
could not express grief for my loss of roots. My soul
was not filled with anguish as my death had brought
with it peace. Jesus heard my thoughts. He warned
me not to utter those words aloud and I did not argue
with him.

᯽ ᯽ ᯽ ᯽ ᯽

'Geordie decided to approach my father. My
parents' door was shut in Geordie's face many times.
Eventually, my father ordered Geordie to keep away
from his door, his house and his daughter,' I spoke
slowly.

'So cruel, why? Għaliex kellu jkun daqshekk krudili?'
Nina asked.

~why would he be so cruel?

'My father's actions were brutal and unfair, yes cruel,
you are right. But I have been told that his behaviour
was animated by love and concern. I do not know. I

150

was my parents' favourite child, you see. My mother once said that I was so generous that, "Elena would give her knickers to anyone in need." We would all chuckle.' I laughed, but my sounds had no weight.

'Il-qalziet ta' taħt tiegħek!' Nina laughed after her words.

~your knickers!

The laughter was short and forced. I wondered when she would realise that she had not lost her mother tongue as I had, that she had returned to the island in time.

აჵა აჵა აჵა აჵა აჵა

'Yes, I know, but they were right. I would give up what I could for others. In Malta I had character, a feistiness I suppose, and I even think that I had intelligence. I was respected, before and during the war. That never happened in Newcastle. In Newcastle I was foreign and nothing beyond that. It was the way at that time. I guess that my father wanted only the best for his daughter and that he knew that my life off the island would be difficult.'

'Iva, yes,' Nina nodded; she agreed or perhaps it was that she understood. I saw into her mind. For Nina it was never about desiring respect, I could see that it was more about searching and needing but not being able to belong. I heard Nina's thoughts as she turned to her broken roots. I understood.

❧ ❧ ❧ ❧ ❧

I continued, because Jesus told me to.

'I can recognise my father's anger; now, of course, I am an adult, I can see reason. I had fallen for a man who was not Roman Catholic. You know how important the foundations of our faith are. St Paul preached and taught Christian values from within a cave and –'

'And you believe that?' Nina interrupted.

'Without doubt,' I said and then continued, quickly. 'And added to Geordie's lack of Catholicism, he was foreign. And so, in a desperate attempt to interrupt my love story, my father was stern and informed me that if I wanted to marry an Englishman, then I would have to leave his house with only the dress that I was wearing as dowry. '

'U allura, int m'obdejtx?' Nina asked.

~and so you were disobedient?

'Of course,' I answered defiantly that I would do just that. 'I was overwhelmed with love for Geordie. I

152

still am.'

I heard Geordie inside of me. He told me that he was overwhelmed with love for me too. He spoke slowly and calmly. If my heart had been working, then it would have skipped a beat.

❦ ❦ ❦ ❦ ❦

'I married Geordie at St Aloysius' College's Chapel,' I continued. 'The small reception took place in my parents' garden.'

'With all of your family? Ma' ħuk u ħutek il-bniet?'

~with your brother and sisters?

Nina asked and I knew that she was interested in me.

'Yes they all came. No one dared challenge the authority of the head of the family. I heard that my father was left heartbroken. But being the authoritarian that he was, sadly he kept his word. I left my family home with little more than my dress.'

My eyes were dry and I wanted to cry. I closed my eyes, expecting a release but then I realised that I had no further tears to shed.

'Initially, Geordie and I lived in a small flat in Rue d'Argent. My mother did not care about honour and shame, the foundation of Mediterranean culture. '

'Nifhmek, esperjenzajtha dik il-mistħija,' Nina
whispered, but I still heard her words.

~I know (I understand), I experienced that
shame.

'All that my mother cared about was her daughter
and her daughter's new husband, whom she already
loved. So, without telling my father, my mother
would secretly go to the market, buy provisions and
take them to us at Rue d'Argent.'

Nina lowered her head.

'As I tell you this, I feel quite sure that my father
realised that something fishy was going on, and that
his funds were suddenly draining faster. He was no
fool, but I am sure that he was purposely closing both
his eyes. If he did not know, then he need not act and
so his honour would still remain intact.'

'Unur. It always seems to come back to honour,' Nina
whispered, softly, her words were almost thoughts but
still I heard them all.

~honour.

'Yes, but we need honour for strength and guidance.
On the eve of the feast of Santa Marija, in 1942,
the starving people of Malta were saved by a food
convoy. As a people, we had combined, we had been

united by an unbroken spirit. I do not know if my Geordie understood. My people have chronicled talk of invasion, empire, rule and siege. Under British influence, our island became the Nurse of the Mediterranean, we had honour, pride even. '

I paused, my teeth ached. My mouth was overcrowded and words were becoming difficult to form. Nina watched me in silence.

I continued, 'People still come here to heal in our pot, even the Romans called our island Melita, honey. There is a spirit, a community that exists within a strength of will. Malta is a honeypot, we open up, attract and then we make better.'

'I like that, ġarra għasel,' Nina said and she smiled, again.

~a honeypot.

સ્⁀ સ્⁀ સ્⁀ સ્⁀ સ્⁀

'Once the war was over, Geordie left the army, but jobs were few and hard to find. We had to start from scratch with no help at all. So he worked as an occasional plasterer and as a labourer at the Farsons' beer factory.'

Nina looked distracted. I saw into her thoughts and I could see Matt. I saw an image of her lying naked in a small bed. They were both young. Christopher was not yet growing inside of her. I heard Christopher. He was telling me to remove the image. I laughed, Geordie laughed, Jesus laughed. I would have laughed tears if I had had them.

Nina looked slightly confused.

'But soon the heat proved too much for my Englishman,' I continued. 'We decided to emigrate to Newcastle, to England, to live with Geordie's parents and we talked of making our fortune and of one day returning to Malta with wealth. My father's worst nightmare was materialising. '

'You were leaving Malta? Rejecting your culture. I did this too,' Nina whispered.

'I know that you did, my Nina. Our stories connect through generations,' I told her. 'Stubbornly, my father held tight to his word as the head of the family. And then I found out that I was pregnant. '

I paused. Nina looked into my eyes, she wanted me to continue. She said no words.

'We were leaving Malta. We had no money and we needed to save on our rent. I begged my father to keep us until we finalised all the arrangements to go to England. My father gave in, but to show that his word meant something, he only gave us the room on the roof. This had glass all around and so it was very hot in spring and summer and very cold and noisy when it rained or hailed, in autumn and winter. Not much time passed before I gave birth to a healthy, blonde baby girl.'

'Bless her. Imbierek Alla... Kemm hi ħewla,' Nina recited without intention.

```
~(blessing given to a newborn baby girl).
Praise God, what a pretty girl.
```

'Sadly, her Maltese grandparents hardly had the time to enjoy their granddaughter. We were to leave the island eight months later. My father's strong ego did not allow him to bless our union. He feared that should he accompany us to the Grand Harbour, it could seem as if he approved. He could not be seen to have turned back on his word. And so not only did he not go to the Grand Harbour to see us off, but he specifically prohibited his wife and his other children from going to bid us farewell.'

I paused. I was covered in an urge to cry, but still the tears could not fall. I was dry. I had so much to learn of the spirit world. Jesus refused to explain; he talked quickly, full of impatience and he urged me to carry

on. He told me that he would fill in details and that
I would learn all that I needed to later. He told me
that my soul was not in anguish and so my range of
emotions had narrowed. This was all truly new to me.
I heard Jesus urging me to continue. I answered by
thinking that I had been thrown into a task, before I
could understand who I had become.

≈≈ ≈≈ ≈≈ ≈≈ ≈≈

'And so, I found myself boarding a crowded ship,
clinging to my husband and hugging my small baby.
I looked out, over the ship's railing, seeing the many
people that had gathered on the quay to throw kisses
and tearfully wave their loved ones away. No one was
there for me. My heart snapped,' I said.

'Qalbek inqasmet. Naf,' Nina whispered.

~your heart snapped. I understand.

I knew that Nina was thinking about her Matt again.
I knew that her Matt had a heart that had snapped in
three and I wished that I could share my knowledge
with her. I wished that I could show her images of
Matt, of his broken heart and his desperate clinging to
Molly. Nina had left a trail that was broken.

Jesus warned me that I must not tell Nina of Matt and
Molly. He warned me of layering guilt. He told me

that Nina had to find her own path. I nodded.

～～ ～～ ～～ ～～ ～～

'The journey by boat was horrific, with a small child and my being repeatedly sick. We travelled for days and mostly all that I can remember is my violent sickness and the depth of my grief,' I said.

'I understand,' Nina spoke and I knew that she did truly understand my pain.

'My life in Newcastle was not as rosy as I had expected it to be. My mother-in-law considered the new wife of her son as an inferior foreigner and thus unworthy of her son's love,' I explained. 'I never did belong. We never did make our fortune. I sacrificed my identity for love.'

～～ ～～ ～～ ～～ ～～

'Now I have come back to Malta, a spirit. I am a stranger. I speak a different language, I have developed new customs,' I told her.

'But my mother says that in Malta people heal,' Nina tells me.

'I also need to repent,' I told her.

'Repent?'

'I did not speak with my mother tongue in my

English home. My children do not know how to speak Maltese. I affected them, do you understand? And after sixty years, my English accent is broken and when I have dreamed I have always spoken in a struggling Maltese. I tried to deny my roots, but in doing so they grew stronger and strangled me. And then when Geordie died, I think that I stopped living too. My life had no purpose without him and I wasted the end. So I need to repent my denial in life.'

'You came home,' Nina tried to reason.

'With death, I arrive here to find my Geordie. You understand that I have been asked to guide you? And here in Malta I will heal, I will mend with my Geordie, before we begin our next journey. Geordie is my perfect match, my true love. I will travel with him.' I smiled.

I wanted to add that Christopher is not her match, that she should leave him to be, to grow, to learn, but, of course, I did not.

'Your next journey?' Nina asked.

'Reincarnation,' I told her. 'I've been told that my life on earth is not yet complete.'

Nina looked confused.

'Jesus told me that life is a progression,' I explained.
'He said that we are living to learn, mature and find
ourselves before we leave physical life. Do not forget,
my dear child Nina, death is an illusion, do not be
afraid.'

'I fear life,' Nina told me.

'Your fear is too great and it clouds your existence.
You are wasting, you are not growing. I feel that you
are rotting in your core, my Nina. You must change.
Soon, I will enter into a new body on the first breath.
But for now I am going to take in the sights, relax,
remember and love. The company here is good,' I
spoke my words quickly and then laughed.

'I have a husband too and another child, Molly,' Nina
told me.

'I know. I have visited Matt but he did not see me,'
I said.

Jesus screamed at me to stop talking.

'My Matt?'

'He is broken until you make well,' I told her. Jesus
shouted inside of me, making my false teeth rattle. He
was angry. He told me to end my conversation.

'I don't know how to heal,' Nina cried.

'Look to your island. Malta is a sanctuary but Christopher is the key,'

I told her and then I left –

Tlettax

~thirteen

Elena Smith
birth: 29.06.1922; death: 10.02.2008.

Elena walks away.

I watch her. Her brown sandalled feet, her American tan tights, her slightly pleated navy skirt walk away from me and down the slope.

I know that she is going to meet with her Geordie.

I watch her, each step offering a skip, a hop.

Nearly at the corner, Elena stops. I watch her, curious; she coughs, she bends forward, practically touching her brown sandals. She coughs.

>she.

>*~c – ough.*

>*~c – ough.*

>coughs, then standing upright, lifts her arm to
her face.

I watch her, sweeping her arm to the side.

>and then, something.

>*~cl – at – ters.*

>onto the cobbles.

Then, I watch her; Elena turns the corner and she is gone.

◎

I stand up from the cold step.

I am stiff, cold in my bones, shiver shiver, shiver shiver.

Leaving my flip-flops I pad, slowly, carefully, down the wet slope.

Nearly at the corner, I stop, I look to the floor.

◎

I see Elena's false teeth.

◎

I make my way back up the slope, smiling.

I get to the step, the front door is open; the chain and padlock lie on the cobbles.

I see Christopher, inside my mother's house, smiling.

He walks to me.

'Shall we sit together a while?'

He says.

I nod.

We sit down on the step, my mother's front door open behind us; he sits where Elena had been.

'Did you bring your guidebook with you?'

Christopher asks.

'Of course,' I say.

'Jesus said to tell you that you should use it. He said it would show you.'

Christopher says.

'Show me what?' I ask.

'The beginning. St Paul.'

Christopher says.

'I don't know if I believe in St Paul,' I say.

'It's true.'

Christopher answers, quickly.

'Which bit?' I ask.

'All of it!'

He says, he smiles, he laughs.

'You're too young to understand,' I tell him.

'Jesus told me that it's true.'

Christopher says.

I have no further argument.

◎

We sit in silence, watching no one.

◎

Like Bees to Honey

Matt,

You have stopped sending me old women wrapped in your essence. Instead, I see you there, with me, next to me as I rerun my days.

As I sleep I replay, slowly, my day and the connections that I have made. I am restless. You are with me, a figure. You never speak, we never touch. You are, without the pleasure that you have always brought to me.

I am beginning to realise that I have two languages and that neither offers the weight of words that I need to express this pulling that I have within me. I ache in my chest, for you. As I close my eyes, as I attempt to fall into a sleep, there are echoes of expressions inside of my head. I am told, repeatedly, that people come to Malta to heal. The words offer both comfort and confusion. I do not know how to heal. I wish that you could help me, that you would speak, that you would move into focus.

I worry that I never will be whole, I worry that I enjoy spending my days with the dead. I worry that I am longing to join them, to pass over to them, to leave you, truly. I feel that I am suspended between two worlds, that I have been for years, but that in Malta it is stronger, more enticing. I do not know which way to move. I am filled with a new fear. I alarm myself. It would be easy to tempt me into death. But in leaving you, and Molly, my passing life would be filled with a longing for the real, the physical. I am torn. I live with regrets and I am not sure how to rid myself of them.

I am beginning to think of the guilt that I am carrying and of the death of our son. My grief has been selfish, consuming. I realise that I am clinging to Christopher in a desperate attempt to alter my treatment of him. I was not as a mother should have been and now that he has passed I am attempting to mother a spirit. And now when I think of my island I think of the hundreds of thousands of spirits swarming. I do not see them all, but I know that they are there. They are attracted to this place, they are all drawn to a small mound resting in the Mediterranean.

I think that I am beginning to find me, to realise. And with each small step I am longing for you. My life is so very empty without you. I am half, of nothing. I wish that I could send my words to you. I wish that I could tell you, that you would begin to understand. I wish that you would wrap your arms around me and pull me into your world, into your space. I am beginning to realise that there is no reverse, rewind, retelling. I move forward or I pass.

My love matures, stronger with each neglectful day. I am truly lovesick with and without you,

Nina x

Erbatax

~fourteen

Malta's top 5: *In Valletta*

✳ 5. The Royal Opera House

Designed by Edward Middleton Barry, the elegant Royal Opera House was damaged in a sweeping fire in 1873. It took over four years for the reopening in 1877, only for further desolation to strike during an air raid in 1942. Over fifty years later and the dilapidated building serves to remind the Maltese people of their heritage.

Caroline Smailes

I am resting, slumped back in the chair in my mother's parlour, my legs stretched out in front of me.

Tilly is floating around, around, around the room. I cannot look to her, her movements make my stomach turn.

As she floats, she is flipping faster, backwards, forwards. I can tell that she needs to talk, that much troubles her, but my mind is elsewhere, in another time.

That guidebook is lying on my outstretched thigh. It is full of Malta's top fives. The narrow rectangular pages are jam-packed with glossy photographs taken from obscure angles. I bought that book for Matt in preparation for our first trip to the island, as a family, with a young Christopher.

That was eleven years ago, now.

◎

The photographs seem out of date, aged. Eleven years are many. The years have been full, since the rejection, that final ostracism.

◎

My fingers stroke the smooth guidebook. My mind shifts, flicks, back to a certain time, summers ago. That was our only visit as a family, my last visit.

◎

170

Of course, I knew that I had broken my mother's heart, I knew of the anger and resentment, but I thought that time would have healed. I was a married woman, we had the gift of Christopher. I had hoped that forgiveness, that healing would have occurred.

I was wrong.

I guess that when I was out of sight, my parents had denied, blocked my very existence. It was easier, that way. I had brought such shame to the family name, to them.

Yet I still hoped and I had planned.

My plan was simple. We were to visit Malta over the summer, to stay for a week, for my family to fall in love with Matt, with Christopher and for them all to live happily ever after. I had bought Matt the glossy guidebook, to prepare and to excite. I had wanted him to fall in love with my island. We had booked a package deal, flight and half-board, so as not to impose, not to expect.

But twentieth-century fairytales are rarely simple.

I had telephoned my eldest sister Sandra, our conversation short and polite. I had told her of our flight arrival.

I had expected.

I was flying to Malta, expecting a welcoming crowd full of extended family members. I had told Matt to expect a loud, energetic throng. I had described faces, pronounced names, explained family connections, ties, divisions, taboos.

I could not help but be excited.

The journey to the airport, the flight, Christopher's first flight, it all passed in a blur.

I remember general tiredness, eyes that felt sticky, tick tacky and then that the flight arrived.

I remember pushing out onto the aisle. I remember walking ahead, Matt with Christopher following, out from the plane. I remember the blast of heat, the warmth from my Lord's smile covering me as I stepped out from the plane's door. I remember climbing down each metal step, feeling the warmth covering my exposed arms, breathing in the dust, smelling my island. I remember that we had to catch a bus from the plane, to the entrance, to the arrivals terminal.

I remember Christopher's eyes wide, anticipating, absorbing.

◎

Inside, I remember.

I rushed to the toilet, applied mascara, combed my hair. I remember that my hand shook as I attempted to drag a lipstick over my too thin lips.

My mother used to tell me, 'Qalbi, inti għarwiena mingħajr lipstick.'

~my heart, you are naked without lipstick.

Yet I could never find a colour to suit, to match with my tones, with my lips that seemed to thin with age. I remember that Matt and Christopher had collected the luggage onto a metal trolley that squeaked and needed to be hauled, dragged. I returned to them, ready. I remember tightening my hand grip with Christopher, as we walked through customs. I remember that Christopher was apprehensive, dragging his feet.

I remember that I made Matt abandon the metal trolley, impatient, not wanting to join the queue for a lift. We struggled with our bags, with Christopher too. And then, as I stepped onto the escalator, I looked down into the crowd that stood waiting for people to arrive. I held my breath, I smiled, I expected.

◎

But there was no welcoming crowd of extended family members, for us.

I had been ostracised, I remembered.

A family governed by religious rules that seeped back to a specific person, an exact time and place, had rejected a daughter and her family.

I had disgraced my family name.

I had broken my mother's heart.

I had underestimated, expected too much.

Yet still, I longed to hear my mother's voice. I needed for her to meet Christopher, for her to see him, know him. And I remember that right then, in the airport, my sense of being, of worth, of belonging, fell from me. And nothing that Matt could do could bring me back.

I had to know, for sure.

◎

And so we caught a taxi.

Matt and I climbed into the back, Christopher on my knee. I remember the heat, longing for merciful Mother Nature to send a cool breeze. Matt and Christopher had never experienced such temperatures, the height of summer in Malta. I remember a smell of dust, of decaying rubbish that had been punished by the sun's rays. It was a smell that was familiar, warming.

The taxi dropped us near to the bus terminal in Valletta. I had refused to go directly to our hotel; I needed to see my parents.

I remember stopping, the intense heat was bothering my English son. I bought him a glass of milkshake, from one of the small kiosks that lined the bus terminal. I think that Christopher chose pink, strawberry. I did not take a drink, I was anxious, my feet pitter pattering. I think that Matt bought a bottle of mineral water.

I remember our walking through the City Gate and into Valletta, within the walls, and then the Renaissance streets opening up before us and sheltering us from the heat. It was blistering warmth. I remember that Christopher was tired, and that Matt could not carry him. The early morning journey and the high temperature were taking their toll. We had our luggage, gifts too. Christopher was dragging behind us, no hand to hold, no comfort to be found. We turned right, past the crumbling Opera House.

I remember Christopher asking me why the building was broken.

I remember ignoring his question, walking up again, then down again. The streets sloped down to the harbour. It was busy, packed with tourists wearing as few clothes as possible, yet still dripping in sweat.

Our suitcases had no wheels; I remember tiring, bumping down each of the stone steps, making my way down the slant of the steep streets. The roads were narrow, they sheltered us, shaded from the overpowering heat of the summer, yet still I dripped sweat. I remember that Christopher moaned with each step. He wanted to go home.

◎

I remember that Matt did not complain.

◎

My mother and father's house was behind a green front door in Valletta.

◎

I do not know if my parents expected me to arrive, I never asked.

I think, well I know, that part of me was hoping that there had been a misunderstanding, that there had been confusion over the date, the time. I had hoped that we would all laugh, ha ha ha. I had hoped that my father would look at Christopher's blond curls, dash of freckles, blue eyes.

I had hoped that my father's heart would open to us.

◎

It was Matt who asked, 'Is this the house?'

We had not spoken during the walk through Valletta, his voice shocked me.

'Yes,' I whispered.

'Shall I knock?' he asked.

'Yes,' I whispered.

◎

I remember standing, very still; I was holding my breath. I wanted to see my mother, my father, my sisters. I needed to feel their warmth.

Matt knocked.

~kn – o – ck.

~kn – o – ck.

~kn – o – ck.

on the door.

No one came.

I could hear shouting, voices, loud then quiet, hushed but no one answered.

I remember that I knocked.

~kn – o – ck.

~kn – o – ck.

~kn – o – ck.

on the door, louder, anger rising.

I wanted to be inside. I wanted to show Matt and Christopher my life, in marble, in rich embellishments, in beautiful paintings, in elaborate chandeliers.

No one answered.

again, I knocked.

~kn – o – ck.

~kn – o – ck.

~kn – o – ck.

louder, loudly, with my fist.

'Why are you angry, Mama?' Christopher asked.

'I want to be inside,' I shouted.

I remember that it was my sister, Sandra, who opened the door.

Sandra turned and walked away, no welcome, no hug, no

eye contact with me or with her nephew.

She left the door open.

I remember looking to Matt, searching; he gestured, an upturned palm into the house and then shrugged his shoulders. We walked inside, leaving our suitcases in the hallway, close to the green front door.

My father was waiting, straight ahead, in the kitchen doorway.

We walked towards him, his face red, volcanic.

◎

I remember standing in the entrance to the kitchen. Matt and Christopher were beside me.

My father had moved into the kitchen, was standing at the head of the wooden kitchen table. He stared at me.

'Daddy, vera qed nieħu pjaċir narak.' I stepped forward.

~Daddy, it's so good to see you.

'No!' his voice was harsh. He stood, he walked past me, out through the kitchen doorway; Matt followed him.

I did not move.

I remember that Christopher was being unusually quiet.

I asked him, 'What's wrong Ciċċio?'

He looked up to me and whispered, 'Can you see the mejtin too, Mama?'

~dead people.

I remember looking at my five-year-old son, shocked, confused, thrilled.

'Dead people,' he translated. 'Can you see the dead people too, Mama?'

'You see mejtin?' I repeated.

~dead people.

'Yes Mama, but I cannot touch the dead people.' Christopher did not appear disturbed.

'Who do you see?'

'I see my new friends.'

'Do they have names?' I asked.

'I see Jesus and I have a new friend. His name is Geordie.'

'Ciccio, honey –' I started to explain, as Matt and my father walked back into the kitchen.

◎

'We should go,' Matt said.

'Why? No.' I felt desperate. I looked to my father. He was steam filled, explosive.

'Inti diżunur għal din il-familja. Minn issa, mhux se nqisek aktar bħala binti. Itlaq minn dari!' my father shouted.

~you are a disgrace to this family. From now on, you are no longer my daughter. Leave my house!

I began to weep.

Matt held out his hand to me. 'We should go. Christopher deserves more than this.'

And so we did. We walked back to the green front door, we picked up our suitcases. Christopher did not speak. And we left.

◎

I remember that I sobbed all the way to the hotel.

◎

I refused to leave the hotel room for the whole week. Matt would take Christopher to the outdoor pool. I would lie on the bed, windows open, letting in only the smallest amount of noise and air.

No one came to visit.

No one came to wave us goodbye.

And all the time, every hour, I remember longing to hear my mother's voice.

◎

And yet here I am, back on the island that had caused my heart to ache.

I sacrificed for love, my roots flap yet all the time I long for a sense of home. A dull and constant ache lives in my bones, in my heart.

I lift the glossy guide to Malta from my thigh. I sit up, still within the chair in my mother's parlour.

I am a tourist, searching for answers.

I open my book, I begin.

Ħmistax

`~fifteen`

Malta's top 5: *Churches and Cathedrals*

✳ **2. St Paul's Collegiate Church, Rabat**
Built upon and to the left of St Paul's Grotto, where St Paul was shipwrecked and the Church of Malta was born.

In Anno Domini 60 it is claimed that St Paul preached and taught Christian values from within a cave, in Malta. This single event was to influence the island, both spiritually and architecturally. The cave became a place of wonder, of origin, of conversion and for three months it is said that St Paul offered prayer. He became the spiritual father of my people and the Church of Malta did flourish.

I know that it is that church, the one that St Paul formed, that covers the roots of my pain. I am lost, buried under a religion that believes that intercourse outside of marriage contaminates all those whom it touches. Christopher being conceived before marriage ensured that my relationship with him was tinged in misery and that his death was inevitable, predestined.

I blame St Paul.

@

'I'm going out,' I tell my mother, as I move to the front door, clutching my guidebook.

She does not answer.

I hear Tilly.

~b – ish.

~b – ash.

~b – ish.

~b – ash.

banging around upstairs.

I look up the grand sweeping staircase, Tilly is floating, over the top stair.

'Where you going?'

She says.

'I need to get out. Clear my head,' I tell her.

'You lucky cow.'

She says, then flips like a Slinky, down, down, down the stairs.

Her anger frightens me, the familiarity, the depth.

I turn, I hurry, I open, I move out through the green front door.

The door closes behind me, I hear a key turning.

and a.

~cl – unk.

as the barrel revolves.

I look, the chain and padlock are connected, have reappeared.

I am forced out onto the cobbles. Tilly cannot follow.

◎

I cannot face another bus journey, I do not want crowds; it is late in the day.

I flip-flop down the slope.

I hail a passing taxi.

◎

The car is rust filled, creaky, it smells of stale alcohol.

The taxi driver does not speak. I see him watching me through the rear-view mirror, not focusing on the road, the traffic. I catch his eye and he winks.

I feel uncomfortable.

My fingers lock, together; I place them on my lap. I fix my eyes on my hands. I find myself praying to my only Lord, for safety.

◎

We arrive, the taxi stops. The taxi driver climbs from the car. I watch him. He moves to the window next to me, he bends his knees to the floor, he presses his lips to the glass and then the rest of his face. His features squash, distort. His movements are quick. Within the minute, he unpeels his face, leaving no mark, no condensation, he stands and then he runs. He is gone, quickly.

I wait, possibly for ten minutes.

He does not return.

I place five euros on the backseat and then I leave the taxi.

As I am walking away, I hear the car horn beeping, a harsh yet tuneful melody.

I turn, the taxi driver is back in the front seat, holding a glass of beer in one hand, the other hand is off the wheel. He waves, he winks. The taxi moves forward, drives, without the man touching the steering wheel.

I watch until he is out of sight, gone.

◎

I use the guidebook. I find my way to a church, dedicated to St Paul, in the former capital of Malta, Rabat. Just outside of the city walls, St Paul's Church was built to the left of, over, above St Paul's Grotto.

This was where it all began, where the religion that rejected love and union outside of marriage was born.

◎

I stand, not quite on the pavement that surrounds the Baroque church.

I stare, the church welcomes, homely, smiling, almost.

I do not want to be received by St Paul.

◎

I think about the pilgrims who rush to Malta, to glimpse two most treasured relics, the right wrist-bone of St Paul and part of the column upon which, it is claimed, the saint was beheaded in Rome.

I do not seek the viewing of relics. I do not believe in relics.

◎

Beneath the focal church, I know that there are two small chapels. It is claimed that the first two Sacraments on the island were held, in there. Publius was baptised there and also consecrated first bishop of Malta. Yet, before these chapels were to become a place of worship and wonder, they were used as a prison by the Romans. I have seen the loops in the stone, used to suspend chains and ropes for harassment. They can still be seen.

The two images, the chapel, the punishing cell, they link.

I smile.

◎

St Paul's Church looms in front of me.

The sun is falling, people will be starting to leave their homes, to promenade, passeġġati.

~leisurely evening stroll.

I offer echo as I flip, as I flop.

~fl – ip.

~fl – op.

~fl – ip.

~fl – op.

up to the church.

I stand on the pavement, in front of, before the limestone building. I curse St Paul.

'You've fucked up too many lives,' I whisper.

'Skuzi?'

The voice jumps over my right shoulder. I turn to face a Maltese mother, late thirties, dark features, angry, clutching a child with each of her hands. The children are gazing at the statue-filled alcoves. The mother drops her children's hands and raises her upturned palms to the darkening sky.

'Oh God. I'm so sorry. Really. I didn't think anyone could hear me. Fuck. Oh God,' I ramble.

'Ssh. No English girl. You cannot use such language on sacred ground. He will not leave you unpunished if you take His name in vain.'

She points towards the heavens and flicks her long bony index finger as she speaks. Her breath smells stale, lingers, familiar.

I follow her finger.

'He?' I question.

'Your only Lord.'

She says, before grabbing her children's hands and steering them through the wooden entrance into the church. She does not look back to me; one of her children, a boy, turns and winks.

I do not move, I do not enter the church.

I am not English.

◎

I wonder when I stopped being Maltese.

I wonder how this church is number two in my guidebook and the Rotunda of St Marija Assunta, Mosta, is number five.

There is no sense.

◎

I stand where the bus will stop.

I am catching the bus back to Valletta, this time.

190

The yellow bus arrives, I climb the metal steps, I scan the seats.

The bus is almost empty and then I see him, Christopher.

◎

He is on the back row, tucked near to the window. He smiles.

I walk to my son.

'Jesus wants to share beer with you.'

He tells me.

I smile.

I sit next to my son, our arms form a link. With my other hand, I lay my fingers over his. He is cold, our thin fingers match.

'Għandek swaba ta' pjanist, ' I say and then laugh, softly, ha ha ha.

~you have the fingers of a pianist.

Christopher curls his cold body closer to me, he sleeps; we travel in silence.

◎

Let me set the scene.

I am sitting in Larry's bar, on Strait Street, in Valletta.

I have not had a drink of beer, yet.

There are empty glasses on the table, they are still cool. Jesus is at the bar, head close to a young blonde. I think she is a barmaid, or possibly Larry's wife. I have not seen her before; she may have recently passed. She is beautiful, her whole face reacts as she laughs, smiles. I have counted thirty empty pint glasses on the table. I think that Jesus must have a new drinking record; I wonder if he is drunk.

Jesus walks. His movements are slow, his feet bare and his toenails painted in multicolour. I think that some jewel art has been applied to his largest toenail. I smile. He comes to the table, he places two pints of Cisk in among the empty glasses. He pulls out the wooden chair, twists it so that the back faces the table, then straddles the seat. He reaches for one of the pints of Cisk.

~Cisk lager was first available in Malta in 1928. It has an alcohol content of 4.2 per cent.

> **Jesus:** You shall not take the name of the Lord your God in vain.

> he lifts the glass of Cisk to his mouth and gulps.

~*gul – p.*

~gul – p.

~gul – p.

gulps down half of the liquid. His gulps are loud, open throated. I watch as he places the glass next to the other, the still full pint.

'I'm sorry. I'm confused,' I say. 'Do we always have to talk religion?'

Jesus stares into my eyes. He is searching. I look to the still full glass of beer, longing.

> **Jesus:** Why do you question my existence, my Nina?

'I'm not. I'm talking to you, aren't I?' I say.

He does not answer, straight away. Instead, he picks up the other full pint, the one that I long for and gulps the liquid loudly, three times. He gulps down half of the liquid. Then, he replaces the glass on the table, out of my reach.

> **Jesus:** You blame him.

'Him?' I ask, but know the answer.

> **Jesus:** The Lord. Your only Lord.

'He took my Christopher, He punished him for my sin, for the sexual acts that I performed outside of marriage. I don't question your existence, I question your Lord's purity of heart,' I say, but I cannot look to his face, my cheeks are flushing.

Jesus: My Nina, look at me.

I look to his face and then he winks. I watch as he takes both glasses of Cisk. He pours the contents of one into the other, making a full, a perfect pint. He lifts the glass up to eye level, connecting his eyes with mine and then with the glass.

he drinks, he gulps continuously.

~gul – p.

~gul – p.

~gul – p.

~gul – p.

~gul – p.

~gul – p.

until the pint is consumed.

Jesus lowers the empty glass from his lips and hands me the empty pint glass. I lift my hand, to meet his and as I take the glass from him, the liquid reappears, the liquid fills the pint glass.

Jesus: Drink, my Nina, be my first.

And I do. I sip at the cold Cisk, feeling the liquid enter me, warm me.

> **Jesus:** My Nina, my child, consider the division between life on earth and the afterlife. On earth people are affected by the acts of those around them, their punishment is temporary. It is only in the afterlife that punishment is truly received.

I begin to shake; I hold the glass with two hands.

'I don't understand. You talk in riddles,' I say.

> **Jesus:** Consider hell on earth, consider what you do to those around you, how they suffer for your guilt. I mean your pupa, your Molly. You feel guilt for your sexual acts outside of marriage, yet you have been forgiven and there will be no punishment for that in the afterlife. You do not move forward, instead you are pushing punishment onto Molly and Matt. You are punishing them from your personal guilt.

Anger bubbles, I stand.

'You know nothing!' I shout, I scream.

Jesus remains in the wooden chair. He is calm.

> **Jesus:** My Nina, I know everything. I can hear your every thought. Christopher died for your sins. Is that what you wish to hear, my Nina? It is not true. Your

only Lord is not vengeful. Focus on the now, my
Nina. Remove yourself from the hell in which you
live.

My knees tremble, I feel faint.

Jesus: You carry more guilt, unvoiced guilt. There is
much that passed between you and your son before
his death. The anger and resentment that you felt
towards Christopher was seen by your only Lord.
Railing against your only Lord is covering you in
anger and sadness.

'You see all,' I say, through my sobbing.

Jesus: Sit, my Nina.

I sit.

Jesus: Find the acceptance that you need to move
forward in your world. This earthly life that you live is
short. But now, drink your Cisk and let us talk about
the Paul O'Grady.

'Paul O'Grady? Jesus?' I ask, confused.

He smiles, he winks. I feel my cheeks flush.

Jesus: Relax, my Nina. Drink your beer. I have much
to ask you.

Sittax

~sixteen

I am waiting for my food to cool, slightly, sitting at the wooden table in my mother's kitchen. I am watching my mother as she sways, slightly, to a song that I cannot hear.

'Tell me, Mama, why does my only Lord allow bad things to happen?' I interrupt her swaying, I ask.

My mother is washing pans, a knife, a fork, glasses. Tonight she has prepared bragioli.

```
~beef olives, although there are no olives. It
is minced meet, bacon, Maltese bread, sliced
egg, onions all rolled up and stuffed into
meat.
```

She turns to face me, smiling.

'So many times I have snarled to God and asked of him, "How could you?"'

She says, twisting to turn the cold tap to off, before wiping her hands on the front of her housecoat, turning the pink slightly darker in colour.

'And you received no answer?' I ask.

My mother pulls up a wooden chair to sit beside me. I am sitting with the plate full of steaming bragioli. I am holding my fork, into the meat. My mouth is watering, anticipating. I have not yet tasted.

'The death of a child was often hidden from you, qalbi.

There was much tradition to give answers to questions that we could not answer. When the child of our neighbour Maria died, Sandra asked me how God could allow that to happen. There was folklore that surrounded the death but it made little sense to an intelligent child. I could not answer my Sandra as I could not understand why our God that is all love would allow such pain. I would not even look to the altar while at the funeral of Maria's child.'

My mother says.

'I never knew,' I say.

'You knew of the death, the twisted child. You remember, qalbi?'

~my heart.

'I remember the child. I still remember your words. "Int għidtli mhux il-waqt u mhux għal erbgħin jum wara u li xi darba jien se nifhem,"' I say.

~you told me this is not only the right time, and not even for the next forty days, and that someday I'll understand.

'It was tradition, qalbi. There were many questions that you never asked. Sometimes, even though you were a young girl, I think that your mind had wandered from our island.'

My mother says.

I am covered in sadness by her truth. She places her cold hand upon my shoulder, squeezing, slightly.

'Before I passed, my cousin died. He was fifty years old and waiting for the birth of his first grandchild. I asked God the same question that you ask of me. I was full of anger. There are many times that I have asked this and the list goes on and on and on.'

'So there is no answer?' I ask.

'To be honest, qalbi, I have asked many priests to explain to me why God allows bad things to happen. I never got a straight answer; instead, I got theological sermons that never truly convinced me. Then one priest told me a story about a St Thomas Aquinas. Listen, qalbi, you should ask Jesus about him. '

~my heart.

'Thomas –?' I ask.

'Aquinas. Issa kul qabel tmut bil ġuħ.'

~now eat, before you starve.

She tells me and then watches, waits.

I lift a forkful to my mouth, the rich smells fly up my nostrils; my senses, my taste buds, my entire being tingles.

I open my mouth.

I am full of bragioli, curled on the chair in the parlour.

Tilly is.

~b – ish.

~b – ash.

~b – ish.

~b – ash.

banging around upstairs.

I do not shout up to her, not this time. Tonight my thoughts and my mind fix on the words that Jesus offered. The pain, the depth, attached to acts that were never voiced, that passed between Christopher and me. There is much that I had thought to be buried, hidden with my dead son.

Yet, I am told that my only Lord has seen it all.

I pull my legs in tighter, into me, curling in my mother's chair. I think to television programmes watched, to conversations overheard, to stories read in novels, in magazines. People would talk of the wonder of motherhood, of being fulfilled, of finding purpose, of finding identity with the cutting of the umbilical cord.

I did not experience that maternal joy. Motherhood came

as a shock; perhaps that is an understatement. Motherhood unleashed me. I was not prepared for the overwhelming feelings, for my inexperience. Christopher came into the world, bruised, battered, misshapen. He was not how I had expected a baby, my baby, to look.

I had spent hours writing a birth plan. I had read numerous magazines, taken advice, made the birth my thesis. It was my distraction. I requested music to be played, a water birth, no pain relief. The key points of my plan were highlighted, in yellow, ready for my due date.

My due date passed.

Ten days overdue, after a sweeping internal, labour progressed, quickly, beyond my control. And as my blood pressure soared and the pain became intolerable, I screamed out for help, for injections to numb me. A water birth was beyond question, the injection was given too late.

Christopher ripped out from me, without control.

He had decided to arrive.

And that marked the beginning of our relationship.

I called him Rokku for two days.

He was Rokku Aquilina for two days.

On day three our pale child, my Ciċċio, was registered Christopher Robinson.

He belonged to England.

◎

I suffered blisters on my nipples, mastitis, fear of cot death, so much more. I could tick each box that indicated postnatal depression, but I did not, of course. I missed my mother, I longed for help and guidance, I feared in a British way.

Matt's parents were not really interested; they were not keen to see the baby that had been made with a foreign girl. They did not come with gifts, with open arms, they did not come. Christopher was seven weeks old when they first met him. There was never a bond.

And so we struggled.

◎

We were twenty and twenty-one years old. Matt was still a student, separate from his student friends, heavy with responsibility. We struggled, financially and socially, but always together.

◎

As Christopher grew I found him harder to deal with, to please.

As a toddler, he was defiant. His speech was limited but his tantrums were brimming in frustration. He would bite and kick; he would react to noise, to change, yet hated routine. He would not sleep when light could be seen.

I had no break from him, no release, no outside life.

At two and a half, he was diagnosed with speech problems, but his eyes flicked and his hands attempted to communicate with us. His anger and frustration came from his inability to be understood, by us, by me.

We tried, of course we tried, but somehow I think that he blamed me.

I was his mother, I should have recognised, understood his attempts to communicate.

I could not understand him, I tried, I really tried.

I thought that he hated me.

He would stare into me, piercing, screaming at me, willing me to read his thoughts and to understand all that he was trying to communicate. But I could not. Our bond was never that way, never strong.

At three, we thought it best for him to start nursery, to learn to socialise. As I left him, he would cry, then scream and kick out. I would watch through the window, I would see the helpers struggling to control him.

He never joined in.

Twice a week for six months, he would sit sobbing for the two hours during nursery. I did not have the courage, the confidence, to stop his attendance. I would sit in the car waiting, in case they needed me. I would wait, for two hours, staring out from my car window, panicking.

I was told, promised, that his behaviour would stop, that he would begin to join in. He never did.

◎

At four, he told me that I was not his real mother. He said that his real mother and father had been killed in a car crash and that he never wanted to drive a car. He told me that his house was white, had lots of stairs, more than ours, that there were three floors. He talked of heat, of sand, of roads that were bumpy. He tried to tell me place names, but his speech was still limited, his sounds and blends never came as he wanted, anticipated. His frustration continued to grow.

◎

I began to wonder if I was his mother, if I ever could be.

◎

And as his frustration grew, my anger and resentment grew too. He was my life, my insular world. I guess that I absorbed Christopher in a sense of home and security, in an almost terror that I could not give him all that he needed, the solid roots that I no longer had.

But with each act, each choice, he would react, rebel, almost.

I was convinced that he hated me, that he despised that I could not peel back his head to unpick the jumbled words and sounds. He demanded my time, my constant companionship. He panicked, reacted when I was out of sight. He wet the bed, climbing into my sleep, invading my time.

I could not be what he needed, I was never enough.

◎

At five he had his only holiday in Malta.

And from the sadness that layered that trip, something broke from me.

◎

When my Ciccio was five years old, I began to hit him.

◎

He would continue to disobey, he would react, he would counter. He would cower in a corner. His hands on his head. I would kick, scream, slap, hit, fall to the ground.

It was never for long, perhaps I offer this as justification.

As it ended, then we, my Ciccio and I, would cry into each other, bonded from the release. I would hug him close and in those despairing moments, I would feel connected to him, understood, accepted.

I think that he hated me.

I sometimes think that I hated him.

I almost wished his death upon us, an escape.

He was needy, more than normal children. He invaded my space, made demands, unreasonable demands. And as he grew, his respect for me diminished.

I tried to care, to support. But there was no respite, no let up, no other family to take him from us.

At nine, he looked at me with hatred. He still cowered from my anger, but he had learned to answer with words, cruel words. He would tell me that he hated me, that he wished that I was not his mother.

And inside my head, I would have the same wish too.

He would stand tall, defiant, angry.

He would make me attack him.

◎

But when he slept, after the violence, the explosions, then I would hold him close. There were moments of tenderness, hidden within the fusing, the explosions that our characters created.

◎

Matt would try to calm us and Christopher would shout and scream at Matt. Telling Matt, his daddy, that he needed protecting from me.

I was a monster.

Ciccio made me that way.

I had never raised my hand or my voice to another being, until Christopher came into this world.

And when Christopher died, the volcano seeped from me.

◎

At ten, Christopher stepped out in front of a car. My Ciccio died.

And I crumbled to the floor, unable to right my wrongs.

And then there is the truth, that hidden truth, that secret that I've carried for all of these years because at some point, I cannot pinpoint when exactly, but there was a passing moment, there was a flicker of relief.

And for that, for that one fleeting thought, I feel that I can never be forgiven.

Sbatax

~seventeen

Malta's top 5: *Drinks*

✳ Cisk Lager
Cisk lager was first available in Malta in 1928. It has an alcohol content of 4.2 per cent.

✳ Kinnie
Kinnie is a distinctive tasting drink. It is golden in colour, prepared from bitter oranges and mixed with a selection of fragrant herbs.

✳ Wine
Maltese wine-making travels back to the Phoenician interludo. White, red and rosé wines are all produced on the islands.

✳ Bottled Water
Tourists are advised to drink bottled water, rather than the local tap water which has been desalinated and could lead to stomach complaints.

✳ Hopleaf Pale Ale
Farsons' Hopleaf pale ale has an alcohol content of 3.8 per cent. In 2006 a stronger Hopleaf Extra was created, with an alcohol content of 5 per cent.

Tilly wakes me.

>she throws something onto the floor, making a.

~s – m – ash.

~b – ash.

I jump, I open my eyes and she is in front of me, sweeping around the chair, a human-shaped cloud. She never stays still, her movements make my stomach turn.

'Tilly!' I shout.

'Thought that'd wake you.'

She says, she laughs, ha ha ha.

'Couldn't you say my name or gently shimmy over me?' I ask.

'Nah. I'm in a hurry and I've better things to do with me time than be your friggin' secretary. Jesus wants to see you in Larry's bar when you get yourself tarted up.'

She says, still circling the chair.

'Thank you,' I say, uncurling, searching for my flip-flops.

'You're a friggin' lucky cow.'

She says and then spins off in her grey wispy cloud.

◎

I apply mascara and lipstick.

◎

Let me set the scene.

I am sitting in Larry's bar, on Strait Street, in Valletta.

I have not had a drink of beer, yet. There are empty glasses on the table, they are still cool to the touch. Jesus is at the bar, talking with Larry and the young blonde. In front of me, on the table, I have counted thirty-five empty pint glasses. I think that Jesus must have a new drinking record and, again, I wonder if this time he will be drunk.

◎

Jesus walks from the bar, carrying a tray with four full glasses upon it. His movements are slow, his feet bare, his toenails painted black. The colour suits him. I think that some jewel art, possibly diamond flakes, has been stuck to his smallest toenail. I smile. I wonder if Jesus realises that his feet are truly unattractive. The toes are crooked, the middle toe sticks out beyond the natural shape of the foot. He comes to the table, he places two pints of Cisk near to me and two pints near to where he will sit. He pulls out the wooden chair, twists it so that the back faces the table, then straddles the seat. He reaches for one of the pints of Cisk.

~Cisk lager was first available in Malta in 1928. It has an alcohol content of 4.2 per cent.

Jesus: That is why I wear the nail polish.

'Sorry?' I ask.

Jesus: I am conscious that my feet are ugly, my Nina.

'Not ugly,' I say, but I know that Jesus has read my mind. My cheeks flush red.

I look to his face and then he winks. I watch Jesus lift his glass of Cisk up to eye level, connecting his eyes with mine.

then he drinks, he gulps continuously.

~*gul – p.*

~*gul – p.*

~*gul – p.*

~*gul – p.*

~*gul – p.*

~*gul – p.*

until the entire pint is consumed.

Jesus lowers the empty glass and places it among the other empties.

Jesus: I think I prefer your ruby red.

He points to my chipped nail polish. My feet look poor, unattractive in their pink plastic flip -flops.

'I left the jar at home,' I say and Jesus smiles.

Jesus: You have a question, Melita tells me.

I lift the fresh glass to my lips and I sip at the cold Cisk, feeling the liquid enter into me. I am comforted by the liquid, by the familiarity that now surrounds me. I replace the glass, on the table.

'My mother told me to ask you about a St Thomas –,' I say.

Jesus: St Thomas Aquinas.

'She told you?' I ask.

Jesus: Of course. I know everything, my Nina.

I nod. Jesus smiles, winks. My cheeks flush, beyond my control. He continues.

Jesus: Are you sitting comfortably, my Nina?

I shift in my seat, I nod, I smile.

Jesus: Good, then I'll tell you how St Thomas Aquinas was a saintly man who asked the very question that I know you are seeking answers for, my Nina. He would ask why God would allow appalling things to happen.

He lifts his remaining full glass of Cisk to his mouth.

and gulps.

~gul – p.

~gul – p.

~gul – p.

down half of the liquid.

His gulps are loud, open throated. He does not replace the glass onto the table, rather moves it, away from his lips, to talk.

> **Jesus:** One day, St Thomas Aquinas was by the sea, contemplating the questions that you ask, when he saw a little boy playing with water. The boy was filling his pail with water up to the brim and the pail was overflowing but still he kept adding water.

Jesus pauses; I take another sip at the cold Cisk. I nod because I feel that I should.

> **Jesus:** 'What are you doing?' asked St Thomas Aquinas of the little boy.
>
> 'I am trying to put all the sea into my pail,' answered the little boy.
>
> 'But that is impossible!' answered St Thomas, very quickly. 'Your pail is too small!'

Jesus says each word with conviction, truth, depth. I am engaged, enthralled. I am wanting to stay with this man for ever, to listen to his story telling, for ever. Jesus has stopped talking, he is looking at me, into me, reading my thoughts. He moves his eyes to meet mine and then he nods, he winks. My cheeks flush red, again.

>**Jesus:** At that moment, the boy turned to St Thomas and said to him, 'You are doing just like me. You are trying to understand your only Lord, using your small, human brain' and then he promptly vanished.

Jesus laughs, guttural, low. I laugh, ha ha ha.

Jesus lifts his glass of Cisk to his mouth and gulps.

~gul – p.

~gul – p.

~gul – p.

down the remaining liquid.

When he is finished he replaces the empty glass among the others, lost.

>**Jesus:** Your only Lord does not punish, my Nina. You have free will and perhaps that is one of your greatest challenges. You get to choose and your only Lord does not interfere. It is those choices that model your life. Many ask me, they send prayers, 'Why does God allow good people to die even though we pray so hard for them? Why does He not listen to us?' I can but smile and simply tell them to stop

trying to understand God with a human mind and
from a human perspective.

I move my full pint of Cisk to Jesus. I sip from my other
pint. My sips are small, delicate, controlled. Jesus does not
touch the glass; he looks to it, then to me.

>**Jesus:** To your only Lord, you are eternal beings.
>You never really die, you simply evolve from one
>form to the next. Look around you, my Nina, you are
>a seer, the spirits circle you.

'But what if I see only what I wish to see? What if I am
insane and this is all but the imaginings of my crazy
mind?' I ask.

Jesus laughs, loud, guttural. I feel my whole body rattle.

>**Jesus:** My Nina, please try to listen to me with a
>mind that is open. As soon as a baby is born, that
>child releases a cry, feeling as if it has died. It has
>been expelled from the comfort of the safe womb.
>We both know that the baby has not died, rather that
>it has evolved to the next stage, one of birth and
>independent living. When a human dies it is only the
>physical body that dies in the eye of your only Lord,
>as that person lives on and evolves to a much better
>quality of existence. They are free to return home to
>the open arms of their loved ones who have passed

on before them, having learned what they were to learn in the physical world.

'But how do I know that what I see and what I hear is true?' I ask.

Jesus: Perhaps this explanation does not warm you, my Nina, but I have no other words. This explanation speaks the truth. I urge you to look beyond your question and to cease your railing against your only Lord. Look to forgiving yourself, my Nina. Look to living your life.

His words seep into me, become me.

Jesus: Now, drink your Cisk and let us talk about reality TV.

'Reality TV, Jesus?' I ask, confused.

He smiles, he winks. I feel my cheeks flush red, again.

Jesus: Tonight we will share many beers together and talk of *Come Dine with Me*.

Tmintax
~eighteen

Tilly Rose born 15 July 1974.
Tilly Rose died 2 December 2007.

I am sitting at the kitchen table, writing to Matt, trying to find the right words.

Tilly is flipping and spinning, around, around, around the room. She is being uncharacteristically friendly. The room is small and her spinning and flying are making the walls close in. I cannot look up, at her, her spinning makes my stomach turn.

'Some idiot decided that they'd drink a bottle of whisky and then kill themselves. Fine, each to their own and all that bull. And to give the idiot credit, well he did a spectacular job of it. He drank his whisky, drove through a red light at a zillion miles an hour and smashed right into me and me Ford Fiesta.'

She says.

'Oh my goodness,' I answer, not looking up from my paper, trying not to encourage her to talk. It is not that I do not like her; rather that I want to write my thoughts from my time tonight, with Jesus, while they are still there, here, in my head.

'Flamin' idiot he was. And I was on me way to meet Jen. I'd bought meself a new skinny top from one of those trendy retro internet companies. It said "I heart ET" on it. I'd shaved me bits, put on some make-up and twiddled me hair into looping curls. I'd made a right effort.'

Tilly says, spreading the sound around the room as she floats and spins. I do not ask about Jen. I know that I should, that I can offer no excuse why I do not, but I want to write, not talk.

'Of course, you had,' I say. I realise that I sound dismissive, uninterested, but my thoughts are for Matt. I am trying to focus on my words, to Matt.

'When that flamin' idiot, driving at a zillion miles an hour, came racing at –'

She stops talking mid-sentence; I know that she is testing me to see if I listen, if I care. I do not look up, I do not encourage her to continue speaking. I want her to go back upstairs, to bash, to bish around. I am beginning to like the noise.

'They said that I was dead. But I'm not, am I? I mean you can hear me so I'm not like really dead, just a little bit dead? You can see me? Nina! Nina!'

Tilly raises her voice; I look up from the kitchen table, from my paper. She throws a glass vase towards me.

it goes.

~s – m – ash.

at my feet.

My mother rushes into the kitchen, screaming and

shouting at Tilly.

'Ieqaf minn din ir-rabja, ja Ħares miġnun!'

~stop with all of your anger, you crazy ghost!

But before the sentence ends, Tilly has already flown, quickly,

up the sweeping staircase –

Tilly

Nina's sitting at the kitchen table and writing her soppy letters that she doesn't have the balls to send.

'Some idiot decided that they'd drink a bottle of whisky and then kill themselves. Fine, each to their own and all that bull. And to give the idiot credit, well he did a spectacular job of it. He drank his whisky, drove through a red light at a zillion miles an hour and smashed right into me and me Ford Fiesta,' I tell Nina.

'Oh my goodness,' she says, but I'm not really sure that she's listening to me and that really pisses me off.

I mean I listen to her moaning and sobbing. She annoys the hell out of me, but I still listen to her. I feel sorry for her lad Chris, he's like stuck with her most days. She's controlling him and not really letting him be dead. If I was him I'd have topped meself by now.

'Flamin' idiot he was. And I was on me way to meet Jen. I'd bought meself a new skinny top from one of those trendy retro internet companies. It said "I heart

225

ET" on it. I'd shaved me bits, put on some make-up and twiddled me hair into looping curls. I'd made a right effort.'

I want her to ask 'bout Jen. I mean I'm dying to tell someone 'bout Jen, but no one's interested. It's like all that doesn't even exist any more. It's like what's happened to me is so unimportant and all we have to do is focus on poor little Nina and her woe-is-friggin'-me bollocks. Melita, her mam, has already told me that I'm doing meself no favours. She tells me that I should help Nina. It's all 'bout Nina, friggin'-woe-is-me Nina. I mean, I just want to talk 'bout me a bit. Is that too much to ask for?

But it's always 'bout the living, always 'bout those who haven't passed and this particular living person seems to be wallowing in her own shit and not living at all. It pisses me off; in fact, that Nina makes me lose the will to live. I really am funny! If I was Nina I'd be happy and I'd live each day to the friggin' full. I'd be with the person I loved and not feeling sorry for meself in a crumbling old house in a too hot country. I mean, what the frig am I doing here? Why the frig am I in Malta? I'd never even heard of the place before.

'Of course, you had,' she says, but she's writing and not really really listening.

She's actually getting on me nerves now. Jesus told
me that I had to talk to her and that I had to help
Nina to find her friggin' way. Of course, Jesus didn't
use the word friggin' and I'm not even sure if I've
heard him swear. He's not really with it but he's not
old school boring. Everyone likes Jesus; he's like
the most famous of all the spirits, apart from John
Lennon. Melita told me that John Lennon hangs out
in TGI Friday's in St Julian's. I was shocked by that,
cos I didn't think he'd hang out in a place like TGI
Friday's. I thought he'd be kinda cooler and more in
a fancy cave kinda pizza place. I'd like to go and see
John Lennon, before I go back to Jen and when I'm not
trapped in this friggin' house. I'd get his autograph
and then sell it on eBay. Jesus keeps telling me stuff in
me head and I've met him just the once and I thought
that he was pretty cool. But now he's in me head all
the time, going on and on 'bout friggin' Nina and
how helping her will help me and it's like I've got no
privacy any more. I daren't even think rude stuff any
more in case he can hear me.

Anyway, it seems to me that Nina's found her way and
I'll tell Jesus that, when I next see him. He's been telling
everyone to talk to Nina and she's like Mrs Popular,
but the selfish cow hardly even listens to people. I'd
kill to be her. Jesus reckons that I've got to learn to

accept stuff and that I've got to let-friggin'-go. Anyway, it'd be nice if he could sort me out and help me find a way back to Jen. I'd kill for a pint, but I'm trapped in this friggin' house in Malta and it's doing me head in. Nina's all settled writing her letters and heaven forbid she actually stops the woe-is-friggin'-me act.

'When that flamin' idiot, driving at a zillion miles an hour, came racing at –' I stop talking a bit to see what Nina'll do. I'm like checking to see if she even cares that I haven't finished me sentence and then I realise that she really isn't listening. Nina carries on writing her letter to her bloke and I'm left thinking that this spirit world is just as rubbish as real life. I mean I was ignored most of me life and no one really got me cos I was a bit different. And then, just when things started going me way, just when I was actually making decisions and sorting out me head, when I'd met the lass who made me nipples tingle, well some drunken git goes and fucks it all up and now I'm stuck in this in-between kinda place.

'They said that I was dead. But I'm not, am I? I mean you can hear me so I'm not like really dead, just a little bit dead? You can see me? Nina! Nina!' I try to shout, but me voice never really gets loud. I want answers and her ignoring me is driving me insane. I want to know what's going on and I want to know when I'll wake up back near Jen. I mean I can't walk and I'm not like those other spirits who visit here. I'm just like I was, but floatier and spinnier. I reckon I must be in a coma or something. Oh God, I wonder if Mark and Jen are at me bedside. Friggin' hell.

Jesus came here a bit before Nina arrived and he told me that I'd have to help sort Nina out first, hinting like I'll get some sort of reward for a job done. It's all a bit screwed up. I just want to get back to me old new life, to Jen. It's been ages now, I'm not sure how long, but I think ages. So I'm supposed to talk to Nina whenever I can and I'm really really trying to make her not want to be a spirit, but I don't think I'm doing enough. I really hate it here. I hate that I float and I'm not like the other spirits. I'm so friggin' angry all the time. I want to go home and I'm pissed off that Nina won't hurry up and sort her friggin' head out.

Anyway, Nina's still not really listening to me and I'm pissed off, so I throw a vase at her head. It misses, mainly cos I didn't really want to hit her and anyway I've not quite figured out how to throw yet. So I'm doing all these girlie girl throws. The vase smashes down to the floor, near to Nina's feet and, of course, that makes her jump and she screams out at me and

her mam comes rushing into the kitchen and shouts at
me in foreign, but I'm off. I'm not waiting around to
get a bollocking off some crazy Maltese woman.

૨ઙ ૨ઙ ૨ઙ ૨ઙ ૨ઙ

So now I'm back upstairs. I'm smashing stuff just cos
I can and really hoping that Nina will come up. I'd
slit me wrists if I thought anyone would notice or if I
had skin that weren't see-through. I mean I'm like this
stereotypical flying ghost thing and it's all I can do to
stop meself from going wooooo wooooo hoooooooooo
all day. I don't get what's happening and I don't get
why I'm all airy fairy and not quite anything any
more. I'm friggin' pissed off with it all.

I try to smash a window but I can't cos I'm not strong
enough. The best I've managed is that crack in the
basement window, but I reckon Jesus had something
to do with that too. I mean I can't manage to crack any
of the other windows and it's like a bit convenient.
Anyway, I throw around a few books and I smash
another glass onto the floor. I'm getting a bit repetitive
and it's boring me to death. Nina doesn't come
upstairs. I mean, of course, she doesn't. She's so self-
absorbed and totally wet. She needs a good slapping.
I'd give anything to be her, but with me tits and not
her tits.

🐝 🐝 🐝 🐝 🐝

I go back downstairs. I mean I float downstairs. The whole floating thing is weird cos all of the other supposed-to-be-dead people walk. I know I get stuck on that but it's like that makes me think that maybe I'm not really proper dead, like I'm really in a coma and that's why I'm so friggin' angry and frustrated and stuff. So I drift and float and spin a bit downstairs and into the kitchen. Nina looks up at me. I mean she doesn't smile or anything, but she puts down her pen and she looks straight at me.

'Tilly,' she says. 'Do you have any regrets?'

I mean she just blurts it out and cos she's listening and cos I can't help meself and really want to talk, well I find meself dying to spill 'bout me life and I want to tell her everything that I can think of.

🐝 🐝 🐝 🐝 🐝

So I do. I mean I start talking and I tell her that I'm thirty-three and I tell her that I'm married. She looks a bit shocked so I explain me life and all the shitty decisions that I've made.

I tell her that I've always known that I was different. When all the other lasses were talking 'bout blokes and 'bout footballers who they fancied, I was thinking 'bout Jet from *Gladiators* and Anneka Rice in *Challenge Anneka*. I'd think 'bout them both when I was lying in bed and I'd touch meself and I'd like the feelings that I got. I tell Nina that if I tried to think 'bout blokes when I was lying touching meself, well it didn't work and me mind would wander back to Jet in her leotard and Anneka bending over in her shorts. I'd never tell anyone. I'd go for sleepovers at me best mate's house and I'd lie in bed with her wishing that she'd touch me and that we could try stuff. She never did and she started to fancy that bloke from the film *Cocktail*. Friggin' hell I can't even remember his name any more.

I tell Nina that I used to think that there was something wrong with me head, so I'd try to make it better. I tell her that I went out with blokes. I'd let them touch me and I'd let them do more than most other lasses would, cos it didn't matter really. When lads did stuff to me I just switched off from it all. So I got a bit of a reputation for meself around the Estate and I probably didn't help matters when I started charging the lads on me Estate a quid for a wank; I must have been 'bout fifteen.

'Is that what you regret?' Nina asks and her listening shocks me.

I mean, I know that I'm talking to her and stuff, but in
the days that she's been here she's mainly screamed
at me or ignored me. I don't even know if anyone has
ever listened to me before, not really and I like it. I
mean I like that she's interested.

I think 'bout the quids that I got for wanking off lads.
They'd be a queue some nights. But I don't think that
I regret it, I mean it was a growing-up thing. We used
the bedroom of Dave, a lad off the Estate. He'd take
a 10p cut of me money and I'd give him a free go at
the end of the night. But then one day there was some
spunk on his bed and his mam freaked. He told her
all 'bout what I did and she went bombing round
to me mam. Me mam was so shamed, but I don't
really regret it, not really really. I mean I felt bad for
being found out and for making me mam shamed,
but nothing really happened. Me mam was too busy
shagging her latest bloke and telling me that he was
me new uncle, which meant she was shagging her
brother. I mean it was all a bit sick and really she
couldn't complain 'bout me wanking off a few lads.
I was getting paid for it unlike her and her shagging
any bloke that gave her a bit of attention. So, after
'bout a week me mam got over the shame and I just
started doing the wanking in Simo's place instead cos
his mam and dad worked nights.

'Oh Tilly,' Nina says. 'What do you regret then?'

I look at Nina's face and she looks sad. I mean I've never told anyone 'bout the whole wanking business and suddenly I find meself thinking 'bout me mam and me childhood and wishing that I'd told me mam how crap she was. I mean she never protected me or really bothered with me. She was too busy shagging blokes and hoping they'd turn into princes. Bugger the kissing a frog thing, Me mam used to get right in there on the first night.

'Tilly?' Nina says me name and then pauses. 'Are you all right?'

I look at her and I see that she's worried. It throws me. It makes me spin around and around on the spot at some stupid speed and we're in the kitchen and I keep banging me feet on the ceiling. But I can't help meself from being bothered that she's actually caring a bit. I find meself thinking that the lass is a bit like me and I suddenly want to help her. I mean I really really want to help her. So I pull meself together, stop me spinning and I tell Nina the thing that I regret the most. I tell her that when I was twenty I agreed to marry a lad off the Estate.

🐎 🐎 🐎 🐎 🐎

I tell her that the lad was called Mark and that I'd wanked him when I was younger and then when I was nineteen, I started seeing him at weekends. There was naught sexy in it. We'd meet in The Rocket, on the corner of Smithy Lane, and have a couple of pints together. He was me mate. I tell Nina the truth, I tell her that I used to go into The Rocket cos I fancied Julie who worked behind the bar. I tell her that one night I'd had a few too many pints and I was having a piss in the ladies. Julie came in and, well I guess it was the beer, but she came right up close to me. She was saying that I had smudged me mascara and she was all giggly. Anyway, I got the whole thing wrong and I mean really really wrong. I thought she fancied me too and I tried to snog her, full on with me tongue and then she got really pissed off with me. She went back into the bar and started telling everyone that I was a lezza. So that night I shagged Mark under the slide in the kiddies' park and I made sure that enough people knew 'bout it and then me and Mark started seeing each other proper.

I stop talking and look at Nina. She's sitting at the kitchen table with tears streaming down her face and dripping onto her letter.

'You OK pet?' I ask.

Nina nods.

So I keep talking. I tell Nina that 'bout a year later, I found out that I was pregnant and how Mark and me got married and moved into his mam's house on the Estate. I tell her that I was happy to get out of me mam's house cos she'd moved in a right tosser who'd kick her and me around when he felt like it and he was a right dirty bastard. He'd come into me room at night and I'd wake up with him wanking on me face. So I know that marrying Mark was me escape and he was a nice bloke; his mam was all right too.

I tell Nina that I think I pretended that I was happy and after Megan was born, I'd let Mark shag me every now and then. I went through the motions of living a normal life and being a normal person. Everyone thought that I was a miserable cow and I was. I know that I was and I must have been a friggin' nightmare to live with. I mean I hated me life, it was like I was living someone else's life, not mine and although I tried, well I never felt excited 'bout anything. I was like a ghost but, I tell her, I love me Meg, cos she's right bright as a button and the best thing I've ever done.

'You have a daughter?' Nina asks.

'Meg's eleven, she's with her dad,' I say.

Nina looks to the floor and I don't know whether or not to continue at first. I can see that she's thinking 'bout her Molly and I can feel right deep twists in me gut and I know they're from her wanting to be with her kid. I stay silent for a couple of minutes and then Nina looks up at me. Her eyes are full of tears but her thoughts are pleading with me to carry on, so I do.

I tell her that a few months ago, well a few months before I ended up here, I'd sorted meself out with a job and was finding me feet. I was working in an old people's home. I was mainly wiping arses, but I also got to sit and talk with the old people. I was finding me again and I was pretty good at making them feel happy. So I tell her that I reckon that I'm good at listening cos I've done it for years. But when I was at work the old people would be like really happy to see me.

🐝 🐝 🐝 🐝 🐝

So I tell Nina that Jen started working there the same day as me. She was a couple of years younger than me and right away, on the first day, she said that she was a lesbian. It's funny cos when she said it, I mean when she said the words and was kinda proud of it like this is who I am and if you don't like it then piss off, well I knew that I was too. I mean I knew that I was a lesbian. I knew that I wanted to say those words and that I wanted to be proud of who I really was. I went out with Jen after work on that first day. We went for a pint around the corner from the old people's home. I went for a piss and she came in to the toilet and we snogged. I don't think I've ever been so turned on, I nearly came in me knickers just from her snogging me. We stayed in the toilet for twenty minutes, then I went home to Mark and I pretended like nothing was going on. I couldn't sleep that night cos I was so alive. I felt like I could run around the block like a million billion times. I wanted to jump up and down and I wanted to go back to that toilet and do it all again.

I tell Nina that the next day I felt sick. I was going to cancel work. I thought that I'd get there and Jen would have told everyone I was a lesbian and I'd get sacked or something. But I got to work and everything was great, I mean there was no awkward shit or anything. After work, well we went back to Jen's flat and we shagged. I did things and I felt things that I'd never known before. It was like something had been switched on inside of me and I knew that me whole life was going to be different.

I want to tell Nina all the stuff we'd done, like to go into detail but not to shock her, just cos this is the first time I've ever even said the words. I mean, I had all this stuff happening and I had to keep it a secret. It's like there's a whole big most important part to me that people don't even know 'bout.

'And what about Mark and Megan?' Nina asks.

I stop talking and am kinda drifting, doing twirls and looping stuff a bit too close to the ceiling. The kitchen's a bit too small for all me floating shit. I try to control meself and get as near to the ground as possible.

So I tell Nina that I was going to leave Mark and Meg. I explain that things were happening with Jen and the more time I spent with her, well the more I knew that I wanted to live with her and be in a proper couple. I'd talked to Jen 'bout it all and we were sorting it all out. I was looking forward to starting to live a bit, for me. I tell Nina that I know that I was having an affair and that was wrong, but that I don't regret that cos being with Jen made me feel normal. I belonged with her and when I wasn't with her I felt like I wasn't me.

Nina nods, I can see that she's thinking 'bout her and her bloke. I can see she's thinking 'bout the two of them starkers in bed.

Then she asks, 'So what do you regret?'

'I regret that I didn't live a life and that I wasn't true to me, cos if I'm dead, then I'm going to be for a long time,' I tell her.

'You would have left Mark earlier and your daughter?' Nina asks me, even though I've already said the answer.

'I would have been true to me heart and stopped feeling so friggin' guilty all the time. I would have lived. I would have accepted that I wasn't perfect and that I'd screwed up. I would have understood that I'd made shit loads of mistakes. But I would have let meself be loved and I would have made the most of me time living.'

Nina bows her head again.

'Nina, do you love your bloke?' I ask.

'More than I can tell you,' Nina answers and I see into her hazel eyes.

I see that she is hurting herself and I wish that I could make her better. I mean I really really wish that I couldn't see just how really bust she is and see all the dark stuff that's causing her shit.

🙞 🙞 🙞 🙞 🙞

I float away and out the room. I feel weak and like I

would break if the wind blew on me. And then I hear
Jesus saying me name.

And I hear him thank me –

Dsatax

~nineteen

Malta's top 5: *About Malta*

❋ 1. Religion
The island of Malta is a mere 17 miles long, a
mere 9 miles wide, yet has a landscape that hosts
over 300 churches and wayside chapels. Faith
and religion are swarming at the very heart of the
Maltese islands.

'Nina, do you love your bloke?'

Tilly asks me.

'More than I can tell you,' I answer.

My thoughts turn to Matt. I ache. Tilly floats from the kitchen, smoothly, gently, elegantly.

I smile.

◎

~~Matt,~~

~~I can't find the words.~~

~~I can't formulate all that I want to say to you and all that is happening. My head is swimming with messages, with signals and with phrases that are repeated over and over again.~~

~~All spirits travel here to heal, to this tiny island rising out of the Mediterranean Sea. They are tiny lights that sparkle and speckle in coloured patterns through the sky. They are dotted over the horizon, each with a story to tell, each with a longing to fulfil.~~

~~I know that when I die I will come here. When I die.~~

~~When?~~

◎

I am at the kitchen table, still, trying to formulate my thoughts into a letter to Matt. I am having difficulty focusing.

I start, I stop.

I cross out the words with a perfectly straight line. I screw the paper into a tight ball and throw it to the tiled floor.

My mother walks in, past me and towards the backdoor. She stands with her back to me, staring through the window in the door, staring out into the backyard.

'Ma baqax lariṅġ.'

~there are no more oranges.

She says to me, I think.

'Tilly has a daughter and a husband,' I say.

My mother turns, her eyes are filled with sadness.

'She was going to leave them, for another woman,' I say.

My mother nods.

'She regrets that she didn't live a life where she was true to herself, without guilt; her death takes her away from love,' I say.

My mother nods, again. I am speaking too quickly, not allowing her words, her judgement, her opinion.

'I love Matt,' I say. 'I love him truly.'

'Qalbi. Aħna kollha nafu, kollha naraw.'

~my heart. We all know, we all see.

My mother smiles, weakly.

'I miss him, I miss my Molly,' I say.

'They miss you too.'

My mother says.

'Have you seen them?' I ask.

'Taqsamli qalbi.'

~it breaks my heart.

My mother says.

I do not speak.

My tears mark my skin, my cheeks.

   I long, for my husband, for my daughter –

Tilly

I think it's a few hours since I talked to Nina. I've been upstairs the whole time, feeling like I want to sob me heart out. I feel different. I mean I don't really feel angry, it's like I'm full of sad and I'm full of regret, but it's not like straightforward. I mean I know what I am and that I'm a lesbian but then I have me Meg and I wouldn't change that for anything.

I'm thinking 'bout Jen when Jesus appears in front of me. He's wearing an "I Love London" T-shirt with baggy skater jeans and heelies. I swear he looks like he's trying to be a student but he's cool. I mean not as cool as John Lennon, but still he's like such a sound bloke.

Jesus: I'm here to thank you, my Tilly.

He says straight into me head, so there are no words floating around the house.

Jesus: You were chosen to stay close to my Nina. I saw the goodness inside of you. And now you have gained energy from the good deeds that you are doing. You are helping her, my Tilly.

'Energy? What's that mean?' I ask him, feeling like I should be sitting at his feet and not floating and spinning over his head like a friggin' loon.

> **Jesus:** Your physical being has died; accept that your body has gone.

He's staring at me all the time and I know he wants me to stay still, but I'm out of control.

> **Jesus:** Your bitterness, your anger are preventing your journey. You should be taking your love and your knowledge and your memories from earth. You should be holding them close to you and journeying forward. Do not fear this death, my Tilly.

I'm not really sure what to say. I mean he's not talking nonsense or anything. I mean I suppose he makes sense. I'm finding meself spinning and flipping in the air, like I'm losing control of it all.

> **Jesus:** I know that you were happy when you were with Jen. But I also know that your anger, your negativity and your confusion from your earth life have carried with you in your passing. You are a lost spirit, my Tilly. You are trying to communicate, not accepting your change from physical to spiritual. You must begin to accept, to let go of all that you resent

and regret.

'But I was just starting to live, Jesus. It's not even like I can be near them any more. It's shit. Nina's next to her mam and Geordie and Elena are back together. It's not even like I'm allowed to see Jen and me Meg. I don't even know if I'm dead. I mean look at me. I'm not like the others. I'm this stupid woo hooooo ghost thing,' I say, flipping and spinning around the broken room.

Jesus: I am protecting your family and your love, keeping you from them.

I try to stop me spinning but I'm getting madder all the time.

Jesus: I fear that you would scare your child, your love, that you would cause injury in your need to be physical.

'I would never hurt me Meg or Jen,' I try to shout out the words but I'm spinning backwards and feel like I'm going to pop in anger.

Jesus: You need to let go of your earth life, my Tilly.

He says into me head and he's all calm and soothing and this helps me and I stop me spinning.

Jesus: This state of being is not natural.

'What do you mean? Am I dead or not?' I ask.

Jesus: Your body is dead, my Tilly. Your soul is angry, but it must return to God. When you mature, when you accept, then you will grow. You will be.

He's talking in riddles. I mean I don't even know if I believe in God. I mean I think I've been to church a couple of times but it's not like I pray or any stuff like that.

Jesus: In helping my Nina, in guiding, you are experiencing purification. It is not a selfless act that I expect of you, there will be rewards.

He continues but I still don't understand. I mean he's using big words and it's all a bit much to take in.

'I really don't get it,' I tell Jesus. 'I mean, I really don't understand what you're telling me. It's like you're talking foreign.'

Jesus: Give it time, give it time, my Tilly.

Jesus smiles.

Jesus: Now, my Tilly, what do you remember of reality TV shows?

૨ૐ ૨ૐ ૨ૐ ૨ૐ ૨ૐ

So I talk to Jesus 'bout Simon Cowell and 'bout reality TV. Jesus listens carefully and he asks questions that I don't always understand. I like him. He's a funny bloke and he smells of pubs, but some of the words that he uses are far too long and right difficult.

🐝 🐝 🐝 🐝 🐝

A bit later he asks me if I'd like to talk 'bout me dying and what's going to happen to me next. I nod and say that I would. He explains.

> **Jesus:** My Nina can see you. She is gifted, just as my Christopher was gifted. She sees through to our dimension, but not all humans can.

'Can Jen?' I ask.

> **Jesus:** No. But she is eager to reconnect with you.

'I don't understand,' I tell him.

> **Jesus:** We offer proof of an afterlife, which can offer an ease of emotion for grieving loved ones. In all of your anger and frustration, you have not considered the grief, the loss of those in the human world. Their longing, their inability to accept could be eased by you. Your selfishness is preventing your own growth and the peace of your loved one, of Jen.

'Jen –' I stop. I want to cry. I start back flipping and looping. I am out of control.

> **Jesus:** Calm yourself, my Tilly. You must accept the guise of your body. You are lost, my Tilly. Your

unfinished business on earth is preventing your progression.

'What should I do? Tell me,' I shout as I flip.

Jesus: I will take you to Martin. We will meet Jen there. But my Tilly, I must warn you that I will not let you frighten her.

Jesus looks older, more mature as he shakes his right, thin index finger at me.

'Take me to Martin. Please.'

᚛᚛ ᚛᚛ ᚛᚛ ᚛᚛ ᚛᚛

As I say those words, me feet touch the ground and I can walk. It's like friggin' amazing to have me feet on the floor again. I look at me skin and I'm still see-through but I don't care cos I have me feet working. Jesus holds out his hand and together we walk through the walls of Nina's mam's house and through the earth.

᚛᚛ ᚛᚛ ᚛᚛ ᚛᚛ ᚛᚛

Jesus and me are standing on the opposite side of the main road that passes through the village. The road's busy with loads of cars parking on double yellows and loads of others looking for somewhere to stop. I recognise the place straight away and I know that I'm

'bout twenty minutes from Mark's mam's house. Jesus
points at the shop opposite. It's called Crystal Zone
and has a huge fake gold Buddha in the window. I
remember me mam going there when I was a kid. She
bought me a bag of chips and said to wait outside
the shop, but it was raining and one of the lasses
told me to step inside. Then me mam started going
every week and so I'd sit with me chips and talk to
a lass called Alison who worked behind the counter.
The place hasn't changed much. I mean it's probably
had a paint job and tarting up, stuff like that, but
seeing as I don't know how long I've been dead and
shit like that, well it's probably a bit better looking
than I remember it. Jesus stops his pointing and he
doesn't say anything else, cos I guess he's reading me
memories and he knows that I know why we've come
to see Martin.

Martin's a psychic and some people think he's a bit
dark and stuff. He talks to dead people. He's really
well known around the Estate and loads of the lasses
used to go to him for readings. I mean me mam was
practically addicted to the bloke. He was pretty cheap
and right accurate. He has a shop that sells mainly
crystals and mini Buddhas, then a couple of rooms out
back for treatments and readings. The shop always
smelled of ciggie smoke cos loads of lasses from the

Estate used to go there for a fag and a chat. Martin
was right popular, but he always used to creep me out
a bit. Me mam stopped going cos some other lass from
the Estate said Martin put his hand up her top and
squeezed her tits.

The next thing I know, I feel Jesus getting hold of
me hand and I'm walking through a wall, into a box
of a room. Jesus goes like within a minute, saying
something 'bout him not wanting to be seen during
treatment but I'm sure it's something to do with
Martin and him having a falling out. I say friggin'
hell and then Jesus is gone. The room's pretty basic
with a couple of sofas that have arse imprints in them
and there's a coffee table with a pack of tarot cards,
another pack of playing cards, a squashed packet of
ciggies and an ashtray that's right full. I would kill for
a ciggie. I'm not sure what goes on in here, but there's
naught to distract me, naught to fiddle with and
naught to smash. I don't know what I'm supposed to
do, so I focus on me feet and wonder if I should have
put some shoes on.

🐎 🐎 🐎 🐎 🐎

The door opens and an old man walks in, he's right
small and skinny and dressed in a brown suit. He
tips his flat cap to me and smiles; then he moves

over beside me and looks towards the door. I'm a bit freaked by him cos he's like small and doesn't speak. I look at the door too and in walk Martin and Jen.

I rush over to Jen and I try to hug her and I try to snog her a bit and she carries on walking. I'm like clinging to her as Martin tells her to take a seat on the sofa. I let go and she sits on the edge, her knees are tight shut, like right close together and her hands are locked and resting on her knees. I reckon she's shaking and she looks like she's lost loads of weight and she looks like she's 'bout to burst into tears. I sit down right close next to her on the sofa.

Martin starts talking and already he's got his hand on her knee. I try to push it off and then he stares right at me. I'm so creeped out. The bastard can see me, but he's not saying anything 'bout it to Jen.

'I can tell you're scared pet and I'm sure that it'll be a canny reading,' he tells Jen. 'Now I want you to shuffle these cards.' He hands her the pack of tarot.

Jen takes them and I can see that she's shaking even more. I put me arm around her and try to pull her close to me but I've got no strength and it's like she doesn't even know I'm there. I'm trying and trying but I'm just not strong enough. Then I try to climb on top of her and try to kinda bounce a bit so that she sees or feels me, but there's no reaction from her at all. I'm so pissed off.

Then Martin starts asking her 'bout how she's been since her girlfriend died and Jen starts crying. I know that Jen's like not really sure how he knows that she's a lesbian and how he knows 'bout me dying. Then the bastard Martin starts describing me to her. He's like saying that I had blonde curly hair and brown eyes. He says something 'bout me having a kid and being married. And I'm thinking he's a cheeky bastard cos he knew me and me mam right well and he clearly recognises me. I bet me mam's been in here too telling him all kinds of shit 'bout me.

So I say to Martin, 'Me name's Tilly, you bastard.'

Then Martin tells her that Tilly is right next to her and Jen kinda jumps a bit. I mean he doesn't tell her that I've been practically jumping up and down on her lap or that I'm like all over her, but Jen's like totally freaked out by it all. So Martin puts both his hands on Jen's knees and I'm trying to push his hands off me lass's knees and I'm getting angrier and angrier. I mean the bastard's got no right to be touching me lass and it's pissing me off that she's not even trying to see me. I hate being ignored. I friggin' hate being ignored. Then the cards start flying around the room and I know that I've really fucked up when Jen starts screaming. I mean I know that it's really really shitty for her but I can't control me emotions. Then I'm floating off the sofa and I start doing back flips again and then I'm spinning in the air and I can't get me feet to touch the ground and it's all out of control.

So Martin tells the old man to take me out the room and the next thing I know me arse is being pushed out through the wall and I'm doing a loopy loop in Melita's upstairs back in friggin' Malta. I look down and I see Jesus and Nina.

Jesus: That went well, my Tilly.

Jesus holds out his hand to me –

Għoxrin

~twenty

My girlfriend went to Malta
and all I got was
this lousy sticker

I am in the chair, in my mother's parlour. Jesus appears in front of me.

Jesus: My Nina, help me please.

He points a long thin finger up, to the ceiling. His face is serious, ghostly.

He rushes to, up, the sweeping staircase. I hurry after him, bare feet, scared.

I am just in time.

◎

I see Tilly emerging head first, spinning, through the wall and into my sister Sandra's bedroom. She twirls at a speed that I have never seen before. I look to the wall, to where she has materialised from, through. I see a wrinkled hand sticking through into the room. I move towards the hand, it retracts, is gone.

Tilly slows, into a continuous looping loop. She looks down, sees me, sees Jesus.

Jesus: That went well, my Tilly.

Then he holds out his hand to try to steady her to a smooth float.

'Oh Tilly,' I say, crying for her.

Tilly stares, glares at us.

'Leave me the fuck alone.'

She says.

I look to Jesus, he nods, lets go of Tilly's hand sending her twisting in frenzy, then he walks through the wall. I turn and walk past my sister's doll's house and out from the bedroom, slowly, looking back to see Tilly flipping into a fury.

I walk, slowly, down the stairs. I hear Tilly's feeble screams.

> I hear glass.
>
> ~s – m – ash.
>
> ~b – ash.
>
> to the floor.

I do not turn back, I do not return to talk to her. I know that she will emerge, again, eventually.

Wieħed u għoxrin

~twenty-one

Malta's top 5: *Churches and Cathedrals*

✸ **1. St John's Co-Cathedral**
Designed by Gerolamo Cassarthe, the cathedral's interior offers spectacular splendour.

✸ **2. St Paul's Collegiate Church, Rabat**
Built upon and to the left of St Paul's Grotto, where St Paul was shipwrecked and the Church of Malta was born.

✸ **3. The Parish Church of Mellieħa**
Dedicated to the birth of Our Lady, a hidden gem.

✸ 4. ~~**Ta' Pinu Basilica**~~, ~~**Gozo**~~ Il-Madonna tal-għar.
~~Thousands travel here, hoping that Our Lady of Ta' Pinu will heal them.~~

✸ **5. The Rotunda of St Marija Assunta, Mosta**
A magnificent dome, said to be third largest in Europe…

Caroline Smailes

Another night has passed, another night that saw me curled in my mother's chair, in my mother's parlour. My mother wakes me. I twist my shoulders and arch my sides, attempting to bend my body out from the curl and back into shape.

'Listen, qalbi, your own bed is better.'

My mother says, her eyes full of concern.

~my heart.

'No Mama, here is better,' I say. 'There are too many ghosts in my bedroom.'

My mother smiles, turns and walks back into the kitchen.

'Come eat,' she shouts.

◎

My guidebook tells me that the number three church, in the top five churches on the island, is in Mellieħa. My guidebook tells me that Mellieħa Bay is a family resort, popular during the summer months. I am told that a visit to the sandy strip that decorates the bay is a must for all families.

Christopher is not with me, today. I will travel by yellow bus, again.

◎

I dismount in the village of Mellieħa, the journey has seemed longer, today. I am restless, fidgety, wanting to be in the open. The bus pulls away and I glance down the steep slope. The view catches my breath. My island is beautiful.

I think to the hotels and the sandy strip that so many tourists have worshipped. I will see them, later, from a higher view. For now, I do not search for the number three church, instead I seek the hidden, the almost secret Il-Madonna tal-għar.

~Our Lady of the Grotto.

◎

I flip-flop.

~fl – ip.

~fl – op.

~fl – ip.

~fl – op.

past the sign that points, WORLD WAR II SHELTERS.

My Lord's smile is burning down, yet merciful Mother Nature sends a cool breeze to relieve me. The wind sweeps my cotton dress around the shape of my thighs.

I turn.

Something makes me turn, a flash of light within my vision.

>I flip-flop.

>*~fl – ip.*

>*~fl – op.*

>*~fl – ip.*

>*~f l – op.*

>around a corner, down steps, down and down.

I stop, the main road is busy, with swirling dust, with noise, with buses, with vans, with cars with horns that bark. I turn, quickly and I see that still she is following me. I am not afraid. I cross the road; traffic stops, for me.

◎

I flip-flop down more steps, down, down, down to the chapel secreted within the rock. I grab the metal handrail, feeling the island steady me, guide me, cover me. Caper trees are overgrown, curling onto the steps, decorating, bowing with the slight breeze. They have no smell; they taste of Malta.

◎

The metal handrail is cold, wet without moisture. The

steps are patterned with a fading tile, of wear, of age.

I stop.

I look down the remaining steps, into the darkness of the cave. I think of all those who have searched into this cave.

I flip-flop down the remaining steps.

~fl – ip.

~fl – op.

~fl – ip.

~fl – op.

and each – fl, each – ip, each – fl, each – op, they echo and rebound.

I am alone, at the entrance.

The walls of the cave lean in, enclose, engulf, enfold a darkness. Before me, a small aisle leads, invites into the cave, to a statue of Our Lady. She is surrounded by a railing that is covered in trays of candles, the candles flicker, give needed light, unite. The wooden benches frame the aisle, they are all empty.

I enter into the dark cave that is Il-Madonna tal-għar.

~Our Lady of the Grotto.

I do not feel welcome, I am filled with an anxiety that I barely recognise.

This place is said to be of miracles. My family would talk of here in hushed tones but I heard tales of family members who had experienced miracles. My cousin once told me of her cousin's cousin who had tried for a baby for sixteen years. The woman had suffered ten miscarriages and thought that she was sinful in her being. She had taken a Babygro, a desperate gift to here, to Our Lady, and within the year a healthy child was born. It is said that those who bestow with goodness will be rewarded.

As I flip-flop in, I am covered in the sense of ending, of loss. I feel grief seeping from the rock, climbing onto my skin. My throat aches; I fear that I will burst into desperate sobs.

◎

The cave is dark. The stone walls are decorated in printouts of photographs, of faces, of words. They have been placed into plastic wallets for protection from the dampness that spills out from the rock. Each tells a story, speaks with desperation of last chances, of needing miracles, of hope. I flip-flop around the cave, avoiding the central aisle. I read the words that tell of children who need our prayers, the words tell of prolonged life, battles with illness, lost children, miracle births, too short lives.

I am alone in the cave.

I am cold in my bones, I shiver shiver, shiver shiver. I miss the heat, I miss the sunshine on my now pale skin.

I see the Babygros, the knitted shawls, the first teddy bear that was never held. My eyes fix on the Babygros, covered in plastic for protection, stuck to the wall, nailed to the wall. I look at, I read a white serviette, scribbled onto it there is the name of a four-year-old British girl who has been lost for almost a year.

My eyes flick to a photograph, a girl, her head is bald, she is said to be nine in the photograph. She is ill, a form of leukaemia, her family came to offer prayer to Our Lady. There are updates, added in pen below her photograph.

I read the updates.

> still ill,
>
> still ill,
>
> hanging on,
>
> slightly better,

treatment working,

death.

The positives are prolonged life, the negative death.

My stomach begins to churn. My eyes search, absorb, weep.

◎

We cannot run from death. We blossom, we wither.

◎

I move to Our Lady.

A railing surrounds the statue; she is white, lacking the usual or even expected ornate luxury that is seen elsewhere on the island. She is chipped, flaking, weathered. Trays hold candles in red pots, the candles flicker; I search for a candle to light. I am unsure if this is from habit, or need, but there are none.

There are no spare candles.

I stand before Our Lady. I feel that my prayers cannot be heard.

◎

I hear her behind me; I turn, a flash of white.

She curves to my ear, cold breath blowing onto me. I do

not move, yet I am not afraid.

'Death must come to us all; dear Nina. She cannot bring the dead back to life. The miracle is often in the prolonging, the being. You do not see it all.'

She whispers the words; I move, I blink, a split second.

She is gone.

◎

As I walk the stairs, I turn and bow my head to Il-Madonna tal-għar. I will cross out Ta' Pinu Basilica in Gozo from number four in the top five churches on the island, I will write in its place Il-Madonna tal-għar, Mellieħa. I walk back into the sunshine. The steps are difficult; I am left breathless as I reach the top.

◎

I cross the road without looking, caring.

◎

I walk through the courtyard, under the arch; I hear the church bell toll.

I flip, I flop.

~fl – ip.

~fl – op.

271

~fl – ip.

~fl – op.

over a road that slopes, past a graveyard, that is full.

I search, for the café, our café.

◎

The sun shines; my only Lord's smile warms me, today.

I see my café, perched on the edge.

◎

I used to tell Christopher about a special place, about the café that I would visit with my mother, after school. I would say that we would sit near to the window; we would talk and look down onto the bay of Mellieħa.

There was a time when my mother would take me to here, to eat. We would come when school ended, without my sisters and without my father. It would be our place, somewhere for us to escape and talk. My mother would share so much with me about her family, the extended family, about my father and about neighbours. I would sip my Kinnie through a straw and listen, wide-eyed, at all the secrets that my mother had gathered. We would share ftira biż-żejt and qagħaq tal-għasel.

~Kinnie is a distinctive tasting drink. It is

golden in colour, prepared from bitter oranges
and a selection of fragrant herbs.

~ftira biż-żejt is a Maltese flat bread seasoned
with salt, with peppers, with tomatoes, with
capers, with olives, with olive oil.

~qagħaq tal-għasel is a pastry ring, filled with
a sweet honey mix.

Today, I sit at the table nearest to the window. The wind
lashes at the plastic trimmings that decorate the outside.
I stare out, over the green slope and down to the hotels,
the sandy strip, the blue sea. There are new hotels; the
landscape has changed much in so few years.

Old sits next to new; they do not blend.

◎

The island has moved forward, without me. A whisper of
a cloud is beginning to decorate the blue sky; the wind
is whipping the sea into waves. I look down onto the
bay and I remember late afternoons, under parasols, my
sisters chatting, my cousins singing, laughing, fighting
over who would sit on a cool box containing watermelon
and a rusting knife.

I smile.

◎

The owner appears, the same, unchanged, plump, groomed black hair that is stacked high into a beehive. Her nails are red, her clothes covered in a layer of flour. A string of pearls clings, tight, into the folds of her neck.

I order ftira biż-żejt and qagħaq tal-għasel. I order a can of Kinnie.

The owner scribbles onto a pad, does not look into my eyes and then turns, scurries, into her kitchen.

And then I see her, standing on the outer side of the doorway. She has followed me from the cave.

I watch her pass through the door, moving towards me. She comes to my table, stands beside the chair. She is dressed in a white smock, more Jesus like than Jesus, yet clearly female, young, perhaps sixteen, seventeen, radiant. Her hair is an unusual blonde, sun bleached but sparkling. She is pure, divine. She clasps her Rosary beads within a clenched hand and, before me, in the rhythm of the Hail Marys she recites in sets of ten.

I speak, 'Nista' nara l-ispirti. Meta nagħlaq għajnejja nisma' l-vuċijiet tagħhom.'

~I can see spirits. When I close my eyes I hear

their voices.

'I see you too, dear Nina.'

She whispers and then she lowers, elegantly, into the chair beside me.

She has no wings.

◎

The owner reappears.

She leans over the spirit beside me, not asking what food she would like and places my order onto the table.

I smile, the familiar ftira biż-żejt, the mouth watering qagħaq tal-għasel.

The owner takes a cold can of Kinnie from her pocket, opens it and places a stripy straw into the liquid.

I smile.

'Melita told me that you would come.'

The owner speaks in English then she winks at me, smiles at the spirit, hands the cold Kinnie to me and scurries back to her kitchen. Music begins to play, instrumental 1980s hits, taking me back, comforting.

◎

'Who are you?' I ask.

'My name is Flavia Bellini.'

The spirit speaks with a voice, pure, sweet, honey.

I stare at the food in front of me. The smells are rich; they transport me back to happier times, to times of safety, of belonging.

'Eat. I will tell you my story, as you chew.'

Flavia tells me.

I do as I am told. I break the ftira into a smaller mouthful, I lift the food to my lips.

I feel myself floating, drifting –

Flavia

For the entire day, I have been following Melita's youngest daughter and finally it is in safe hands to approach her. She rests in a café that is seeping memories.

Dear Nina is full of hunger and the rich foods in front of her are tempting her into a sheltered state and so I tell her, 'Eat. I will tell you my story, as you chew.' And so, as dear Nina eats, I speak the words that I have been chosen to bestow.

✻ ✻ ✻ ✻ ✻

I begin.

✻ ✻ ✻ ✻ ✻

I say, 'Mine is a story that combines with that of the most honourable of women to have ever lived. I am blessed. I have been watching you, dear Nina. I see your sadness, I know of your sacrifice and of your loss. I have been watching you from afar and wondering when you will let your son be free to experience his own death and to grow within this spirit-filled world. Jesus has told me, he spoke his words into my mind, that I must share with you my story. I hope that you can listen to each word and that Our Lady will honour you with Her strength.'

I say, 'We all know of Her story, but when I speak the words out loud I am covered in a sense of honour that She should have chosen me, that She should have chosen to appear before me. I know that my life has been blessed.'

I say, 'I need to go to the beginning, to the moment when once there was Mary who was a normal fifteen-year-old girl facing adolescence and all the problems that this brings. As if adolescence was not enough, Mary was engaged to a man named Joseph. I do not know if you know, but he was much older than She was. In fact, I think that he was in his fifties, yet the Bible does not say much about him. Mary and Joseph were in a relationship, seeing each other I believe is the term and, of course, extra-marital relations were a big no no. In fact, it was the way that if a woman was caught either in the act, or bearing evidence of it, then she would be stoned to death by the village authorities.'

❋ ❋ ❋ ❋ ❋

I say, 'It is said that Mary was a God-fearing young
lady. She obeyed the Jewish tradition and prayed
constantly. One fine day, while She was praying, an
angel, Gabriel, manifested himself to Mary. Do you
know that angels have no gender? Many consider
Gabriel to be a he although it isn't rare to find Gabriel
referred to as a she. I am often fascinated by this.
He announced to Mary that She would bear a child
and call him Jesus. He told Her that Jesus would
save humankind and that She would squash evil. Of
course, Mary was very frightened. Would not you be?
I would have run a mile from the angel and feared
for my sanity. But instead of running that mile, Mary
said, "Let God's will be done."'

❋ ❋ ❋ ❋ ❋

I say, 'Mary was mature and Her faith was strong.
Needless to say, this resulted in Her being pregnant
and when Joseph learned of this, he was furious. I
mean, what kind of an excuse was She giving to him,
"An angel appeared and I am now pregnant. Please
forgive me." Yet, Joseph loved Mary and did not
wish Her any harm and so he left quietly. Then, and
this is the bit that I like, while he slept in a field, an
angel appeared and told him that Mary had not had

relations with another man and that She was carrying the Son of God. Joseph was told that he was chosen to be Jesus' adoptive Earth father. And so, Joseph went back to Mary and I am sure that you know of the nativity story.'

✻ ✻ ✻ ✻ ✻

I say, 'Jesus can fill in the blanks on all that you are missing from his life, on all that was not fabricated and all that was not documented. He drinks beer in Larry's bar. I think that I have seen your son with him, or rather I have seen from a distance.'

✻ ✻ ✻ ✻ ✻

I say, 'And so Jesus, with thanks to Mary and Joseph, had a normal but very humble childhood. He would help his father and so he learned the trade of a carpenter. Yet, when he reached and passed the age of thirty, then he took up his real mission. It is said that Joseph had died earlier. He was old, remember? And when Joseph died, it is said that Jesus cried because he was human and he missed his Earth father. Jesus must have known that Joseph was safe on the Other Side. I have not met with Jesus over here and doubt that I will. I have seen him and he has smiled at me, but he has not invited me to share beer with him. He speaks to me, inside of my head and if I am honest with you,

I must say that I long to sip beer with him. I have much that is unanswered in my life. It is said that those who sip with Jesus in this world will be blessed when they are reborn.'

I say, 'Mary, Our Lady, was Jesus' number one fan and supporter. She followed him around, except when he decided to spend forty days in the desert, there he went alone. I have never been a mother, God did not bless me with children nor with old age, and so I cannot imagine the anxiety that Mary must have felt when Her crazy son was preaching about love and forgiveness and accusing the high priests of being corrupt hypocrites. She would have watched Jesus performing miracles and I am quite sure that the authorities would have described them as dangerous sorcery. Yet, Mary was fearless and She followed Jesus while he was carrying the cross up Mount Golgotha and stood underneath the cross next to the apostle John and Mary Magdalen. She is all that a mother and a woman could be.'

I say, 'It has been said that while Jesus was breathing his last, that there underneath the cross, in his very final moments, it is said that Jesus turned to John and nodding at his mother, he said, "Here, this is your mother." Then, it is said that Jesus turned back to his mother and nodding at John, he told Her, "And this is your son." Do you understand what this means? Do you comprehend the message and the power of the words? What this meant was that Jesus was giving humanity Mary, to be our mother and to be Our Lady.'

❋ ❋ ❋ ❋ ❋

I say, 'When it was time for Mary to pass on to the Other Side, Mary was awarded a very special concession. She passed on to this side with Her earthly body and soul. Our Lady Mary has been interceding for humankind's benefit ever since. I have yet to meet Her on this side and I must state that this confuses my very core. I search for Her and this search has brought me here, to Malta. Do you see all the spirits that hover, that crowd, that walk this island? We are all searching for something.'

❋ ❋ ❋ ❋ ❋

I say, 'I am a Catholic, as are you, and so the Mary that we both know is the same. She is Our Lady and blessed is She. We call Her this to bestow honour and respect upon Her. She is, after all, the mother of our saviour and She is the cause of our joy. Of course, it comes naturally for us humans to pray to Our Lady

when we find ourselves in the direst of needs. That is
why many people are particularly devoted towards
Her. She was human, like us, very young, powerless
and She was a woman. She lived in a man's world,
with few resources and yet She gave all that She had.
She gave the ultimate, Her only son. Her power, Her
compassion and Her open heart mark Her. In my
life and in my death I am devoted to Her. Can you
imagine how it feels to have your life guided into the
fidelity of another human being? She came to me with
reason and in my death I still search for Her truth, for
my purpose. I fear that I will search for eternity, or
until Her son speaks to me face to face.'

I say, 'My village is far from this island, but still the
landscape is familiar and the heat that rises from the
land is offered by the same Lord. Do you know my
name? Do you know of me? I am branded, my seeing
documented and tested. In my village there is a sign
that has been completed from a piece of wood. The
wood has been nailed to a post that directs others
onto the mound. The sign speaks my name with that
of Our Lady in black paint that did dry in the midday
sun. Many years later, when my death was part of the
village history, a statue was erected in honour of my

memory. The statue was positioned on the mound and it offers the image of me, as the young girl that I will always be, looking upwards, my palms held above my head, as Our Lady bestows Her love and blessing upon me.'

I say, 'My story begins when the light was falling. It was early evening, during my fourteenth year and I was walking through my village when I heard a voice calling my name. "Flavia Bellini." She called to me from the top of the mound that bordered our village. As I climbed, I saw Her beauty. I asked of myself, "By what fortune have I found myself in heaven? Do I dream? Where am I?" I continued to climb, believing that I was entering heaven. As I stood on the top of the mound, Our Lady did show Herself to me. I looked to the sky and I saw Her beautiful face smiling down onto me. There was not a glow surrounding Her, She was simply the most radiant of beings calling my name. I reached up my arms to Her, bold, fearless, feeling myself brimming with purity, with love and with hope. I was modest, perhaps weakened by Her beauty, by Her elegance. I fell to my knees below Her, my face bowed to the dusty ground. I breathed in the dust of my village and felt my whole body shaking as

if in fright. Our Lady must have kneeled to the floor,
She placed Her open palm onto my back and my
whole body warmed as if by the midday sunshine.
This being the only time that I felt Her physical touch,
that She journeyed into my space. Our Lady, She told
me not to fear. I spoke my words to Her, declaring, "I
am not afraid. I am humble." And so, She told me that I
must come to that very place and that I must come on
the same date and at the same hour for the next seven
months. As I stood to leave Her, She asked me to keep
my sighting within my own mind. I did not promise,
perhaps because I knew of my own weakness.'

I say, 'There were others within my village who
claimed that they had seen Our Lady somewhere.
I remember that one elder was mocked by many,
as he claimed that Our Lady visited his bedside at
night. As children, we were told to avoid him, that
he was foolish in the mind. And so, as I descended
the mound, I knew that I must keep my conversation
with Our Lady close to my heart and within my
tight lips and mouth. It was then that I met with my
oldest friend, my cousin. As we walked through the
village and back to our homes, I swore her to secrecy.
I described and I spilled all that I had vowed to hold

within me and, of course, she talked, because that is
what children do.'

❊ ❊ ❊ ❊ ❊

I say, 'And so, as is the way of my people, within
days a sign was made from a piece of wood and that
wood was nailed to a post. The words "Flavia Bellini
il Monte della Nostra Signora" were on it. My name,
Flavia Bellini, directed others onto the mound of Our
Lady. And at the same date and at the same hour of
the following month, a crowd moved onto the mound.
I do believe that all from my village were there, as
people left doors open and shops unmanned and
then there were others, from neighbouring villages.
Word had spread and many were curious as to why
a teenage girl would be blessed in such a way. I had
spent a month being asked questions covering every
aspect of my life and still they could not find a reason
for my madness. As I walked to the mound, I must tell
you that I knew that Our Lady would not abandon
me. I knew that She would accept the inadequacies
of a child and the speaking of words that I had been
asked to hold secret.'

❊ ❊ ❊ ❊ ❊

I say, 'But during that month I did begin to consider
why I had been blessed. Those learned from my

village spoke in whispered tones, but I heard and I understood what they were discussing. They suggested that my apparition was for personal comfort and then another spoke that they would foretell. They were both correct in their words.'

I say, 'For it was true. Did you know that my second sighting, my second blessing came with a forewarning? The others stayed at the foot of the mound, as I climbed. Again, I heard Her voice calling to me, "Flavia Bellini" but the others did not. As I climbed, I looked to the sky and I saw Her beautiful face smiling down onto me. I saw Her beauty and this time I knew that I was not stepping to heaven, rather that She had words that I must hear. I did not ask of myself any questions. Instead, I climbed to below Her and I fell before Her, onto my knees. It was then that Our Lady told me that my mother would be moved to a hospital ward with greying walls and disease-filled air. She told me that there my mother would die on the fourth eve but that her soul was pure and I should have no fear for her. Our Lady told me that my mother should pass, that I was not to be riddled with guilt that my power could not save her. As She left me, I lifted myself from the dusty mound, I looked to the sky and saw the faded image of Her beautiful face. I turned to the crowd. It was then that I spoke all that I had been told, in language that was beyond my years. The crowd hushed, my mother wept and soon I was shepherded into a safer place. I was taken from my family and kept by the religious men, who told my mother that I had the form of an angel.'

I say, 'And so my mother travelled to hospital and passed on the fourth eve. Many did say that I was filled with sorcery, others that I had cast the evil eye upon her. I found a human strength to ignore the evil that leaked from their mouths. I wept, for I am human and my mother held my love. But my sorrow was selfish, as Our Lady had told me my mother's soul was pure and that she had passed to this side. I had no fear for her; rather I had fear for myself, fear for what I would be told and the responsibility that the words would carry. The learned men and the religious leaders argued of how or even how not my apparitions had been sent to offer comfort. I would listen and I would know that their raised voices were in vain. I was not to be riddled with guilt that my power could not save my mother, as I did not know of the power that I possessed. Do you know of it? Have

you heard the words that talk of the miracles that
I performed?'

✳ ✳ ✳ ✳ ✳

I say, 'And so, at the same date and at the same
hour of the following month, a crowd moved onto
the mound. The crowd had grown in size with the
passing of a month. People travelled to see me and
many wanted to touch their skin onto mine. I walked
with religious men, they sheltered my human form
from the crowds and then I climbed alone to the top
of the mound. Our Lady, She did show herself to me. I
looked to the sky and I saw Her beautiful face smiling
down onto me. For those who would look to the sky
and not see Our Lady, I would shed tears.'

✳ ✳ ✳ ✳ ✳

I say, 'Word continued to spread across the country
and into other places with exotic sounding names.
Soon there were crowds of seekers, and a cross was
erected to mark the position where I would fall to my
knees. And at the same date and at the same hour
of the following month, a vast crowd moved onto
the mound. The crowd knew to separate, to let me
pass as I walked with religious men, sheltering my
human form. And then I climbed alone to the top
of the mound and to the cross. Again, I heard Her

voice calling to me, "Flavia Bellini" but the others
did not. I looked to the sky and I saw Her beautiful
face smiling down onto me. I fell before Her, onto my
knees, positioned by the cross. This time Our Lady
told me to look into Her. I looked up to see the face
of Our Lady. I heard Her instructions that we should
pray for reparation for those who have sinned, for
repentance and purification of the soul. I began my
recitation of the Holy Rosary, sending devotions
to Her Immaculate Heart. It was then that my life
altered again. You must have heard of this tale, it is a
mythology, it has become part of history.'

✳ ✳ ✳ ✳ ✳

I say, 'It was during this visitation that Our Lady began
to tell me names, sometimes it was part, sometimes full
and I called out to the crowd below. Then the crowd
parted and those chosen they came to me. I prayed
before them, that they would receive healing within
their heart. And then Our Lady, She told me that I
should place my hands onto the chosen people and
so I did. I laid my hands upon people whom I did not
know and I told them that they would heal.'

✳ ✳ ✳ ✳ ✳

I say, 'I know not how, dear Nina, yet I healed hearts,
limbs and minds. It was always a miracle and each

was rejoiced. The healing passed over hours, until my physical body could no longer stand. It is said that doubters would not heal, that their minds were conflicted and riddled with thoughts that prevented my powers from penetrating their core. My healing could not penetrate those who could not believe. There were many who came to curse me, to spit and to say words that carried hatred and harm. They would say that I was trying to take the sight from my village, trying to trick people into blindness by looking directly at the sun. They spoke of how I would injure them and then steal from their homes. Their words hurt me, but Our Lady told me to continue, that my faith and power would speak louder than any words that they could throw at me.'

❈ ❈ ❈ ❈ ❈

I say, 'Did you know that there were times when those healed would offer to pay me for the miracle that I had performed? My family were of little means and few resources, but I could not take payment for God's work. Those healed thought that money would repay the miracle, the blessing that I had been able to bestow upon them, but I would say to them that God's work could have no bill and with those words they would withdraw and they would understand. There were others who would seek to find their own rewards. They would bring cameras, blinded by a need to capture and to prove Her very being. Our Lady would never smile down onto those blinded by financial gain. Mine is a story of purity of heart and of sacrifice. Can you begin to understand my words?'

I say, 'It is noted that I had seven visions before my death. During the seventh apparition, Our Lady told me that I would die in my sleep, a painless death and that I would leave the physical world. She told me that I should have no fear and that one day I would return to my island in the physical form, as so many who have passed do. She told me that I should explore the Other Side. That I should see sights and that I should search out the honeypot for those who have passed on. I asked Our Lady if I would go to heaven and She said that I was pure and deserving. Ten days did pass before my death. And for years I have searched for the honeypot, not knowing that the island of which She spoke was at the heel of my country. Here, your island, is where spirits and lost souls come.'

I say, 'I have been told and now I will share with you, although I must ask you to promise secrecy. It

292

is said that if you open my grave, then you will find that my body has been preserved as if I sleep. In my physical body I am still fourteen years old, I have aged not a few years in my passing. It is said that my physical body shows no signs of deterioration at all. I am blessed.'

I say, 'And here I am, still searching this spiritual honeypot. Did you know that there is a man who claims that he is seeing Our Lady, here, in Malta? He claims that She appears each Wednesday at 6 p.m. on a mound in B'Żebbuga. There is a wooden sign that points in the direction of the mound and on it, in black paint, it reads "Il Madonna ta' Lourdes". The man has been interrogated by many priests and still in his mind there appears no evidence of madness. Some people are sceptical but I would say that most believe him. I mean, who would be so crazy as to put his reputation so much on the line? People are flocking to the place where he says he sees Our Lady. I assemble there too, but I have still to see Her.'

I say, 'I must admit to you that I do not understand why I cannot share his vision. I mean that I would not say that it is very common to see Our Lady, but I have

heard of at least five Maltese people who insist that
they did and that they do see Her. This has been in the
last thirty years that I have been here and so I remain.
I am searching for Her, but not finding and no longer
seeing. Who am I to contradict them, those people
who claim to see? I know that I have been witness
to some incredible things and, if anything, I have
learned that much occurs that we cannot see. I have
yet to meet Our Lady on this side and I must say that
this confuses my very core. My only hope is that She
appears before me. One day I can but hope that Jesus
allows me to share my first beer with him in Larry's
bar and then he will answer my questions. I feel that
my searching has reached an end. I am no longer sure
of my purpose. I have seen and I have been around
the world and I am ready to leave this side. I am
wanting to live in the human form again. And before I
leave and before I give up my final hope, you are sent
to me and I to you. I do not think that I am supposed
to share these thoughts with you and now I see that
you are close to the end of this meal.'

❄ ❄ ❄ ❄ ❄

I say, 'This island is your home, dear Nina. Here
is the centre of healing, here is where your sense
of belonging can be found. I beg of you to not lose

sight of the greater focus, of all that happens that the human eye cannot see. You have such a gift, you see and you hear those who have passed. You have been chosen, dear Nina and with that blessing, you have sacrificed your only son. Take comfort from Our Lady, She knows of your loss –'

Tnejn u għoxrin

~twenty-two

Malta's top 5: *Beaches*

✳ 2. Mellieħa Bay
One of the largest sandy beaches on the island,
with shallow clear waters, good facilities and direct
transport networks, Mellieħa Bay is an ideal spot for
parents with small children.

'You have been chosen, dear Nina and with that blessing, you have sacrificed your only son. Take comfort from Our Lady, She knows of your loss,' Flavia says, places her cold hand onto my shoulder, but I do not look to her.

I have been looking at the plastic table cloth for at least ten minutes. The lingering taste of olive swims around my mouth. The plastic cover is white, with swirls of blue that blend into filled circles as my eyes focus in and out. Flavia has stopped talking, an echo, a wisp of her last word tings within the air.

I look up, to meet with her sparkling eyes, but she is gone.

It has all gone.

I am in an empty café, no plates before me, no owner bustling around, no 1980s instrumental music.

I am alone, at the only remaining table in a stripped room where no life exists.

I am covered in dust.

My only Lord's breath whips at the torn plastic that decorates the outside of the café.

The tang of olive clings to the roof of my mouth.

I look to the door.

◎

I see my son.

◎

Christopher walks through the door and to me; he sits on the floor beside my chair, crossing his legs as if a schoolboy.

'I used to talk of this place, do you remember?' I ask.

'This is your special place. I recognise it from your description. I was watching you, Mama as you ate with the angel.'

My son speaks, his voice lower, quieter than usual.

'I used to come here with my mother, after school. We'd sit here, near to the window; we'd talk and look down onto the bay of Mellieħa. We'd eat ftira biż-żejt.'

~Maltese flat bread seasoned with salt, with peppers, with tomatoes, with capers, with olives, with olive oil.

'I have tasted it now.'

My son says.

'You have?' I ask, my stomach tightening.

'Elena made it for me.'

He speaks the words, in an almost hush; my stomach knots from anxiety, envy, loss.

'I gave you words without flavour, without texture,' I say. 'I thought that there would always be a tomorrow, but I was wrong.'

'And that is why you should be with Molly.'

My son says, anger seeping from the words; then he stands and runs through the door.

◎

He is gone.

◎

The dust sticks to my white cotton dress, to my skin, to my hair, to me.

I have not changed my clothes, for days, perhaps.

I leave my special place, the café, alone.

I look to the uneven pavements, roads, as I.

~fl – ip.

~fl – op.

to the bus stop.

◎

I look out through the window of the bus, I watch the

sea.

The bus travels over smooth roads that I have never seen before, the island has progressed. The bus hugs close to the lip of the island. Il-grigalata is burly today, angry, whipping the waves up and onto the path.

~strong wind.

The bus driver swerves to avoid a wave that jumps up, onto the road. The salt water will damage his shiny new bus. He thinks of his bus, first, swerving onto the wrong side of the road. Cars beep, the bus driver holds up his hands into the air. He is blaming the heavens.

'Affanjiet li jiġru l'Malta biss!' I say.

~only in Malta!

I look up, to the sky, to the spirits that can float. I see outlines, on different levels. My eyes adjust to see all those who swarm to Malta. The spirits look so small, yet still they come, like bees to honey.

I smile.

◎

The bus pulls into the terminal, into Valletta. The bustle of people waiting, chatting, shouting; the clamour of buses, of cars, of taxis. The noise of Valletta warms me.

I smile.

I look to the kiosks, skimming for Christopher, hoping to see him clutching a glass of strawberry milkshake. He is not there. There are no children there, they are at school.

I think to Molly.

◎

I walk, I flip and I flop.

~fl – ip.

~fl – op.

I think to my son, to his being with Geordie, with Elena, with Jesus. They will be telling him of their world, of his new world; he will be learning and living as a spirit should.

I think, Christopher has been near to me less and less. Since we arrived in Malta, I have been self-absorbed; my son has had a freedom. And with that taste of independence, he has moved from me, almost beyond my reach. His anger, resentment, disappointment are unhidden, growing.

'My son is dead,' the words escape from me, they force me to catch my breath.

I inhale sharply, trying to suck back my voice.

'My son is dead,' I say, again, louder.

I walk, my eyes full, blurred with tears, trying to watch the pavement. My words roll from my tongue in a loop.

The road, the pavements that lead through the City Gate and into Valletta are uneven. I wonder if they will try to make these pavements smooth. The new roads are progress, but something is being taken and covered with each new construction. They are burying dust into the roads. The island of Malta should never be smooth, perfect without blemish, there is too much history, too many marks, injuries, memories.

The island breathes, has character.

I walk into Valletta, within the walls. The Renaissance streets open up. I look up to crumbling balconies, to chipped frames and flaking façades. Each building has a story, each building breathes through history, space and time. They speak many languages, blending into the story of invasion, of desire to control. The buildings are proud, they exist; they speak their own words into an island that carries the story of my family.

I will always belong, here.

Each building breathes out the same dust that forms my heart.

I turn right, past the crumbling Opera House, up again, I feel my fitness level improving, then left, then down again. I long for an ice-cold Kinnie. The streets slope down to the harbour. I stand at the top of the slope, looking down my mother's street. I see the bumps, the cobbles. I think of how the rain glides down, of how slippery the street becomes. I have fallen, my mother has fallen, my grandmother has fallen, here.

⊚

I feel younger, lighter, today.

Here the heavens shine, my only Lord is happy, no wind whips the cotton dress tight to my thighs. The narrow streets of my home offer protection, of sorts.

I am warm, warm in my bones, I am covered in dust.

I reach my mother's green front door.

⊚

I stand, very still; I think about holding my breath.

I long for my sisters, Maria and Sandra.

The images of them, as children, have appeared in my head, before my eyes.

I have no sense of them as adults. I wonder where they are living, now.

I think about how we would play games here, on this slope. I think about how the slope would ruin, make each game almost impossible, but still we would play, together. Cousins would visit, cousins of cousins would visit and together we would play up and down and up and down the slope. We were a family, close, belonging. I think of a childhood that was filled with laughter, with noise.

I think to Molly, to all that she is missing, to all that she needs, to all that she deserves.

'I wish that I could go back to that time, start again, relive, compromise, find a way,' I say, to no one.

But of course there is always a someone.

> **Jesus:** Your longing is for a home that no longer exists. It is your need to belong that is shrouding your vision.

I turn, a full circle. He is not here, rather reading my thoughts, placing words inside of my head, covering me in the smell of stale alcohol.

'I need my family,' I say, to someone.

> **Jesus:** You have your family, your Matt and your Molly. Think to the future and stop this dwelling in a past that is no longer yours.

'You have no idea!' I shout, to someone.

> **Jesus:** Oh my Nina, your argument is so weak. I know everything.

'Tkellimniex aktar!' I say.

~stop talking to me!

> **Jesus:** You must stop your needing to belong to the dead.

'Iskot!' I scream.

~shut up!

The smell of alcohol drifts away from me; he does not continue with his words.

◎

> I bang.
>
> ~*b – ang.*
>
> ~*b – ang.*
>
> with my fist onto my mother's green front door.

I hear a key turning.

> and a.
>
> ~*cl – unk.*
>
> as the barrel revolves.

The chain and padlock come undone, unrelated.

I hear the chain clunk.

~cl – unk.

~cl – unk.

to the floor.

And then it is gone.

I do not care that it has gone. I need to be inside.

Tlieta u għoxrin

~twenty-three

Malta's top 5: *Gastronomic Pleasure*

✳ **2. Imqarrun**
A baked dish made with macaroni, a meat and tomato ragu-style sauce, egg, and then made to an individual family recipe. A layer of grated cheese is added to the top which then melts and, along with the egg, helps to fasten the ingredients during baking.

I walk into my mother's house, I slam the door. I stand, back to the door, filled with anger.

I scream.

~*sc – re – am.*

~*sc – re – am.*

~*sc – re – am.*

~*sc – re – am.*

till my throat pulls, aches.

My mother walks to me, from the kitchen.

'Nina, qalbi. You are home. Did you like Flavia? She is wise, yes?'

~my heart.

She holds out her arms, wide, and as I move towards her, as I reach her, as she wraps me into her, I become enveloped in her scent.

'Jien qiegħda d-dar,' I whisper.

~I am home.

'Come, qalbi. Come eat with us.'

~my heart.

◎

My mother turns; I follow her into the kitchen.

She moves, near to her cooker, six plates, a bowl, six forks, a knife and a large silver spoon are laid out, ready. I see the imqarrun, in a large metal dish. I smile.

```
~a baked dish made with macaroni, a meat and
tomato ragu-style sauce, egg, and then made to
an individual family recipe. A layer of grated
cheese is added to the top which then melts
and, along with the egg, helps to fasten the
ingredients during baking.
```

That baked macaroni recipe was passed down through my mother's side of the family. I would cook it for Christopher, for Molly, but away from my mother's advice I could never quite capture the taste. I think of how my children would love the flavours, I think of how English I made the dish. I used to alter the recipe, buy specialist pastes and sauces, but could never quite reproduce my mother's perfect taste.

'Zokkor, grazzi. Jien nieħu zokkor.'

```
~sugar, thank you. I add sugar.
```

My mother reads my thoughts.

I smile.

'The recipe alters with each generation, qalbi, you should

not be this hard on yourself.'

~my heart.

My mother begins to cut the baked macaroni into squares, then she scoops and serves them onto each of the plates.

'Who will eat with us?' I ask.

'Christopher has invited some friends. He is at home here.'

My mother tells me; my stomach tightens.

I lean my bottom onto the back of one of the wooden chairs; there are six surrounding the kitchen table. I watch my mother, her expertise, the presentation of the dish. Steam spills from the macaroni, the rich tomato smell floats into me. I lick my lips.

In the centre of the table, the crystal bowl remains empty.

Christopher arrives with three others. I had expected to see Geordie, Elena, even Jesus, but no, not tonight.

Christopher is finding his feet in his world.

He introduces me, Sophia, Toby, Paul. I smile. They are all young, sixteen, seventeen, perhaps eighteen. Within seconds, they are seated around the wooden table, chatting to each other, to my mother. They talk of other spirits, neighbours, performances, concerts, shopping, all in their dimension. Sophia is excited that John Lennon will be performing at TGI Friday's. I am quiet, listening to the altered voices of people who no longer breathe. They talk over each other, interrupting, laughing, gossiping about spirits who have recently moved into the area. They are happy.

I smile, because I am expected to smile.

I do not fit into their world, not now, not quite.

I feel lost.

◎

The chatter continues. I eat.

I stop pretending to listen, to nod in the right places, to be enthusiastic.

Instead, I search, I look to their bodies for signs of how they left the physical world.

I wonder how they passed and with that thought silence falls into the room, heavy. They each stare at me, each having heard my thoughts, my questions, my queries.

'He killed me.'

Sophia tells me. A flashing image startles my mind.

'I fell asleep.'

Toby stares, he does not smile.

'M6 crash, my father was driving.'

Paul speaks the words and I am covered in sadness.

I have no right to rake over ashes past, events gone, events that have not prevented their progression, growth. They all look the same age as my son, yet their life experiences and learning would each have been so very different.

The silence is lifted.

Sophia talks of how Jesus and John Lennon compete to be the most famous spirit. The table, the walls, they all rattle, with laughter, merriment, genuine connections.

Christopher is smiling, beaming, he is relaxed; he jokes with my mother, she squeezes his shoulders before leaning over to kiss his cheek.

I begin to fade.

I know that in this form, I have no sense of belonging here. I am lingering between two worlds and the end is nearing.

◎

Tilly stands at the doorway to the kitchen. Her feet are firmly grounded, somehow; her arms are crossed over her chest. She looks angry.

'What yous doing?'

She asks.

'Eating, come join us, Tilly,' I say.

She looks around the room and tuts, then looks some more, then sighs, loudly.

'There's no friggin' room.'

She shouts, then stomps up the stairs and slams an upstairs door.

I stand to go to her, but Christopher places his hand onto my arm.

'Jesus will go.'

He says.

I look at my son. I see that he is ageing, growing more handsome each day. I smile; I place my hand over his. He feels cold.

'When will you leave here?'

Christopher asks me.

We are in silence, all around the table, waiting for my reply.

'I don't know if I will,' I tell him.

'You must.'

He raises his voice.

'Molly needs you. It is not your time to be here.'

I stand. 'I cannot leave you,' I tell him.

'I left you, Mama. Soon I will need to leave you again.'

He says.

I cannot speak.

I turn, I say to my mother, 'Int għidtli naqta' qalbi u issa
nifhem il-kliem tiegħek.'

~you told me I cut my heart, I lose hope and
now I understand your words.

'Nina, qalbi, you must let go of the past, ta.'

~my heart.

~ta is a tag that seeks confirmation.

My mother tells me, firmly.

'Qalbi maqsuma fi tlett biċċiet,' I say.

~my heart is broken into three.

'But Nina, qalbi, you can heal. Think to your Molly, think
to her loss.'

~my heart.

My mother stands, moves away from her position at the

head of the table. The others are silent, they watch as my
mother walks to me.

She places her arms around me

　　　and I curl into her soft breast –

Tilly

I'd rushed downstairs, cos I'd wanted to show Nina
and Melita me feet, but then I found them all sitting
round the table having a friggin' ball without even
thinking to ask me. So I'm standing in the doorway
and feeling pissed off.

'What yous doing?' I ask them, but I know really.

'Eating, come join us Tilly,' Nina says all gooey like
but I can't be arsed spending the night with a bunch
of dead student types and there's no friggin' room for
me anyways.

※ ※ ※ ※ ※

I storm upstairs cos they don't give a shit 'bout me
or me feelings. It's always 'bout poor friggin' woe-
is-me Nina. I'm sitting on the floor in the corner of
one of the upstairs bedrooms in Melita's house. I'm
feeling shitty. I mean, it's like everyone else is sorting
out their friggin' lives and passings and I'm left
here, stuck in some friggin' house in the middle of
nowhere. They're all downstairs talking shit and they

318

didn't even think to ask me to join them. They're all
a bunch of bastards anyway. I've got me legs back, I
mean I can walk and I'm not like a flipping loon any
more, but it's not enough. I mean I just feel so friggin'
sad.

🐝 🐝 🐝 🐝 🐝

I look up and see Jesus is there. I hate how he can
enter rooms without anyone knowing.

🐝 🐝 🐝 🐝 🐝

Jesus: Why are you cheerless, my Tilly?

He speaks with such a lush voice and before I can stop
meself an image of Jen pops into me head. It's the one
where I'm in Crystal Zone, after Jesus had left, it's the
one with Martin and Jen. I mean it's the one where I
flipped. In me head the cards are flying around the
room and Jen is screaming. I would feel sick and I
would feel pains in me gut, if I wasn't dead. I mean I
just couldn't control me emotions back then and me
whole self was reacting to it all. I mean I'm better now.
I'm sad and shit like that, but at least I've accepted
that I'm dead and at least I know that Jen cares
enough 'bout me to go and try to find out where I am.
I just regret scaring her, when I could have told her
that I was OK and that I loved her and stuff like that.

319

That's what I'm thinking, but I'm not saying the words out loud or anything. It's more 'bout pictures in me head.

૨૬ ૨૬ ૨૬ ૨૬ ૨૬

So I've got all this stuff inside me head and I'm showing it really fast. It's like I've pressed a fast forward button on me remote control. Jesus is just standing there, staring at me but I know that he's listening and I know that he's seeing it all too.

૨૬ ૨૬ ૨૬ ૨૬ ૨૬

Then, the next thing I know, Jesus and me are standing on the opposite side of the main road that passes through the village. I mean I am there again, right far from Malta and Melita's house. We're standing on the pavement, me still without any shoes on. The road's virtually empty which is kinda weird, but it's dark so it must be pretty late at night or something. I mean usually there are loads of cars parking on double yellows and loads of others looking for somewhere to stop, but it's different today. Then I realise that it's raining but I'm not getting wet and I mean I can't even feel the water on me bare feet. Jesus points at the shop opposite and I look to see Crystal Zone with the huge fake gold Buddha in the window. There's a light on inside and I can see

Martin, sitting behind the shop counter. He's smoking a ciggie and keeps looking at his watch.

᙭ ᙭ ᙭ ᙭ ᙭

'How long's it been since I was last here?' I ask Jesus.

Jesus: Time is insignificant, my Tilly.

He says the words, smiles, then looks at a bright red Mickey Mouse watch which I reckon is new cos I've not seen him wearing it before and I reckon it's the kinda thing I would have noticed. I really don't understand why he can't just give me a straight answer. I mean friggin' hell, I was only making conversation.

᙭ ᙭ ᙭ ᙭ ᙭

I don't get why we're still outside and I can't be arsed to ask Jesus, so I keep quiet and have a good look around. The place hasn't changed much since I died or since I was last here. I mean it could have been a few hours or a few days or even a few months. I mean I don't know and that's kinda weird. It's funny I mean cos I've been stuck in Melita's house for what feels like ages and I've been thinking loads 'bout home. I've been seeing it like it's the best place on earth and like I'd give anything to be living here again. I mean I've been missing normal stuff like me Meg and Jen, but then there's like other stuff I've been missing like smells and tastes and stuff like that. I'd kill for a bag of chips from the Chinese chippie, or a bacon stottie with loads of red sauce on it or a bowl of Mark's mam's homemade leak and tattie soup with crusty bread. I mean there's so much that I'm not ever going to taste again and it's shit when I think 'bout how much I took for granted, but I know that's what we do. I mean none of us really live each day thinking we could die at any minute. If we did, like we'd never work or shit like that.

🐾 🐾 🐾 🐾 🐾

I'm standing here, in the rain and I can't feel a thing. I mean I want me clothes to get wet and I want to shiver and feel really really cold. But I'm not going to again, cos some idiot drunk decided that he'd down a bottle of whisky and then kill himself. I mean, I know that his life was shit but he didn't have to kill me too, but he did. I was thinking, the other day or time, how hard it would have been if I hadn't been killed. I mean I would have left Mark and me Meg, but it would have been hard on them. I reckon that cos I'm dead I've actually protected them a bit and saved them from loads of shit.

Jesus: Death is just an illusion, my Tilly.

Jesus interrupts me thinking. I mean I can't even have a private thought when he's around. It's like he thinks it's OK to read me mind all the time.

Jesus: You have grown; you are nearly ready to pass through, to proceed onto another level of existence.

'I know,' I tell him. 'I've changed. So me standing in the rain that I can't feel, well it's like I'm here to understand what I've lost but I kinda know there's loads more lush stuff to come.'

Jesus nods his head and then starts splashing his bare feet in a friggin' huge puddle beside the kerb. He's got green nail polish on his toenails. He's a funny bloke. I laugh right out loud and me whole body rattles a bit. I mean it kinda shocks me.

Then, Jesus points away from Crystal Zone to a parked car a little further down the road. I see Jen climbing out of a red Mini. I rush across the road screaming out Jen's name. I fling me arms around her. I try to lift her from the ground and spin her around, but I can't. I haven't any strength. Jen keeps walking, tugging at her coat sleeves. She's left her umbrella in the car and her hair is getting right wet. I love her hair. I hurry along next to her, trying to stroke her arms, but she's moving too quickly and each time

I stroke her she pulls at her sleeves even more. She stops outside of Crystal Zone. Martin sees her through the glass front and smiles; then he looks at me and smiles too.

🐎 🐎 🐎 🐎 🐎

Martin opens the door.

'Come in out the rain, you two lasses,' he says.

Jen begins to take off her coat. 'Is she here today?' she asks him.

'She's right next to you, keeps stroking your arm. I'm surprised you can't feel anything,' he tells her.

'I did outside. I felt like me clothes were like suddenly a bit tight,' Jen says. 'I couldn't believe it when you phoned tonight. I mean I didn't think that you worked Sunday nights.'

'I don't,' Martin says. 'But I was sent a message to get you here. And it was the kind of message I knows better than to ignore. Now come on through, both of yous,' Martin says and looks right into me eyes.

🐎 🐎 🐎 🐎 🐎

The next thing I know, Martin is holding open the door and I'm walking through into a box of a room. He closes the door after me. The room's the same as last time. I mean there's nothing much in here and that's maybe cos Martin doesn't need fancy tricks and stuff. I mean he's clearly like a proper psychic. Jen sits on one of the sofas and I don't know whether to sit or to stand. Martin puts his ciggies on the coffee table and I reckon I would kill for a ciggie. Then Martin sits on the coffee table.

'Can I have a ciggie?' Jen asks.

'When did she start smoking?' I ask.

'Tilly wants to know when you started smoking,' Martin asks Jen and then smiles at me. 'Sit down, Tilly,' Martin points to the sofa that Jen's sitting on.

Jen takes a ciggie from the pack and lights it. I look at her smoking and I can't remember having seen her smoke before. I mean there must be loads of stuff 'bout her that I'll never know. I sit down next to Jen.

Then Martin's granddad walks through the closed door. He tips his flat cap at me and smiles; then he moves over to the back wall, so that he's facing Martin. I see Martin smile at him and the old man tips his flat cap again.

I put me arm around Jen.

'Is she still here?' Jen asks Martin.

'She's got her arm around you, she's on your left,'
Martin tells her and at that Jen turns to me and smiles.

'Now shall we get started?' Martin says and we do.

⁂ ⁂ ⁂ ⁂ ⁂

Jen asks Martin questions and I ask Martin questions
and we kinda talk through Martin. Sometimes he
makes up what I'm saying a bit and I shout at him.
He's kinda dark but I like him. I tell Jen everything
that I can think of and everything that I should have
told her when I was still alive. Some of the stuff I say
is a bit embarrassing and personal. I mean I talk 'bout
her taste and stuff like that. I reckon Martin's finding
some of the stuff a bit horny really, but I'm not going
to miss this chance to say everything I can. I mean,
I'm not wanting to regret anything else. I ask her 'bout
Meg, but she doesn't really know anything. She tells
me that Mark never found out 'bout me and her and I
think that's best, it's like I don't feel extra guilt. I mean
I know that the affair thing was wrong, but I'm glad
Mark didn't have that to deal with too. Then Jen tells
me 'bout me funeral and she cries like with real snot
and stuff.

⁂ ⁂ ⁂ ⁂ ⁂

It's been like ages and Martin's been pretty great

passing on our messages. But then I reckon that he's getting to be a bit pissed off, cos he stops talking and looks at his granddad.

'You all right?' Jen asks him, but Martin doesn't answer.

'I think he's talking to his granddad,' I tell Jen but she can't hear me.

I reckon it's ages before Martin speaks, but I don't know for sure cos it's like I've no idea 'bout time any more and no one wears watches apart from Jesus and that bright red watch that he's managed to get hold of. I wish I had a watch.

Then Martin speaks.

'I'm going to let yous do something special,' Martin says and I don't really know what to expect. 'Have yous heard of something called transfiguration?'

Jen says no and I'm pretty impressed that Martin knows such a friggin' big word.

'It's where I let the spirit use me face and me body,' he says.

'I don't get it,' Jen says.

'I'm gonna let Tilly use me face and I'll let her talk to you,' he says and then he holds his palms up to the

327

ceiling and starts chanting something 'bout seeking protection from the Holy Spirit. I mean I'm kinda shocked cos I didn't think Martin was religious, but then I don't think I've really thought 'bout it before. I mean who am I to argue or to say owt, cos what he's doing for me and Jen is friggin' amazing.

Martin's granddad walks over to me and he holds out his hand; I mean he never talks to me and I can't hear him saying anything inside me head. He takes me hand, I stand up and he guides me to right behind where Martin's sitting. He then puts me one hand and then me other hand onto Martin's shoulders.

The next thing I know I'm in Martin's body.

I mean I've heard 'bout this kinda thing before, you know where a spirit takes over the body and face of a medium, but I always thought it was a trick, like the grieving person was only seeing what they wanted to see. But it's not a trick, I mean I'm inside Martin's body, I really am. I mean I'm a man and I can hear Martin's words and I can feel stuff, like actually feel stuff. I mean it's like I'm in the room proper.

I reach over and I use me hand in Martin's hand to touch Jen's leg. She's staring right at Martin's face, so I guess she's staring right at me. I touch her leg and I can feel her leg. She puts her hand onto mine and then she starts crying and then I start crying.

'It's you,' she says.

'It's you,' I say and then we hold each other for ages.

🐝 🐝 🐝 🐝 🐝

Jen and Martin have gone out the room. Martin's messing around through there and Jen's probably gone to the pub or something. I'm back sitting on Martin's sofa and I'm thinking. I mean I'm really thinking. I reckon I forgive the drunk bloke for killing me. I mean the poor lad had had enough. And I reckon I'm done with having regrets; I mean I did what I did and I am what I am. Jen now knows that there's something after you die and she's left hoping that I'll go and see her again and maybe I will. So I reckon I'm ready. I mean I'm ready to accept who I am and move forward. I reckon I've finished all me business here.

I look up and Jesus is there. I hate how he can enter rooms without anyone knowing.

> **Jesus:** It is time for you to walk into the light, my Tilly.

'Walk into the friggin' light!' I say and giggle. Jesus laughs too.

Jesus: Death is but an illusion, my Tilly. You have survived physical death and now you must move onto a new level of existence.

'But walking into the light,' I say. 'Isn't that a bit, well isn't it a bit naff? I mean, next you'll be talking 'bout staircases and escalators to heaven,' I say and Jesus laughs.

Jesus: Come, follow me. The light is not what you're expecting.

He walks through Martin's wall and I follow.

❧ ❧ ❧ ❧ ❧

Now I am standing in a field covered in a lush yellow glow. The field is full of sunflowers that are as tall or as small as me. I mean me head is just 'bout the same height as the flower head. All the flowers are looking up to the clear blue sky and to like the most perfect sun ever. Jesus is a bit in front of me. He's running like a loon through the field and dodging in and out of the flowers. His arms are flapping and he's laughing and laughing. The sound of Jesus' laughter is making me giggle too and I want to run like a loon and I want to join him.

Jesus: Come, follow me, my Tilly.

He's shouting as he runs and weaving through the

right lush sunflowers.

I can't help but giggle and smile. I mean I'm dead and I'm in a field of sunflowers with a laughing Jesus, but I feel more alive then I ever have.

'Wait for me,' I shout and then I run –

Erba' u għoxrin

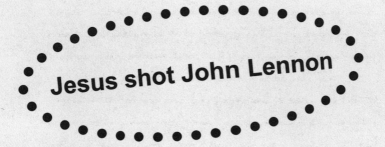

twenty-four

Jesus shot John Lennon

Matt,

I dreamed about you last night; my feelings grow stronger each time that I fall into the darkness. In my dream, I was driving next to the shoreline and a wave came up and over my car. The car began to erode, as the salt stripped away the paint and then the body. I found myself sitting on the road, wet and shaking in my bones.

Then you came to me; you were guiding, helping, an old old woman who staggered and groaned with each movement. She was hobbling, with bare feet and a straw hat. I am sure that she had straw sticking out from her greying blouse. You moved from her, as she began to walk around me, circling with her words and staggered footing.

'Qalbi maqsuma fi tlett biċċiet,' she said the words over and over. 'Qalbi maqsuma fi tlett biċċiet, qalbi maqsuma fi tlett biċċiet.'

I tried to pick out the words, I tried to understand what she was saying to me, but her words were folding into each other. She spoke again, in English.

'My heart is broken into three,' she said. 'My heart is broken into three.' She pointed to her heart, with a finger that was too long and too crooked. I looked to where she pointed and I saw my face, with Molly, with Christopher. I woke from my dreaming, sobbing.

You come to me in the night, you send me messages in words that I no longer catch. You travel with women who speak to me with a tongue that, with darkness, I can no longer understand. And when I wake, I am covered in a longing, in a need to feel safe in your arms. I long for all that I cannot allow myself to give to you. I wish that you could speak to Christopher and that you would begin to understand the sacrifice that I have made, am making. I know that I must leave my son, but I have not yet the strength to say a final farewell.

I am truly lovesick, without you,

Nina x

◎

'She's gone.'

Christopher's words wake me from something close to a sleep.

I am curled into the chair in my mother's parlour. I have turned my knees, my body, so that I fit. I have my mother's crocheted blanket wrapped around my legs, warming my cold bones, yet still I shiver shiver, shiver shiver. My shawl, with tassels, is wrapped over my shoulders. A brown woollen blanket covers my body. It scratches, tickles on the skin that it finds. I fear that nothing is warming me, that dust is covering me.

I look to the floor and see Christopher sitting upright, straight backed, uncomfortable, almost formal, agitated. He is staring into me.

'Who, Ciccio, who has gone?' I ask.

'Tilly's gone.'

'Gone where, Ciccio?' I ask.

'To the sunflowers.'

He says then places a hand to the floor to steady himself. He stands, turns his back to me and runs through the wall, out onto the sloping street.

'Ciccio, where are you going?' I call after him.

'To see Elena.'

I hear his words, but already he has gone.

⊚

As the days pass, Christopher is with me less and less.

When we are together, he seems happier, less distracted. He has stories to tell, he is gaining histories, knowledge, words that talk of experiences that grown men have witnessed. He is ageing before my eyes, maturing.

There is a part of me that feels blessed to have been given this time with my son. Each moment with him is filled with a grasping, an appreciation of this other chance, these moments that should never have been. Christopher is becoming a man, a dead man, yet still his interactions with others who have passed, they thrill me.

He will be a good dead man.

I think, he will be a good father. And then I am covered in a shiver, in a coldness that surrounds my heart.

My whole body shakes.

> I sob.
>
> ~s – ob.
>
> ~s – ob.
>
> sob into my shawl.

◎

My thoughts worry me; I realise that I no longer know reality.

Lines blur between dimensions. I have no concept of how long I have spent in Malta. I have tried to count, to remember, yet I know not of days, of time, of the outside world.

Today I stay in the chair, in my mother's parlour, focusing on who I am, who I have become, who I wish to be. The thoughts stay within me, flashing images around.

I see myself, when I search within, I see myself balancing right on the edge of a diving board. I am sitting with my legs dangling over. Below is the pool, a deep blue, calm, refreshing. Behind me are fragile wooden stairs, I cannot see the bottom, but I know the direction in which I must descend. The fragile, perhaps broken, wooden stairs lead to the unknown, the deep blue invites.

I have been on this edge for some time.

My choices are not as clear as they once were.

'Mhux se taqbeż, qalbi.'

~you will not jump, my heart.

Her voice flicks me into the now.

I look to my mother. She is standing by the door, a look of concern, of love, covers her beautiful face. She is rubbing her hands over her hair, shaping her black hair into a ball. She does this a lot, too much. She looks younger than when I arrived. My days are melting into one, time marked only by the ageing of spirits.

My mother looks so very fresh, alive; her skin is stretched with pinked cheeks. She looks flushed. She looks younger than me. I wonder how I look.

'Nina, qalbi. L-aqwa li ġejt lura id-dar, dak biss li jgħodd.'

~Nina, my heart. You came back home, that is all that matters.

My mother holds out her arms, wide, but I do not move from the chair.

My bones are aching; I feel cold, again.

'Why will I not jump?' I ask.

'Because of Matt, because of Molly, qalbi.'

~my heart.

She speaks in a whisper and then turns back into the kitchen.

'Mama. How did you die?' I call to my mother; she comes back.

'My heart was broken. It was broken from the moment that I was born. We did not know.'

'Am I to blame?' I ask.

'No, qalbi. I lived a life full of miracles. Our Lady blessed my parents with a child who should never have been born. They prayed twice each day at Il-Madonna tal-għar, they prayed for seven years and then I was delivered to them. Each day was a blessing.'

'You were a miracle,' I smile.

'And so were you, ta.'

~ta is a tag that seeks confirmation.

She smiles and her whole face glows, radiant.

'I was not told when you died, not until weeks later.' I look to my knees.

'I know of this, Nina. Daddy would not allow the family to contact you. He wept each night, he prayed for strength. He had hoped that someone would disobey him and contact you, but the family stood together and offered him respect. And you know that your daddy is a stubborn man. You are like him.'

My mother does not move close to me. She speaks her words, smiles and turns to return to her kitchen. She is impatient, distracted, today.

'When did he die?' I ask, quickly.

'Die? Your daddy dead?' She turns to face me, again.

I nod.

'Huwa mhux mejjet, qalbi. Jgħix ma' oħtok Sandra, f'tas-Sliema.'

~he is not dead, my heart. He lives with your
sister Sandra, in Sliema.

She speaks, then turns, walks into the kitchen and I do not ask any more of her.

◎

340

I stay curled into the chair in the parlour. My knees, my body, my bones all ache. I feel stiff, cold, weak. I think back to the last time that I saw my father. I think of his words and of the volcano that became him. But my mind will not dwell on the images of him.

my mind.

~fl – icks.

~fl – acks.

~fl – icks.

is controlled, a photograph album turning rapidly, through images, beyond my command.

The page rests on a reflection, on Molly.

I think of her; my stomach begins to spasm.

⊚

My pupa, my Molly, she is four years old; too young to understand why her mama has left her. I wonder what Matt has explained to her. I wonder if he talks of my coming back or if I have already been erased from their every day.

I pull my shawl tighter around me, until the tassels connect.

I think of when Molly was a baby, before she began

toddling. I can remember her curling into me, her warmth, the security that she gave to me. I can remember wrapping the shawl around us both. We would sit, together, music playing in the background, a television programme flashing across the screen.

My focus would be on my daughter, always.

Molly would fiddle with the tassels, rolling them between her tiny plump fingers, pulling them up to her mouth. With that action she would draw me forward, to her, with her already strong movements. I would smile at her, laugh with her, feel her affection, her love. I was covered in happiness each time that she was close to me. She was a beautiful baby, breathtaking, perfect. Loving my Molly was easy, uncontrollable.

But if I moved out of that moment, away from her physical presence, then I remember that with that ease of love came guilt. With that deepness of love that I felt from her, to her, with that feeling of such emotion, came fear.

I feared that I would forget Christopher, that in loving Molly I was lessening my loss, increasing my vulnerability.

In my mother's parlour, I think of my Molly and of my Christopher and they stand united.

The pieces begin to fit.

Lost within my grief, I failed to see the missing detail. I think, I realise, Molly has a likeness of Christopher, their curls and eyes connect them. Molly is part of us all, part of the history that binds us.

I think of my daughter, my stomach spasms and my heart aches.

I miss her, beyond my words.

◎

I cannot move.

I think back to the airport, to that phone call, to those deep sobs that Molly released into the phone. I think of Matt trying to comfort her, fumbling with words, with fingers.

My Molly, my pupa, my Molly.

~my doll.

I pull my shawl up to my face, I breathe in, I search for a scent that no longer exists.

I long.

I sob.

~s – ob.

~s – ob.

~s – ob.

as I am missing Molly, too much.

☺

Jesus: Do not cry, my Nina.

I lower my shawl and open my eyes. Jesus is here, in my mother's house. He is standing in front of me, a little too close. I look to his waist. His jeans are hanging from him; I think they call them skater jeans. I look down, his toenails are painted the brightest of pinks. I look up and he wears an "I shot John Lennon" T-shirt. I smile, yet all the time I am wondering when he last ate. He looks too thin.

> **Jesus:** This morning, my Nina. I ate your Cadbury's chocolate this morning.

He smiles. He moves, elegantly, to kneel before me. I am still curled into my mother's chair. Jesus rests his hands onto my thigh. I feel the warmth from his touch.

'I miss her, Molly,' I say, tears trickling without control.

> **Jesus:** You are nearly there, my Nina.

His hands move, slowly rubbing my thigh, comforting me with their warmth.

'Where? Tell me where I must go. Please,' I plead.

> **Jesus:** You are considering what you do to those around you, how they are suffering for your guilt. You are thinking of your pupa, your Molly. You are

344

beginning to accept your guilt, Christopher's death, your mother's death. Yet still you must stop pushing punishment onto Molly and Matt. You know what you must do.

'I know what I must do,' I say, I nod, I know.

And then Jesus is gone.

His warmth sweeps up my legs and into my stomach.

'I know,' I say the words aloud, to someone. 'I know.'

'You know what?'

Christopher stands in the kitchen doorway.

'Jesus was just here,' I say.

'Flavia's waiting for him in Larry's bar. Jesus told me to find her.'

'And you found her?' I ask.

'Of course, she's never far from you.'

My son turns into the kitchen. I hear my mother singing in Italian; Christopher's laughter floats to me.

Ħamsa u għoxrin

~twenty-five

Malta's top 5: *About Malta*

✳ 5. Folklore and Tradition

For many years folklore and tradition have guided the people of Malta. The telling and retelling of stories is passed down through generations. These stories mask moral conduct, deepen tradition, tell of customs and of experiences acquired through time. Folklore and tradition have deepened the cultural identity of the island.

Matt,

I feel that my time is ending, that soon I will be making decisions and moving in a direction.

My island is magical, it speaks with wisdom and with beauty. Each word has a depth, a lyrical twist that lingers when spoken. I wonder if I will ever tell you of those who have visited my mother, Melita's home. I wonder if you will listen without raised eyebrows, without tutting, without telephone calls to psychiatrists and the talk of prescribed drugs. I wonder if you will ever accept my gift, my seeing.

Your son is different here; he has a freedom to wander and to grow. You would be proud to see the man that he is becoming. He reminds me of you in so many ways. He is handsome, has integrity, he would make a good father. I know that he never will. I know that he has passed, but still I watch him and I feel honoured to know him. He grew without us, yet still he will always be part of us. It is our love that joined to make him whole.

My mother has explained to me about her death, about the miracle of her birth and I am beginning to understand why I was not told of her passing and how precious a gift she offered to my life, in giving me life. I miss you Matt and I miss my Molly with every part of my being. I ache. There is so much that I need to talk to you about, so many words that we need to share.

I am lovesick. My heart is split into three perfect
pieces and yet I will always belong to you,

Nina x

◎

I am awake; my neck is stiff, twisted into a crook. I do not
know how long I have been sleeping.

I call out to my mother; this time she does not come.

◎

I sit in the darkness.

I think, replay fragments, flashing images prompt my
thoughts.

I think to my life in England, to my need to be British. I
think of my denial of all that is within me, my denial of
roots and grounding.

I think back to being pregnant with Christopher, to the
plans, the reading of magazines, the obscure requests
that we felt we should include in our birth plan. I was
meticulous, in a superficial way. I focused on all that
I read; I ignored what I already knew, what was buried
deep within my roots

◎

I replay my mother's words, about the folklore of the
island, about the many questions that I never asked. I

349

wonder when my mind wandered from this island.

I think to, I remember, the twisted child.

It was back, many years ago, when I was a young girl on the island. Our neighbour had given birth to her fifth child; my mother she said to me, 'Nina, come Nina, come see the twisted child.'

I remember she dragged me down the slope, to our neighbour. My mother pulled at my arm, lugged me to Maria's house and in her other hand she grasped at her Rosary beads. And I remember Maria answering the door. She was wearing a traditional robe, black satin covering, smothering her remaining figure. She did not speak, she lowered her head in what must have been shame. I remember my mother's grip tightening around my arm and my not knowing what I was going to see. I remember wanting to close my eyes and not look upon the child.

'This one was bought in a shop,' my mother told me. Then she leaned over the child. 'Ikun imbierek Alla,' my mother said. I remember counting to ten, waiting for all evil spirits to have gone and then I looked down, upon the twisted child.

~God be praised.

I remember that I released a gasp and my mother pressed her fingers tighter into my arm, making a mark, pinching me to withhold my reaction, emotion.

My mother told me, 'Learn, qalbi. Not during and not for forty days afterwards. One day you will understand.'

~my heart.

I remember that I looked down to see the twisted baby and that I wondered why they had bought that one from the shop. I was confused, but did not want to question or to ask. I wanted to know why they had not picked a good one, a not twisted one. There were so many thoughts that we were not allowed to have near to newborn babies. I remember that I tried to clear my mind.

Maria told my mother, 'I counted wrong, Melita. I met with Pauline on day thirty-six. I thought that it was day forty-one, that I was allowed to go out with my baby. I called at Pauline's house. I thought that it would be safe for us to meet. I was certain that it was day forty-one. She opened the door and I saw her fear. We are both new mothers and now one of us or one of our babies will die. It is all my fault.'

'But you had sexual relations during pregnancy. That is enough. The meeting made it worse for you all,' my mother told Maria and then I remember that my mother kneeled before the crib, holding her Rosary over the twisted child. My mother prayed and prayed.

I could hear my mother telling Maria that intercourse during pregnancy was wrong. I did not understand what she was saying. My mother was calm, caring and Maria was sobbing. I thought that she was sad because her baby was twisted, because her child was deformed and very sick. I thought that her sobbing was because she had counted incorrectly, because she had met with another new mother within the forty days.

I was a naïve child, I never thought to question. I knew only what I was told to believe, what knowledge I was allowed to possess.

◎

The twisted baby did not survive.

◎

I think back to when Christopher was born. I called him Rokku for two days.

He was Rokku Aquilina for two days. I should never have changed his name.

On day three our pale child, my Ciccio, was registered Christopher Robinson.

I thought that he belonged to England, but I was wrong.

◎

I remember our taking Christopher, for his birth to be

registered. We were unmarried, we had to go together, to sign the documents together. I was taking my child out before baptism, within forty days of delivery, at three days old. I knew that my only Lord was angry. Matt had to be there, we both had to be there, to accept responsibility. On the certificate it stated that I was unmarried and unemployed. Eight months later, we married in the same registry office, and with our marriage certificate, they gave us an altered birth certificate.

The shame was erased.

But I know that my only Lord sees all.

I remember when I was pregnant with Molly, I would stare at a photograph of Christopher. I would look at his blond curls and blue eyes and I would long.

Somewhere, buried within me, I knew of the belief that if you stare at the image of a saint or even a famous person when with child, then your child will be born resembling, formed into the image that you wished for. I guess that the same could be said of a cat or a dog or even a rat; if you stare at these animals too long, then your child will be born resembling that animal.

I stared at the photograph of my dead son. I longed, I raked over a past.

And Molly was born in his image, from his image.

I think of Molly and my stomach spasms.

◎

My mother speaks to me.

'Nina, qalbi, tikkritika ruħek wisq.'

~Nina, my heart, you criticise yourself with
much passion.

My mother is standing at the kitchen door. She is not smiling.

'Where have you been?' I ask. 'I called you.'

She does not answer. She looks distant, distracted, her eyes heavier.

'Minn fejn jiġu t-trabi, Mama?' I ask her.

~where do babies come from, Mama?

She looks to me and smiles through her words.

'You came to us on a boat. Maria came in a box and Sandra we bought in a shop.'

I cannot help but laugh, ha ha ha. My mother laughs too, the sound tinkles, tink tink tink.

I used to think that I was so very special, that I had travelled the furthest to be part of our family. I used to

look at the boats in the harbour and wonder which one
had brought me to Malta.

'You should have told me the truth,' I tell her. 'Of sexual
intercourse and of pregnancy.'

'I blame myself, Nina, for letting my child into the world
without education. We never talk of sexual acts, the shame
is too great. And outside of marriage –'

My mother stops talking.

'Ġibt il-mistħija fuqkom 'ilkoll,' I say.

~I brought shame upon you all.

'It is in the past, qalbi, times have changed.'

~my heart.

'I have heard that during pregnancy if a pregnant woman
does not have her wishes fulfilled, then this may lead to
miscarriage,' I say.

My mother nods.

'I often think back to when I visited this island, with
Christopher, with Matt. I do not know if that ostracism,
if that rejection led to the death of my son. There is a
connection, do you see it?'

'Nina, no. There is no connection, no blame to be placed.
You are confusing stories, you are ignoring the purpose.'

My mother speaks; sadness covers me.

'Tell me,' I whisper.

'It is simple, qalbi, the lore of an island offers insight, structure; it tells of the mysterious ideas that have been rooted in our minds through generations, ta.'

~ta is a tag that seeks confirmation.

'Are you saying that it's not true?' I ask.

'No, I am saying that it is within us all. Listen, we are born with these stories and they offer explanation for what science and religion cannot make clear.'

I nod, I let the words sink in.

'Lore binds our people, qalbi, it characterises and it is our cement.'

'And when I was rejected, the bond was removed and I lost myself. I denied all that I was. I lost my language, my personal and my cultural identity,' I say.

'But Nina, look, you never did lose it. Now you must see, your identity is stronger than ever before. Listen, qalbi, you must allow yourself to blossom.'

~my heart.

⊚

I move my legs, untwisting them, letting my feet touch the

tiled floor.

I push my toes into the flip-flops. I stand.

I flip-flop to my mother.

~fl – ip.

~fl – op.

~fl – ip.

~fl – op.

~fl – ip.

~fl – op.

as I reach her, she is gone.

'Mama,' I call out, but she does not come.

'Christopher,' I call out.

My son walks through the wall and into the parlour.

'Come sit with me a while; come talk to me,' I say.

'I can't Mama, I'm talking to Elena.'

He says, he turns, he walks back through the wall.

I am alone –

Christopher

Christopher Robinson sits in Geordie and Elena
Smith's home, in Lascaris, the war rooms in Valletta.

Christopher: She wanted me to talk with her. Jesus
told me not to stay too near to her, but I am hurting
my mama.

Elena: You must do what Jesus tells you to, he is
our guide. Can you see? Can you see that she is
thinking to your death again? Melita must go to her.

Christopher: She thinks to 5 February 2002, I
stepped onto the road and was hit.

Elena: God bless your soul.

Christopher: Ka -pow. Th – wack. Spl – at by a red
car. The girl in the car had only passed her test a
month before and she was talking to her boyfriend
on her mobile. Her reactions weren't as quick as they
could have been, but I was the one who stepped out
in front of her. B – ang. Wh – ap. Sp – lat.

Elena: Listen, but to blame her I think would be

worthless.

Christopher: There is no blame. My mama had called out Ciccio. She was smiling. And then B – ang. Oo – ooff. Oo – ooff. Z – onk.

Elena: Mela, your mama plays this moment over and over, yes?

Christopher: Mama lives in the past; it's been six years now, Elena. She tells me that I was killed on impact. All I know is that I went B – ang. Wh – ap. And Sp – lat. It didn't hurt and somehow I left my broken body and I found myself sitting at a table, in Larry's bar with Jesus.

Elena: And were you scared?

Christopher: I don't remember much, but I know that I was shaking and crying. I was ten then and still a kid. I wanted my mama.

Elena: Hanini, that is the normal reaction.

~my pet.

Christopher: I stayed with Jesus and then with Geordie for ages. They looked after me and explained what was going on and what it meant that I'd passed.

Elena: Geordie has spoken of those days and of

your fear. You have moved far, ḥanini.

```
-my pet.
```

Christopher: I was growing in this world and then one day I could hear my mama speaking in my head. She was talking of when she began to hit me, of how she would hurt me when I was a child. I don't remember this time. Jesus could hear her too. He told me that Mama was losing her battle and that her guilt was killing her, so he sent me back to her. I was only supposed to visit her once.

Elena: And now she will not let go.

Christopher: She used to cling to me. She would focus on me and I would watch Molly quivering from fear because my sister doesn't see the dead and didn't know what was happening to her mama.

Elena: Your sister is beautiful ta, but I think she needs her mama.

```
~ta is a tag that seeks confirmation.
```

Christopher: I need Mama to go back to Molly. I need for her to let me go.

Elena: I know ḥanini, you are doing so well. We are all proud of you.

```
~my pet.
```

Christopher: This is my task; Jesus says it is my journey. I have to help my mama to come to terms with my death and to move forward in her life. So far I'm doing a rubbish job.

Elena: No ħanini, you are doing well. We are all helping you, it is Jesus' wish. You must stay strong.

~my pet.

Christopher: When I tell her that she must leave me, she cries.

Elena: The time will come shortly, ħanini.

~my pet.

Sitta u għoxrin

~twenty-six

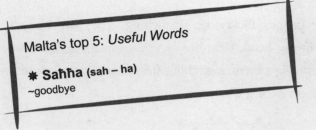

Malta's top 5: *Useful Words*

* **Saħħa** (sah – ha)
~goodbye

Curled in the chair in my mother's parlour, the darkness coils around me.

I cannot sleep.

I have images flickering, disturbing. They are images there, in my head, I cannot escape from them, I cannot stop replaying them, searching for reason, for purpose. I want them to be gone.

'Qalbi, do not fight them. Tell me about that day.'

~my heart.

My mother walks from the kitchen, she clutches a mug. She walks to me, hands me the hot milk, then lowers herself to the floor in front of the chair.

I tell my mother, 'Six years have passed, but still my mind wanders, back. I cannot control the images that flash within my head. Christopher hadn't seen me. He was standing at the main road, waiting to cross.'

My mother nods.

'I called his name, shouted out Ciccio.' My throat begins to ache. 'He looked at me, a huge grin on his face. And then, he stepped out onto the main road.'

'Qalbi, talk to me, tell me.'

~my heart.

◎

'He was killed on impact,' I speak the words and then I sob.

◎

I am curled into the chair in my mother's parlour. My knees, my body, my bones all ache. I feel stiff, cold, weak. I clutch the mug of hot milk, little warmth transfers into my hands. My mother looks up to me, her eyes glazed in sadness, her fingers locked together as if to pray.

'There was nothing that I could do,' I tell her.

◎

'I have said those words over and over and over,' I say.

'There was nothing that I could do. There was nothing that I could do. There was nothing that I could do,' I say.

'I think that I may have convinced myself that they are true, meaningful. I shouldn't have shouted, I should have trusted him to walk home alone, I should have been a better mother,' I say.

'Life can change, can fall, crumble with ease. I made the wrong decision, I did the wrong thing,' I say.

'Mama, a mistake. A split of a second error in judgement.

The weight of consequence is beyond measure,' I say.

◎

'We all make mistakes, qalbi.'

~my heart.

My mother speaks.

'I have tried to change,' I tell her.

'We know.'

My mother says.

◎

'The following day, I walked back to where the accident had happened. I stood in the same place and I watched the school children, with their parents,' I say.

'Why Nina, why were you not grieving in your home?'

My mother asks, folklore guides her.

'I watched the flowers being placed onto the pavement. There was a pile of plastic wrapped flowers, of teddy bears, a football. There were cards, pencil drawings, all for Christopher,' I say.

'He was so young.'

My mother looks at me, her sadness, understanding, comforting me, now.

'Mama, I watched the mothers twisting their children into them, that little bit tighter, that little bit closer. I watched them all,' I speak through my tears. 'I watched that in that moment, in that time, they recognised how very fragile life was. They held the importance of their family, of their lives that little bit closer and that little bit tighter.'

'Ma mietx għal xejn.'

~his death was not in vain.

My mother offers.

'No Mama, my loss was their gain.'

'As the days, the weeks passed by, I continued to watch the children with their parents stepping back into old lives and old habits. The flowers by the side of the road died and then one day, when I walked past, they were gone,' I say.

'It is how it must be.'

My mother tells me.

'No Mama, no. Christopher had been buried, his grave tended daily, by me. Matt went back to work, life moved on. I had nothing, no one,' I sob, snot, tears, streaming from me.

'I should have been there for you. That is my regret.'

Caroline Smailes

My mother says.

Then she moves, stands, gracefully. She stoops, down, balancing on the edge of the chair. Her fingers stroke my hair, my cheek.

Her cold fingers shock me.

◎

'Molly arrived, not by boat. She came out from me with control, with grace,' I smile. 'I have already spoken of my love for her, of her beauty, of the closeness, of the guilt.'

'Is-sens ta' ħtija sejjer jieklok, Nina, qalbi. Trid tħalli l-passat warajk.'

~guilt will eat you, Nina, my heart. You must leave the past behind you.

'The guilt grew. Matt began to notice. He would find me crouched in a corner weeping, sobbing, rocking backwards and forwards. A smell, a sound, a word, silence, everything was filled with my loss. I needed my son, I needed to see him again.'

My mother nods.

'I would speak to him, begging for forgiveness, begging for a sign that he was safe,' I say. 'I couldn't eat, I couldn't sleep. I wasn't functioning. '

'And pupa, Molly, where was she?'

~my doll.

'Molly was growing. A baby, a toddler, beginning to communicate, an only child. Each time that she was not upon me, needing me, I would drown in my grief,' I say.

⊚

'And then one day he heard me.' I pause.

'And I had passed too, by this time. I remember talking to Christopher, to Jesus, about you. Konna kollha inkwetati ħafna dwarek, qalbi.'

~we were all so very worried about you, my heart.

'Matt was at work, Molly was sleeping, I was sobbing in the corner of his bedroom. I was rocking on the floor, clutching a Power Ranger in a tight fist. I felt angry, angry that he was ignoring me, that he wouldn't talk to me. I felt that he had been taken from me to punish me, that I had been tried, sentenced, convicted. Could you see me?' I ask.

'Yes Nina, I hid from you. Your gift, your seeing was not as tuned. Your grief was clouding you.'

'I needed my son,' I say. 'And then he came back.'

'I came with him. I showed him how to travel.'

'He walked through the door and into his bedroom. He sat

on the bed.' I smile. 'Did you hear me scream? I screamed and then I sobbed, even more snot and tears were dripping from my face. I was wiping them onto my sleeve and still the tears were falling and the snot was dripping. I moved to him attempting to touch him, to see if he could be touched. He stayed sitting on his bed.'

'We had told him to stay calm. He was unsure how to react. You were his first apparition.'

My mother is calm, her voice low, soothing.

'He looked older, had aged with time, without time,' I say. 'He was smiling at me.'

'Għandu t-tbissima tiegħek.'

~he has your smile.

My mother's fingers continue to stroke my hair, my cheek.

'I touched him, cold. I hugged him, cold,' I say. 'I remember not caring if I was going insane. I remember waves of happiness rushing through me, to see my son again.'

'Christopher told me that he had heard me speaking in his head. He told me that Jesus could hear me too. He did not mention you. He told me that Jesus had sent him back, to help me, to stop me losing my battle. Christopher spoke of how my guilt was killing me and that he would stay, a while. A small amount of time, until I was ready to let go,' I say.

◎

'That was two years ago,' I say.

◎

'In those two years, we have grown. I have told him about Malta, spoken to him in a language that I thought buried, lost. We have watched films together, laughed, argued. He has taught me to play chess, about music, about his favourite songs and bands whom I never knew existed,' I tell her.

'But Nina, qalbi, in that time he has grown with us too. He lives with us. He belongs in our hearts too.'

~my heart.

My mother tells me, I listen, I nod.

'We hoped that by bringing Christopher to you, that he would ease your grief, help you to move on. Jesus uses this treatment to help those drowning in grief. He underestimated your heartache. In bringing Christopher back to you, we took you further from your family and deeper into your anguish.'

My mother says the words and then sighs, deeply.

Caroline Smailes

'I did not know,' I say. 'Molly could not see him, Matt could not see him. I thought I was the only person who could care for him, that he was alone and needed me.'

'Matt and Molly needed you.'

'I have left Matt and Molly alone, confused,' I say.

◎

'Did you know that I tried to tell Matt?' I say.

'I see Christopher,' I told Matt.

'We all miss him, Nina,' he told me.

'No Matt, I see Christopher. I speak to him, I can see the dead,' I told Matt.

'You need help, Nina. You need to go back to the grief counsellor,' he said.

'Why can't you see Christopher?' I asked Matt.

'He is dead, Nina,' Matt told me.

'But I can still see him, talk to him, laugh with him. Why can't you?' I asked Matt.

'This must stop!' Matt shouted.

◎

'And all the time Molly would be listening, watching, feeling fear, confused,' I tell my mother.

372

◎

'Nina, qalbi, listen to my words. Christopher was sent to save you, but now you must release him. It is best.'

~my heart.

My mother moves her hand from my hair, my face, grabs my wrist and squeezes, slightly too hard.

'When he first came back to me, I needed to grab hold of any time, any remaining time with Christopher. If I could not see him, hear him, touch him, then I was filled with an anxiety, loss,' I say.

'Listen, qalbi, I have watched you. I have seen you. You have changed.'

~my heart.

'He has been fading of late,' I say.

'He is happy here, with us all. He is growing, we all are.'

My mother says and then smiles. Her fingers have stopped gripping my wrist. She moves her whole palm to rest on my cheek.

'Each time he leaves me, I fear that he will not come back,' I say.

'He will not leave you, until you let him, until you tell him. But he too must move on, when his time is right. Soon you will be his mother again, you will let him walk forward, in safety and protected on this side. I will look after him for you, qalbi.'

~my heart.

'I know,' I say and I do.

I know.

◎

'Where is Christopher?' I ask.

'With Elena and Geordie.'

My mother tells me.

'Can you get him?' I ask.

'Call him and he will come.'

She says.

◎

My mother stands, makes room. I uncurl, lowering my legs to the cold floor and slip my feet in the flip-flops.

　　I flip-flop to the kitchen.

　　– fl – ip.

　　~fl – op.

　　– fl – ip.

– fl – op.

~fl – ip.

– fl – op.

· to beside my mother's cooker, I run my finger over the smooth work surface.

I think, Ciccio, I need to talk to you.

And then he is there.

◎

'I need to say goodbye to you, Ciccio,' I say.

Christopher is standing in my mother's kitchen. He is resting against one of the wooden chairs. His blond curls have grown; they are dangling, slightly, over his eyes. He does not speak.

'It is time for you to leave me, to grow, on your own,' I say.

The words are stilted, they are forced.

'Ciccio, I am sorry, for not being the mama that you needed, that you should have had,' I say.

'Inħobbok, Mama.'

~I love you, Mama.

'Will you visit, sometimes?' I ask.

'I promise.'

My son smiles; I look to the tiled floor, tears falling. My son comes to me. He is taller than me, now. His arms wrap around me, cold.

'Love Molly for me.'

My son tells me, then he releases his arms from me and moves to the wall.

And then, my son walks through the wall and he leaves me.

Seba' u għoxrin

~twenty-seven

Malta's top 5: *Resorts*

✳ Sliema and St Julian's
Sliema and the shoreline leading to neighbouring St Julian's offer a vibrant heartland for shopping centres, pulsating entertainment and glitzy café life. A far cry from the quiet and historic, St Julian's and Paceville are Malta's principal nightlife districts, popular with young locals and tourists.

Days pass, not measured in light and dark.

I am alone, truly alone.

My mother is not near. I call out her name, over and over, she does not come.

The spirits that I have met, that were sent to help me, they have moved forward, from my sight. I know that they are watching, waiting for my decision.

◎

I have stopped writing to Matt. I have lost my words.

I do not know what to do next.

I am stuck, undecided, between the fragile wooden stairs and the diving board.

I dare not move.

◎

I am still sitting, in darkness, in my mother's parlour, when she appears, finally.

She stands in the doorway to the kitchen, her eyes are glistening, tear filled but not falling.

'Missierek qed imut, qalbi. Mur għandu.'

~your father is dying, my heart. Go to him.

My mother says.

◎

My Lord spits and then stammers, stutters onto me. The heavens are a dark grey and then they open, my only Lord cries His tears down on me.

His tears are warm.

I flip, I flop.

– fl – ip.

– fl – op.

– fl – ip.

– fl – op.

through the puddles that are beginning to form.

I am struggling to keep up with my mother. She is racing, the rain not touching her being. I have no umbrella. I pull my shawl around me, over my head, over my shoulders, tightly.

'I have left that house now. I cannot go back.'

My mother says.

I nod, but she is not looking at me.

◎

The buses are waiting in the terminal. They are parked, neatly. The drivers are huddled, smoking under the shelter.

We board a yellow bus, climbing the rusted steps. I sit near to the front; the fabric covering the seat is ripped, old.

My mother does not sit with me. She prefers to stand, clutching the metal pole, gazing out through the window, maintaining perfect balance as the bus swerves around corners. There are two others on the bus, a traditional bus, yellow, orange, rusting. I think that the other passengers are spirits; I do not ask, I do not stare. I poke my finger through the rip, the hole in the fabric, feeling the grainy sponge on my fingertip.

I feel sick in the pit of my stomach.

the bus judders.

~jud – der.

~jud – der.

~jud – der.

and shudders.

~shud – der.

~shud ˙– der.

~shud – der.

in a rhythm that alters with each turn.

The driver is small, young, grey, dead.

I wonder if I am going insane. My mother laughs, the sound tinkles, tink tink tink; her eyes lock onto my face.

I count four car accidents.

The Maltese are not used to driving in the rain, the tyres do not seem to grip to the roads. They concertina cars, one into another. There are no injuries; rather it is that the cars do not stop, the roads are wet, without grip, the cars slip together. I watch angry men raising their hands to my only Lord. I watch young men talking into mobile phones, pointing at cars and shaking their fists. The bus driver steers past the accidents, occasionally beeping the horn; no one notices as we swerve. I think about the angry fists and hope that fighting does not follow.

My mother does not speak; her eyes are now fixed through the window, distracted, not quite here.

I know that she is with my father too.

I am cold in my bones, I shiver shiver, shiver shiver.

I know only that we are travelling to the village of Sliema, to Sandra's house. I do not know where she lives, the kind of house, who she lives with, nothing. I know very little of her adulthood, of anything from the family that formed past my leaving Malta.

I realise, I have been detached from my blood.

◎

My mother tells me to pull the wire down; she is with me again.

I pull the wire, I hear a ting and the bus slows down, pulling in to a stop.

My mother first, I follow, carefully, down the bus's rusted metal steps and out into the rain.

◎

The rain is warm to the touch and then it seeps into my bones, I shiver shiver, shiver shiver. My only Lord's tears are becoming part of me.

◎

My mother slows and moves next to me. She links her arm through mine.

'Sandra, your eldest sister, we bought from a shop.'

I laugh, ha ha ha, my mother laughs, the sound tinkles, tink tink tink.

'Four years before I came in on a boat,' I smile.

My mother smiles.

'She was studying Maths at university, here, when I left,' I say.

'She went on to marry a policeman, to have two daughters. She teaches now. We are proud.'

'Maths?' I ask.

'A primary school teacher. She is a good woman, a strong mother, strong in her dealings with your father, qalbi.'

~my heart.

My mother speaks the words, covering them in pride, in satisfaction.

'She had only girls? Is that still mocked, do we still see her as lacking?' I say.

'Times have changed, qalbi, the island has opened.'

My mother says and I nod, I understand.

◎

'Will she close the door on me?' I ask.

'Not this time, qalbi.'

~my heart.

◎

Sliema is different, it has grown. Concrete everywhere; hotels, shops, bars, restaurants. My eyes search for

383

traditional, for old.

My mother guides.

I flip, I flop with her.

The rain begins to stutter and then it stops. People are beginning to emerge for the passeġġati.

~leisurely evening stroll.

Couples, families, are wanting to take their evening promenade along the seafront. People walk by, they look at me, measuring me, some nod; some see my mother, my mother smiles to them.

◎

My mother stops.

Sandra's house is tall. The door is the same green as my mother's.

The door is huge, towering above me, half open. I know that my father has not died; tradition dictates that the door would have been closed if he had. I think that the gap may swallow me up.

I do not press the doorbell.

'Press, qalbi.'

~my heart.

My mother says.

I do not move.

'Qalbi, press.'

My mother says, stronger in her voice.

I press the bell.

My mother walks through the door and into Sandra's house, but still I hear her words.

'Listen, qalbi; remember that if you tell a lie then the tongue will burn from your mouth.'

I wait for someone to answer the door.

⊚

A young girl comes to the door. She smiles at me.

I speak in English, 'Is Sandra home?'

She turns, leaving the door open, runs along the darkened corridor.

'Mama,' she calls. 'Hemm mara Ingliża fuq l-għatba.'

~there is an English lady on the doorstep.

My eyes adjust, along the darkened corridor. Marble, wood, white walls, everything perfectly presented.

At the far end, Sandra steps into the corridor. Our eyes connect, she steps forward, one, two, three.

and then she falls to the floor.

~s – *ob*.

~s – *ob*.

~s -*ob*.

sobbing.

I flip-flop to her.

I curl to the floor, next to my sister. I wrap my arms around her. She is so small, so fragile.

'Go to Daddy,' she whispers from inside of our curling embrace. 'Mur issa, Nina, qabel ikun tard wisq.'

~go now, Nina, before it is too late.

◎

My father is in bed.

The bed is in what looks like a lounge, a parlour. The bed looks out of place, wrong. I see between the people, those collected around his bed. My father is not moving, a white sheet is tucked tightly around his thin body. He seems smaller. Next to the bed, beside my father's head, my mother is stroking his hair. His eyes are closed. He has much hair, greying but still with flashes of black. I look to his face; he is old, creased, his features being absorbed by his skin.

I stand in the doorway, afraid to step closer to him. I am torn. I want to wake him, to shake him, to shout, to cry, to hate him, yet I am filled with a need to see his eyes, one last time.

◎

There are a number of people gathered around the death-bed. My eyes flick over their faces, forming outlines and shapes but failing to place, to recognise. They have opened a space, for me to move towards my father, to join their vigil. There is a priest, of course; his hands are creased, sun kissed, wrinkled. I do not look to his face. He has been called, the end is near.

The priest may have already administered the last rites. I think so, the mood is low, whispered, filled with grief. People, people I have not yet recognised nor placed, recite the Rosary. A single voice, low, hoarse, speaks a different prayer, the words are unfamiliar. I know that her words will help the dying, my father.

I move my eyes from my father, to a dark shape. There is a man, in the corner, reading a glossy magazine and drinking a pint of beer. He looks at me, winks, smiles. He is watching me. I do not speak.

◎

My mother speaks.

'Ġużeppi, ara min ġie lura d-dar.'

~Joseph, look who has come home.

My father opens his eyes, slowly. He fixes upon me, he stares. The man in the corner laughs; the surrounding people scream, gasp, I think that someone faints. The volume augments. There seems to be increased movement, increased clamour. The man from the corner moves out past me, into the corridor. The movements of people rub by me.

'Nina,' my father whispers. His hands flicker.

There are more screams, more gasps; the reciting of the Rosary has lifted in speed, in volume.

I flip-flop to the bed. I stoop down. I place my hands over my father's hand. I lift my father's hand to my cheek. All the time he watches me, his fading eyes locked onto mine.

I hear people enter the room, I do not turn.

'Nina,' my father whispers, hoarse, death filled.

'I came home, Daddy,' I say.

I can hear Sandra wailing in the corridor. I do not turn. My eyes are locked onto my father. His eyes are beginning to waver; his eyes are losing their lock.

His eyes close.

I hold his hand to my cheek. My tears trickle onto him.

'I came home,' I whisper.

Tmienja u għoxrin

~twenty-eight

I move from my father's body, walking backwards, slowly, trying not to flip-flop, trying not to make a noise.

My mother speaks.

'Listen, remember to tell no lies.'

◎

I turn, into the hallway.

I see my sisters, my Sandra, my Maria. Maria looks like me. She is the middle child who was squashed in between the dominant and the most loved. Around us there is noise, phone calls, the priest, a doctor. There are movements, wailing, sobbing, sniffing into handkerchiefs. Around us there is chaos yet we stand together, a three, not speaking.

'How did you know?' Sandra asks me.

'Mama told me,' I say.

'Is your husband with you? Is your son outside?' Maria asks.

'Christopher died, six years ago. I am here alone,' I say.

Sandra has been controlling her grief, but now she lets out a snort, which turns into a wail. Maria folds to me, Sandra follows. Our grief rejoins us.

My sisters understand.

392

My father's body is washed clean, for his journey, it is covered, a vigil is held.

Twelve hours of prayer, before the funeral, before the final farewell to his physical being. We are offered tranquillisers from the doctor. Sandra takes two, Maria declines, I decline.

We have a house to prepare.

I change into black, Sandra's clothes. My father had asked for a traditional funeral. The mirrors are covered in any material that we can find, the photographs are turned, the pictures on the wall are turned too. The feel of the house is dark, grief filled, grim.

The front door is closed, the door knocker removed, the bell disconnected. There is to be no sweeping near to the front door. We, my sisters, me, we work together, scurrying around.

I do what the island's tradition dictates, yet all the time I am thinking to the spirit world, to the happiness, to how my father has joined with my mother again.

I am followed everywhere by the young girl who answered the door. She seeks my hand, in hers.

'What is your name?' I ask her.

'Lucie,' she tells me and smiles.

'You are very beautiful, Lucie, just like your mama,' I say.

'I had a dream about a candle,' she says.

'Did you?' I ask.

'And Ciccio was there too,' she says and smiles.

I smile. I know that she is a seer.

◎

Twelve hours pass.

A traditional burial is coming. I am filled with panic. I need to be strong, but loss, grief, everything combines within me. I wish that I had taken the tranquilliser. Sandra is so very calm, controlled, able to perform. There is an expectation, a duty to show grief outwardly. In Malta this is a sign of respect.

I cannot.

I cannot wail, I cannot allow myself to sob over the death of my father's physical being. I have learned, I know the secret, I have been told that death is but an illusion.

◎

The hearse is pulled by horses, followed by the mourners.

Some of the women are professional mourners, they howl, they sing through their wailing. There are three of them, dressed in the traditional għonnella with black veils covering their faces.

~a type of hooded cloak, usually black and made from silk or cotton. It covered the head, the body frame but not the face. The garment has historical significance and depth, but is rarely seen in modern day Malta.

There is crying, too much crying.

I feel that I am drowning in false grief.

Lucie walks next to me, holding my hand.

'In-Nannu u n-Nanna huma ferħanin issa.' She smiles, she does not cry.

~Granddad and Grandma are happy now.

We are all in black, Sandra wears a veil. I do not cover my face. I know that all are watching, staring, trying to place me. I see cousins, cousins of cousins, neighbours, old teachers, friends of my father, of my mother. They will all know of the shame that I placed upon my family and still I came home. My being here, my coming home before my father's death has erased something, not all, but something.

I hold my head high. Men walk with us. They wear black ties; some wear a black band around one of their arms. The men are not interested in me, they do not gossip through tears. They are here to pay their respects to my father, a good man, a strong and loyal friend. I see my mother's brother, my Uncle Mario. His eyes connect with mine, he smiles.

I wish.

Then I stop my wish.

I think of Molly, of Matt. I long for them. I long for them to meet with all who have surrounded me, all who are here to pay their respects to my father.

I think of Matt, I crave his strong arms, for his strength, his love, his gentleness. I look to Lucie and I can see a resemblance of Molly, vague, flashing. I want them to know each other.

'Death is a return to God, a release from worries,' a grieving voice whispers.

I hear.

But that is wrong.

◎

I need Matt.

◎

The funeral passes, blackness, everywhere. The grief is controlled, performed by me, by my sisters. I speak to neighbours, to cousins, to friends of my father; they all ask how I knew of my father dying.

I tell them, 'Ommi qaltli.'

~my mother told me.

I do not lie; they all look confused, shocked, disturbed. My Uncle Mario laughs, ha ha ha.

◎

And then when all is quiet, when the watching, judging eyes have gone, then I lock myself within the bathroom in Sandra's house.

I turn on the taps, I fill the bath. The crash of water masks any other sound.

As the water flows from the taps, I curl to the floor in the centre of the room.

my grief pours from me as I.

~s – ob.

~*s* – *ob*.

~*s* – *ob*.

without restraint.

◎

Lucie knocks on the bathroom door.

'Auntie Nina,' she says. 'Come have hot chocolate with us.'

She breaks my grief.

◎

Sandra has welcomed me into her home. My sister is good at organisation, at routine, at healing. My days have had structure, again.

Her two daughters, her Lucie and then her Nadia, are keen to learn of my life in England. I tell them of London, of Liverpool and their eyes are wide, wild, wanting.

I sit in their kitchen, at their wooden table, chatting, drinking hot chocolate that is thick and fragrant. Sandra bustles around us, watching, interrupting, attempting to compare the places that I talk of with their small island.

'We have a palace,' Sandra says.

'We have museums,' she says.

'We have history,' she says.

'Our island is beautiful oħti,' I say. 'But there is a world beyond what your eyes can see.'

~my sister.

'My girls will not leave Malta,' she says.

I nod.

'But you must all come and stay with me, for a holiday,' I say.

Sandra smiles.

'Will you have more children?' she asks me.

'I don't think I will,' I say. 'Molly needs me and Ciccio cannot be replaced.'

'God picked that little flower and wanted it to make heaven even more beautiful by its presence,' Sandra says.

The mood has changed, suddenly. I glare at her, arguments forming inside my head.

'Do you really believe that? You believe that God sees children as flowers and picks them for His selfish gain?' I ask.

'It is the way. Listen, Nina, God loved Christopher so much that He wanted your child closer to Him,' she says.

I do not speak.

'The death of a baptised child should be seen as a blessing, Nina,' Sandra continues. 'A blessing from God.'

'You are telling me to rejoice in the death of my child?' My voice is filled with anger.

'No Nina, no. Grief is selfish, over time you will grow to accept that God has taken Christopher for the greater good.'

'Over time,' I repeat.

'Over time,' she says.

I think, six years must be nearing time. I think, we will never truly understand life and death. Instead, I understand, I know all that has been told to me leads me to a conclusion, a state of being.

Life is to be grasped and lived. We blossom and then we wither.

◎

'She is right.'

I hear Christopher, inside my head; he interrupts my reasoning.

'I am too handsome.'

I laugh out loud. My laughter shocks me.

Sandra looks at me, confused. I attempt to adjust my facial expression.

'Remember to say goodbye to everyone before you go home, to Molly and Daddy.'

Christopher says.

I hear his words and I nod.

I am ready to go home, to England.

Disa' u għoxrin
~twenty-nine

Malta's top 5: *Gastronomic Pleasure*

✳ 1. Pastizzi
Delicate diamond-shaped pastries, filled with fresh
ricotta or mushed peas.

Lucie and I, we are eating pastizzi, still warm from the local bakery.

~delicate diamond-shaped pastries, filled with fresh ricotta or mushed peas.

The pastry flakes and crumbles between my fingers. I taste the ricotta cheese, it melts in my mouth. Sandra is fussing around us, slamming cupboards, exiting, entering rooms.

I have told her that I am returning to England. I have told her everything, no lies, no hiding, everything about Matt and Molly, about Christopher, my seeing, my grief. She absorbed all, without comment, without argument, without emotion. Now she fusses around her house, forming packages for me to take home, for my family, her family. She wants me to return, in the summer, with Molly, with Matt. We are all to stay with her, in her home, a family.

I smile.

I have eaten two pastizzi, I could eat more. I am hungry.

◎

'Meta hi t-titjira tiegħek, qalbi?' Lucie asks me.

~when is your flight, my heart?

'I will leave later this afternoon,' I say.

'Before you are going to see Nannu u Nanna?' she asks.

~Granddad and Grandma.

'Yes, pupa. On the way,' I say.

~my doll.

Sandra stands at the kitchen door, her face covered in apprehension, in panic. She does not speak.

'Do not worry oħti, I am not mad,' I say to her.

~my sister.

'Where are you going?' she asks me.

'Back to the house of Mama and Daddy, to say goodbye,' I say.

'I will come with you,' she tells me.

'No, Sandra,' I say. 'I must be alone.'

⊚

I ask Sandra to telephone for a taxi. She refuses.

'I do not want to go by bus. I do not want to drag my luggage with me. I want quick and smooth,' I say.

'I will drive you and I will wait for you,' Sandra says.

⊚

My luggage is placed in the boot of the car.

Sandra drives. We do not talk in the car. Lucie sits in the back, without a seatbelt, reciting times tables in a looping song. She is accurate, clever.

Sandra drops me where the buses terminate. She should not, but she does. I climb from the car and walk towards the city.

'I will be here for you, in one hour. Do not be late or you will miss your plane!' she shouts to me, at me, through her open window.

'Thank you,' I say, without turning back to the car. I hurry through the City Gate.

◎

I flip-flop over the uneven pavement.

I flip, I flop.

~fl – ip.

~fl – op.

~fl – ip.

~fl – op.

My only Lord is smiling. His sun is shining, again, burning down onto my shoulders. I am wearing Sandra's clothes, a vest top, shorts, those pink flip-flops. I have brushed and pulled my thick hair back into a ponytail. I am wearing mascara, lipstick, all from my sister, all to make me presentable, beautiful.

I am full of goodbyes.

◎

It is early afternoon, the streets have filled with tourists. I make eye contact, I smile.

I flip, I flop.

~fl – ip.

~fl – op.

~fl – ip.

~fl – op.

down the narrow stone steps, making my way down the slant of the steep street.

I reach my mother's, my father's green front door.

◎

I knock on the green front door.

'No one lives there.'

The voice is behind me, I turn.

'Look, the door is chained. There is no one there.'

The man is old, grey, wearing shorts, a string vest and no shoes. He says his words and then lifts a pint of liquid, I think lager, to his lips.

I look at the man, a small man, vaguely familiar. I look at his face, he seems sad. I look to the door, there is a chain, a padlock. I look back to the man.

'I lived here, once,' I say.

'You are Nina Robinson.'

He tells me.

'They said you were leaving.'

Then he nods his head, winks and walks down the slope, towards the harbour.

I smile. He is just about to turn the corner.

'Goodbye Jesus,' I shout after him.

◎

I knock again, louder.

No one answers, the key does not turn, the chain does not clunk to the ground.

◎

I look up to the balconies, there are two. The house towers, leans slightly. The wooden balconies look like they will crumble with a gust of wind. I look to the façade, discoloured, flaking plaster, cracks. I look to the green front door, weathered, drained of colour. The rusted padlock, the tarnished chain, to keep those in, those out.

Like Bees to Honey

I need to be inside.

I close my eyes, I call him, I say his name. Christopher.

He was probably behind me, in front of me, over me. I do not really know. I open my eyes and he has come.

Christopher reads my unspoken thoughts.

'Don't worry, Mama, you know how to get in.'

'I do?' I ask.

'Of course, through the cracked window in the basement. It's easy.'

'For you, Ciccio, but not for me,' I say. 'Open the chain, please.'

I hear a key turning.

and a.

~cl – unk.

as the barrel revolves.

The chain and padlock come undone.

I hear the chain clunk.

~cl – unk.

to the floor.

409

And then it is gone.

◎

Christopher opens the door, it creaks, it snags, it jars.

I walk into my mother's, into my father's house.

I see grey.

Dust swirls before me, around me. The hallway no longer exists. I am standing on rubble, among rubbish that is piled, scattered, abandoned. The smell hits me, decaying, riddled. I am in filth, festering, sinking.

'Where is Mama?' I ask, panic rising in my voice.

'She left here. And when she left she could not return.'

Christopher tells me.

'But I need to say goodbye to her, to Daddy,' I say.

'Go to the backyard.'

He tells me.

◎

I walk over, through the rubble and the decomposing rubbish that is scattered across the ground. The staircase has crumbled, down to the floor, no longer vast, no longer sweeping, no longer grand. I look to the ceiling and I see an enormous hole, I see the blue sky.

My mother's and my father's home is hollow, a shell that is falling, decaying, disintegrating.

I walk through the remains of the kitchen, no wooden table, no cooker, no sink. There is no door.

I walk out into the backyard.

◎

The backyard is in colour, vines of green grapes hang overhead. The walls are a perfect white, radiant, the floor a mosaic of coloured tiles.

I hear music, taking them back to the 1960s.

My mother and father are dancing over the tiled floor, spinning, twirling, laughing. My mother is ahead of me, being guided into twirls by my father's hand. She looks young, fresh, rosy. She is youthful, early twenties now. Her figure has curves. Her lips are covered in red lipstick; she is wearing her best clothes, fashionable, for then.

I watch as my father places his arm around her and she folds in towards him. They look to each other and smile. He is young, handsome. His hair is jet black, quaffed and gelled.

They are happy.

◎

I interrupt them.

'I am leaving,' I say. 'I wanted to say goodbye.'

They turn, smile and rush to me with their arms open.

I feel myself crumbling. I try to be strong, but inside I am breaking, again. I want to fall to the ground, I want to curl into a ball, I want to be their child, again.

They hold me, engulf me into their time, their place, for a short moment and then they withdraw. My father places his arm around my mother as she speaks, as she looks into my eyes.

'Il-pupa tiegħek għandha bżonnok.'

~your doll/daughter needs you.

My father speaks.

'Inti miżżewġa raġel sew. Dan, jien rajtu.'

~you have a husband. I have seen that he is a good man.

I look at my mother, at my father. My eyes flick around the backyard of the family home that moulded me into all that I became. My eyes wander, my stomach churns.

In the far corner, there is a wooden table. Upon it, a radio, gloves, my mother's red lipstick, the crystal fruit bowl. I see oranges.

'Take one with you.'

My mother smiles. I do not move.

'Say goodbye to Elena, to Geordie, to Flavia,' I say. 'Tell them, thank you.'

'I will.'

My mother says.

'Jesus loves you.'

My father says and then he laughs, loudly. It rumbles around the bright backyard.

'There is a shawl, on the coat stand, qalbi. It is lace. It was my mother's. Take it with you.'

~my heart.

My mother says.

'Ħudha miegħek meta titlaq.'

~take it with you when you go.

My mother says.

I turn. I fight the churning spins in my stomach, the need to vomit, the need to wail, the need to curl to the mosaic tiled floor.

◎

And so I go.

My mother and my father do not move near to me. The distance is that of worlds, of dimensions that I am not ready, not able to pass.

I flip, I flop.

~*fl – ip.*

~*fl – op.*

~*fl – ip.*

~*fl – op.*

over the rubble, to the front door.

I take the lace shawl that hangs alone from the coat stand that has appeared, again. I wrap the shawl around me, I breathe in the damp stale smell.

◎

I open the green front door and stand onto the step.

The door closes behind me, I hear a key turning.

and a.

~*cl – unk.*

as the barrel revolves.

I am forced out onto the cobbles.

I look, the rusted padlock, the tarnished chain are connected, have reappeared.

414

◎

I flip, I flop up the slope, slowly.

There is a slither of my only Lord's smile, His sun projecting through the buildings, guiding me, warming me.

I am leaving my island, again.

◎

Sandra is waiting in the car, the engine running.

Lucie is excited to see me; she waves her hands out of the open window.

I climb into the backseat of the car; Lucie has my clothes in a neat pile on her lap.

'You have Nanna's shawl,' Sandra says. She has turned to face me.

I nod.

'How?' she asks.

'Melita, my nanna gave it to her,' Lucie says, smiling.

I nod.

Sandra looks to Lucie, to me, then she turns back and grips her steering wheel.

A few seconds pass, in silence.

Sandra makes eye contact through the rear-view mirror.

Her eyes tell me that she is confused, lost for explanation, for scientific reason.

I smile.

'Quick Nina, change your clothes,' Sandra tells me.

I take off clothes that belong to my sister.

I strip to my underwear in the back of my sister's car, as we rush through my island.

My clothes have been washed, ironed, folded.

I pull on jeans, a T-shirt, my knee-length boots.

I pull on my English clothes.

Tletin

~thirty

AIRLINE	TO	FLIGHT	DEP	GATE
ALITALIA – CAI	ROME	AZ 877	17:50	7
AIR FRANCE	ROME	AF 9746	17:50	CLOSED
EMIRATES	LARNACA/DUBAI	EK 107	17:50	CLOSED
AIR MALTA	LARNACA/DUBAI	KM 2155	17:50	CLOSED
LIBYAN ARAB	TRIPOLI	LN 367	18:00	6
AIR MALTA	FRANKFURT	KM 428	18:20	PREPARING
LUFTHANSA	FRANKFURT	LH 3385	18:20	PREPARING
AIR MALTA	MANCHESTER	KM 159	18:35	PREPARING

We arrive at the airport, we park.

I check in my luggage.

We move to the café, to drink coffee, to talk.

I tell Sandra about our parents, about their dancing in the backyard.

Sandra listens, does not comment, controls her emotions.

I do not lie.

◎

The airport is busy. It smells of popcorn, sweet.

I am leaving Malta. I wait until the final flight call.

'You will telephone Matt?' I ask.

'As soon as your flight leaves,' she tells me.

'And you'll explain?' I ask.

'Everything,' she tells me.

'And you'll pray that he'll forgive me,' I say.

'I promise.' She crosses her heart with her fingers.

I look to my sister, to the sadness that fills her eyes and I smile.

I am grateful.

◎

I say my goodbyes.

I hold Lucie close to me and I tell her to write, that I will return, that I promise to bring my Molly with me, next time. She cries; I fear that she does not believe me. Sandra pulls her daughter to her, to comfort her, to help her to understand that I will return, that I will keep my promise to her, that my little girl needs her mama. My sister understands.

I am hugged, I am squeezed. I am loved.

◎

I walk from them. I wave.

I walk into departures, through security without being searched, without beeping, without my handbag being invaded.

Security is not tight, here.

◎

In Malta, after you have passed through the baggage inspection, after the passport showing, you climb an escalator to the gates and to the Duty Free shops.

My sister and Lucie have waited; they wait for me to stand on the steps that move. And as I do, as the escalator carries me to the shops, to the gate, they wave, they shout my name and they shout for me to come back soon.

I wave down to them.

I mouth, I will come back soon. I mouth, I promise that I will come back soon.

Lucie smiles.

I reach the top of the escalator, I am about to walk forward, into the Duty Free, when I see him.

◎

I stop.

I smile.

'Thank you, my only Lord,' I say.

My son, my Ciccio, stands behind my sister, behind Lucie.

My son, my Ciccio, is with my mother, my father, Elena and Geordie.

He is safe, he is loved.

My stomach tightens, my throat aches.

I wave.

They all wave back, to me.

I turn, tears streaming down my cheeks, my whole body shaking, rattling. I wrap my mother's lace shawl around my shoulders, tighter, closer to my skin.

I walk, to gate number 3.

And there I board the plane that will take me home, to my Molly and to Matt.

Wieħed

~one

Nina Robinson (née Aquilina)

Born: 17.10.1971 —

The plane doors have been closed, security measures have been explained.

I am next to the small oval window; a man in a creased suit already sleeps beside me.

as the engines whir.

~wh – hir.

~wh – hir.

~wh – hir.

and as my head falls back to the headrest, the engines whir some more.

~wh – hir.

~wh – hir.

more and more.

The plane darts forwards, upwards, it tickles deep, into the back of my throat.

I swallow, forced gulps.

And then I am gone.

I am in the air, higher and higher.

Through the small oval window I see the light that marks the life, the homes, bars, restaurants, churches on the island. The plane flies over the skyline.

Spirits swarm, becoming lights that sparkle and speckle in coloured patterns through the sky. They are dotted over the horizon, each with a story to tell, each with a longing to fulfil, each having travelled here to Malta, each needing to heal.

I see the vast dome, the number five church, the Rotunda of St Marija Assunta in Mosta.

I hope for a different miracle.

◎

I look out through the small oval window, I look out until the lights fade, until I am truly gone.

I look out, as darkness falls, until my eyelids close.

◎

The air steward's voice wakes me, a monotone booming over the bustle of the tourists.

'Please stay seated until the aircraft is stationary.'

They do not, of course.

The plane is on the ground, they seek an escape.

seatbelts begin to click.

~cl – ick.

~cl – ick.

~cl – ick.

People stand, push into the aisle, pull coats and bags down from the overhead lockers. It is dark outside, the tourists are tired from their journey, impatient, keen to be home, in their own beds. Children cry, babies cry, parents speak with sentences that are clipped, abrupt.

The jetty is being attached. The doors open.

I wait. I do not hurry. I watch the tourists file past.

I wait, then I walk onto and down the aisle.

I smile, I say goodbye to the air steward.

I walk out, over the jetty.

> the heels of my knee-length boots clip-clap.

~cl – ip.

~cl – ap.

~cl – ip.

~cl – ap.

over metal and then the noise sinks into carpet.

I walk, I walk, I walk.

I am tired, drained, anxious.

I walk through passport control, I walk down to baggage collection.

The conveyor belt moves slowly, slowly, slowly, the luggage yet to be placed onto it. The belt groans and moans around and around and around.

I stand, I wait.

I take my lipstick from my handbag and pull it across my cracked thin lips.

The fear, the anticipation, the panic all twist together inside of my stomach. I do not know what will happen next.

◎

'Jien qiegħda d-dar,' I whisper, to no one.

~I am home.

Nixtieq nirringrazzja lil...

~I would like to thank...

My grandma Helen, for telling me her story. And my grandad George, know that I still miss you. And Jacqueline, Mario and Ramon Azzopardi, for welcoming me into their home and for showing the beauty of the island. And you, my beautiful Kugina Jaka, thank you for showing me that Malta is a place to heal (I will be eternally grateful to you). And Karl McIntyre, Matt Hill, Sophia Leadill Taylor, Paula Groves, Margaret Coombs, Richard Wells, Megan Taylor, Nik Perring, Kate Holmden and Jon Mayhew, for making me believe that I could. And Flavia Baralle de Goyeneche, Sandra Scicluna, Stephen Shieber and Vicky Lowsley, for the clever advice and help. And the Novel Racers, my blogging friends and my twittering pals (you know who you are), for being there during the ups and downs. And Áine McCarthy, Mel Sherratt and Clare Christian, for reading it first and for the feedback that made me cry and smile (at exactly the same time). And my agent Cathryn Summerhayes, for believing in my writing. And Joanna Chisholm, for the clever (and patient) typesetting. And Becky Adams, for the exquisite cover artwork. And my

427

publisher Scott Pack and Corinna Harrod at The Friday Project, for their support and absolute faith in me. And Gary, Jacob, Ben and Poppy, for giving me the space to create and the roots to grow (you lot are the bee's knees). And, finally, to Jacob, this one you can read (but don't be too brutal in your criticism, please).

1980

On March 26 1980, I was six years, four months and two days old.
I was dressed and ready for school. It was 8:06am on my digital
watch. My mother was still in bed. I went into her room to wake
her. I found her lying on top of her duvet cover. She wasn't wearing
any clothes. Her ocean eyes were open. She wasn't sleeping. And
from the corner of her mouth, a line

of

lumpy

sick

joined her to the pool that was stuck to her cheek. Next to her,
on her duvet I saw an empty bottle. Vodka. And there were eleven
tablets. Small round and white. And I saw a scrap of ripped paper.
There were words on it.

jude, i have gone in search of adam.
i love you baby.

I didn't understand. But I took the note. It was mine. I shoved it into
the pocket of my grey school skirt. I crumpled it in. Then. Then I
climbed next to her. I spooned into her. Moulded into a question
mark. Her stale sick mingled and lumped into my shiny hair. I
stayed with my mother, until the warmth from her body transferred
into me. We were not disturbed until my father returned from work.
At 6:12pm.

*****

Exhibit number one —
my mother's note.

*****

In the days between my mother's death and her funeral, I noted that someone from every one of the thirty-one other houses in my street came to visit. Some just stood in silence in the hallway. Some drank coffee at the wooden kitchen table. Others sat with my father in the lounge. Smoked cigarettes and drank from tin beer cans. My father liked these visitors the best. There were some neighbours who came each day. Just to check on my father. And between them they decided on how best I should be cared for.

I was six years old. I was more than capable of taking myself to school at 8:30am. My father left for work twenty minutes before I left for school. 8:10am. That was fine. I loved those twenty minutes. I was alone in the house. I was king of the castle. I spent the twenty minutes sitting. Sitting on the bottom red stair. Staring at my watch. Glaring. Terrified that I would be late for school. I loved those twenty minutes. School was a ten-minute walk away. Over only one main road. But a lollipop lady watched out for me. *They'd had a word.* Then coming home from school. I could manage the walk. But. But they thought it best that I wasn't at home alone. My father came home from work between 6:10pm and 6:17pm. So together. Those smoking drinking neighbours and my father. They decided where I should go each night.

2

Monday.	(Number 30)	Aunty Maggie.
Tuesday.	(Number 19)	Mr Johnson.
Wednesday.	(Number 14)	Mrs Clark.
Thursday.	(Number 21)	Mrs Roberts.
Friday.	(Number 2)	Mrs Hodgson.

I had my key. Tied to a piece of string and fastened with a safety pin inside my brown parka. That key was to lock the door each morning and only for emergencies at night. That key would allow me to escape from my neighbours.

During those days. Between my mother's death and her funeral. I used to watch my neighbours slowing down as they passed by my mother's house. I could sit on my bed and watch them from the window. I could open the window. Just slightly. Just enough to let their words fly in. They didn't look up to me. I was already invisible. They never saw me. They never looked for me. Some neighbours would stand talking. Curlers in their hair. Slippered feet. Dressing gowns pulled across their chests. They would point at my mother's house and they would chitter and chatter and yackety yacker. Gossip. Gossip. Gossip. Always about my mother. My precious, my beautiful mother. She was in the tittle-tattle. She was in the chitchat. Her demise. My demise. My mother's house, Number 9 Disraeli Avenue was the centre of the universe. Front page gossip. The neighbours talked of *a pure evil* that was within my mother. They spoke of her *lack of motherly instincts*. They talked about a *murderous past*. I didn't understand their words. But. But they

3

were tinged and tanged with mean-sounding twangs. They talked. I listened. I heard them. Through the open bedroom window.

On the day of my mother's funeral. Five days after her death. My father told me to put on my school uniform. A grey skirt. A blue blouse. A blue and yellow stripy tie. My blouse was creased. Crumply and worn. My tie was stained with baked bean juice.

My mother's coffin was in the box room. The lid had been removed. She looked so beautiful. Her long blonde hair had been styled. She looked like a glamorous film star. She was covered in a white sheet and her bare feet were poking from beneath it. I crept into my mother and father's bedroom. I took my mother's favourite shoes from her wardrobe. I also took a blouse and hid it under my pillow. Her scent still clung to it. Combining Chanel, musk and Mary Quant. Then. I returned to the box room. I took her purple stilettos. I lifted the white sheet to see her ankles. I placed her purple shoes onto her blue feet. Touching her skin sent a throbbing ache into my stomach.

I feel sick. I feel sick.

I fought my weakness. I stopped myself from being sick. I needed her to be wearing shoes. I didn't want her feet to become raw. She was off to hike through foreign lands. My mother was not smiling. Her face was blank. As I looked at her I realised that all expression came from her eyes. I longed for those ocean eyes. *Open your eyes, please open your eyes.* Just to connect with her one last time. My hair was tangled, still matted with her sick. So I sat on her hairdressing stool. Next to her coffin. In the box room. And I counted each stroke as I brushed my hair. *One ... two ... three ... four ... five ... six ... seven ... eight ...* I needed my mother. I needed her to get rid of the tatty tatty clumps. I reached into the coffin. Her coffin. I held her cold hand. I heard people laughing and chatting downstairs. *Ding dong. Ding dong. Chatter chatter. Laugh laugh laugh.* Aunty Maggie from Number 30 had brought rice, Mrs Clark from Number 14 had brought a platter of sandwiches and with each ding dong my father poured drinks and welcomed his guests. I sat. Holding my dead mother's hands. Wishing that she had taken me with her on her journey. Downstairs they talked loudly. And then. Then hushed and whispered. *She hadn't left a note, she was so very selfish, how could she be so cruel to little Jude.* They talked badly of my mother. I wanted to go and scream at them. To stop their evil gossiping. My father said that he wouldn't speak ill of the dead. But. *Sarah was an evil whore and ahm glad that she's deed.* And. *She'd been threatening te dee it for years.* And. She was *an evil lass. A selfish murdering whore. She divvnae care aboot anyone but horsell.* I hated my father. I hated that he fed the neighbours lies. I didn't understand. Liar liar. Pants on fire.

My mother loved me. She did care about me. I didn't understand why my father was telling lies. My mother was magical. She was beautiful and she loved me. Right up to the sky and back. She was thirty-two. She was clever. She was just going to explore the world a little. She would come back when she was done. She had gone in search of Adam. Her explanation was simple. I had no idea who or what an Adam was. She would tell me all about it when she found it. She'd come back then. She'd come back and carry on being mine. I'd wait. I'd always wait. I stroked her long slender fingers. She was cold. Too cold. Back into my bedroom. A hot water bottle. I took it into the bathroom. Turned the hot tap till it was burning. Burning. I filled my plastic hot water bottle. Then I returned to my mother. I placed it under her sheet. I gave her the shiny fifty pence that Aunty Maggie, Number 30, had given me the day before. Just in case. She may have time to buy herself a treat. An ice cream and a ten-pence mix up.

My father shouted for me. I stood. Over my mother's coffin. I looked at my mother. The last time. She did not look back at me. Her eyes were closed. Sleeping. Sleeping Beauty. I would not cry. I could not cry. I had to be brave. They would think badly of my mother. My father had told me. He had warned me. *Big girls don't cry. Do you hear me? Big girls don't cry.* I bent down and kissed my mother. She did not wake. I was not magic.

I sat next to my father in the large black car. I lowered my head and tried to name all the foreign places that I could think of. My fists were clenched. I recited names. I could think of only five.

Spain ...
France ...
Scotland ...

America ...
London ...
Spain ... France ... **Scotland** ... **America** ... **London** ...
Spain ...
France ...
Scotland ...
America ...
London ...

I tried to picture my mother in these countries. The Tower of London. Loch Ness. Disneyland. The Eiffel Tower. On the beach. Sunbathing. And in my head I could see her smiling. Her eyes twinkling with excitement. As she grasped her sketch book, charcoal and lead.

The funeral ended. Mr Johnson, from Number 19, took me to school in time for lunch.

Mashed potato.
Peas.
And carrots.
Mixed together.
Fish fingers.
One, two, three.

Jam sponge.
Custard.

7

The afternoon of the funeral passed quickly at school. Children avoided me. My teacher cried at the front of the class. I sat at my small wooden desk and held my tightly clenched fists in front of me.

Spain ...
    France ...
        Scotland ...
           America ...
              London ...
                Spain ...
                  France ...
                  Scotland ...
                  America ...
                  London...
                  Spain ...
                  France ...
                  Scotland ...
                  America ...
                  London ...

I would not cry. I did not move during afternoon playtime. Teachers walked past the classroom window and peered in at me. My nails dug into my palms, but my knuckles were fixed and I concentrated through the pain.

        Spain ... France ... Scotland ...
        America ... London ... Spain ...

France ... Scotland ... America ...
London ... Spain ... France ...
Scotland ... America ...
London ... Spain ...
France ...
Scotland ...
America ...
London.

I didn't draw an Easter card. I didn't practise my writing. I didn't listen. I didn't speak. Nothing. Nothing. Nothing.

The final bell rang.

I left my desk. Children moved out of the way. Terrified that a touch from me would make them catch the evil eye. I had the evil eye. Mothers at the school gate turned their backs. Talked in packs. Always in hushed tones. No one wanted to look at me. No one could find the words. My mother was fresh in the ground. I was at school. The neighbours were drinking. Eating. Celebrating. I had to walk home alone. Alone. Alone. Alone.

It was a Wednesday. But Mrs Clark was at my mother's wake. In a pub called The Traveller's Rest. A wake. The neighbours were trying to wake my mother. I had tried that too. Given her a kiss. It hadn't worked. She needed a handsome prince. The neighbours would wake her. They were old and clever. Aunty Maggie was nearly one hundred and ninety-five years old. She was the oldest person in the world. She had to be the wisest person in the world.

I used my key and let myself into my mother's house. It was cold. It was silent. I rushed to the box room. Ran up the red stairs. *Quick quick quick.* Just in case she was still there. But. But the room was empty. She was gone. I went into my mother and father's bedroom. I opened my mother's wardrobe. It was empty. She had taken her clothes with her on her travels. She had packed. She had gone. I went downstairs. Into the kitchen. I found her things. Next to the door. Waiting to go into the garage. They were in black plastic bags. Waiting to be thrown into the garage. Ready for the bin man. One bag for her clothes, one bag for her secrets. For her stuff. I took her secrets. A bag full of letters and beads and books and her sketch book and a box. I took that bag. I hid it in my room. Buried within a basket of teddies and dolls. I would keep it for my mother. I wouldn't look. She could show me when she came back. We could take it with us. When she took me away. When she had found herself an Adam.

When it was time.

I took my mother's blouse from under my pillow and held it to my nose. I tried to sniff in her smell. But. But already it was fading. I was forgetting. I curled onto my bed. Onto my blue duvet. I curled into a question mark. I held my mother's blouse tightly to me and I stared out of the window. I stared up to the sky. I watched the

10

day fall into night. My father and some of the neighbours returned home. I heard them chatting and laughing and cheering and singing. I felt their happiness. It kind of stuck into me like a fork. They sat downstairs, smoking and drinking beer out of warm tin cans. They didn't come into my room.

* * * * *

Life entered into a robotic routine. I existed. I grew. I was quiet. A thoughtful child. I had no friends. I carried the world inside my head. I carried the world on my shoulders. In my hands. There was no room for play. There was no way of playing. I sat. I thought. Always about my mother.

Aunty Maggie gave me a shiny fifty-pence piece. Every Monday evening when my father came to collect me. I saved all of them. And eventually. I was able to buy an Atlas. I held the world in my hand. It was a large hardback book. Glossy. The pages stuck together. New. Crisp. I learned of new places. Unsure if my pronunciation was correct.

Spain ...
     France ...
Scotland ...
     America ...
London ...
Libya ... Malta ... Tibet ... Victoria ... Boston ... Greenland ...

11

Spain ...

    France ...

        Scotland ...

            America ...

                London ...

Libya ... Malta ... Tibet ... Victoria ... Boston ... Greenland ...

        Spain ...

        France ...

        Scotland ...

        America ...

        London ...

        Libya ...

        Malta ...

        Tibet ...

        Victoria ...

        Boston ...

        Greenland ...

Spain ... France ... Scotland ... **America** ... **London** ... Libya ... Malta ... Tibet ... Victoria ... Boston ... Greenland.

I placed a small heart-shaped sticker onto a country. Onto a place. Then. I moved it around each day. I plotted my mother's travels. I watched her move through my book. I watched her move around the Atlas. I held the world. I held her world. I carried the world with me. Always. Always with me. My room was tidy. Always. I

12

asked for and received so very little. Yet with the uncluttered space came calmness.

I started to write poetry. I started to draw. I spent hours scribbling words. Or sketching my mother. In different countries. Outlines of her, with signs pointing to her next destination. My drawings weren't very good. They weren't good enough. I had no photographs of her. My father had taken them all. I tried to sketch her. In case I began to forget. But. I couldn't capture her ocean eyes. I wasn't good enough. My drawings were rubbish.

But.

Her eyes.
They penetrated to my soul.
At night.
As I closed my eyes in the cold darkness of my room.
My mother appeared and her eyes warmed me.
I longed for my mother. My precious mother.
As I closed my eyes.
In my darkness.
My mother.
Behind her a signpost.
Pointing.
Four different directions.
All leading to Adam.

All searching for Adam.

Her bag of secrets.

Her bag of her. Still buried. Untouched. Waiting. Waiting for her return.

* * * * *

Context

1. Black Box (*noun*)

a. An informal term for an event-recording device, most commonly associated with aircraft. It is recovered after a crash and its contents examined for clues as to why the crash occurred.

b. An informal term for an event-recording device, used creatively to give voice to Ana Lewis. It has been recovered after the crash of Ana Lewis' life and its contents are being examined for clues to help determine why the crash of Ana Lewis occurred.

2. Crash (*noun*)

a. A collision of moving vehicles, often caused by a catastrophic sequence of events and leading to a total breakdown in ability to function.

b. A collision of Ana Lewis and Alexander Edwards, caused by a catastrophic sequence of events and leading to Ana's total breakdown in ability to function.

BLACK
BOX #01

Flight Recorder
DO NOT OPEN

[55°01'01.54" N 1°27'28.83" W]

Bedroom. Ana's first floor flat in a Victorian house near the coast of Tynemouth. The room contains a wardrobe, a bed and a bedside table. The walls are red. The duvet cover is red. On the bedside table there is an empty glass and an open pair of scissors. Next to the empty glass there are two white rectangular boxes. One of them once contained sleeping tablets. The other once contained painkillers.

~Are you still there?~
You've ruined the end.
Now I know what's going to happen.
The plot has you coming back to kill me.
A twist in the narrative.

[five second silence]

I had cast you in the role of handsome prince.
How strange that you should turn out to be my killer.
But that's an end.
And now I need to find a beginning.

~Are you there?~
~Will you listen?~
~Do you remember?~
I am remembering when we were courting.
It was always cold.
I'm thinking back to when you wrapped your arm around
me as we walked along Tynemouth beach.
I remember you folding me into you.
The image is practically cinematic.
~Do you remember?~

[five second silence]

We wore matching scarves.
I had knitted them and they had holes where I had
dropped stitches.

3

You had laughed at my fumbling attempt.

[sound: a throaty laugh]

I had dropped many stitches.

But you said that you loved them.

~*Didn't you?*~

That they were perfectly us.

~*Do you remember?*~

The scarves wrapped around us.

They bound us together.

You could climb up your scarf to mine.

~*Do you remember?*~

And then you found that knobbly washed-up stick.

And you wrote our names in the sand in those huge
perfectly straight lines.

And those lines stood together and made the flawlessly
straight letters of our names.

ALEX+ANA.

You said that our names and our lives and everything that
we would ever choose to do would be straight.

And I thought that you liked that.

[sound: sniff sniff]

I thought that the neatness and the organisation and the
perfectly horizontalness.

Well I thought that you liked that.

[volume: high]

No kinks and no bends.

A perfectly straight route from here to there.

From there to here.

To nowhere else.

And on that day when you wrote our two names into the sand.

Well I didn't realise that one day.

When you wanted.

That you'd wash away the +ANA that was joined to the ALEX.

[sound: sobbing]

[silence]

But your name would never go away.

It grew fainter, but it is still there.

I still see it there.

I can still see ALEX+ANA.

[sound: throat clearing]

You started a new life.

ALEX+SUE.

But I can't write another name.

There are no other names that are perfectly straight and perfectly able to cover ALEX.

[silence]

But you went off.

And you found that new name.

And it had curves in it because you had decided that you preferred curves.
↑

The lines no longer needed to be straight.

You adapted.

You accepted.

You left me here.

You left me.

Trapped.

[silence]

My room is a box.

A black box.

A sometimes ruby red box.

> *~Is that confusing?~*

You trapped me in here.

[voiced: unrecognisable word]

[volume: low]

I have a front.

I have a back.

They are my window and my door.

My door takes me to my children.

My door keeps me from your Pip and my Davie.

Our two children.

> *~They are your children too.~*

> *~But you know that they are your children too!~*

> *~Am I trying to be too clever?~*

The view from my window is ever changing.

I see the sand.

I see the sea.

And that image is my painting mounted in a chipped red window frame.

A sometimes black window frame.

A perfect square.

A perfect painting.

A painting that holds the memories of you and me.

We met as students.

       ~I know that you remember that.~

We lived in the same halls.

On the same corridor.

And we met in the first week.

You were so quiet.

All the girls wanted to know you.

To know what made you tick.

You were different.

You carried books around with you.

And you read those books.

You had a guitar.

And you could play your guitar.

Your friends were all girls.

You preferred female company.

And although girls flashed their breasts at you and

although girls flicked their flowing hair and offered
themselves to you.
You never accepted.
You had integrity.
It covered you in a bubble.
It protected you.

>*~When did it pop?~*
>*~When did the bubble burst?~*
>*~Was it when you selected that girl from that*
>   *magazine and trimmed her flawless edge?~*

I love(*d*) you.
I used to watch you playing your guitar in the common
room.
And I love(*d*) you.

>*~Did you realise then?~*

We were friends before we were anything else.
We were friends that became something else.

[silence]

But not until our second year
I was chair of the Poetry Society.
You'd come along to listen.

>*~Did you realise that they were all about you?~*

You used to listen.
You never clapped.
And then afterwards you'd always want to walk me home.
Sometimes you'd hold my hand.

And we'd walk in silence.

Words didn't carry meaning for you.

~How many hours did we spend together?~

~How many hours passed in silence?~

And I always preferred your place to mine.

You lived alone.

You preferred it that way.

You liked your own space.

One room – bedroom/lounge/kitchen.

And then a door to your grubby toilet.

Your furniture was shabby.

Your toilet was always grubby.

~No it was filthy!~

But in the corner, just beside the sunken brown armchair.

Your guitar rested against the wall.

But the guitar would wait, as you mixed, rolled and twisted the end of your joint.

Then you'd balance the smooth roll of paper onto your lip and you'd strum.

And you'd sing your sad sad songs.

And the lyrics wouldn't connect with me and with us.

They were of places and experiences that we'd never shared.

But I wanted to recognise myself within your words.

I wanted to hear you recount experiences that we'd shared.

To be singing about a depth of emotion that you had suffered because of me.

And that's why I kept coming back.

~You didn't realise did you?~

I wanted to make you feel something in the hope that you would commemorate me in your words.

Like you had for the Indian Girl.

That you would give me a purpose in being.

Because you stirred me when you sang and you strummed.

You turned something on within me.

You made me want the performer in you.

And I'd wish that you'd sing and strum something that would make my insides explode.

A song to communicate the words that you never spoke to me.

[sound: humming of an unrecognisable tune]

That was before we ever kissed.

I used to think that first kiss was an afterthought.

A something that you never really meant to happen.

That we'd travelled as far as our friendship could go.

And that the only possible next step was a kiss.

A kiss that should never have been.

[five second silence]

But it did.

And we did.

And then Pip did.

And once when I questioned why you sang such sad sad songs about places and times and happenings that I never understood.

You said, **I sing them because I like them**.

And that, **the words don't matter**.

That, **it's about the way things join together**.

How they loop.

How the syllables become beats.

How the beats have to fit.

It was a timing thing with you.

It was a red thing with me.

The view from here is red.

       [sound: humming of same now vaguely recognisable tune]

I had short hair when we met.

       -Do you remember?-

I spiked it with cheap gel.

That was then.

Now my hair grows long.

If you call out at my window, I will let my hair fall down to you.

I must remember to *blink*.

My eyes are dry as I stare out of my window.

Red eyes.

I want to dip my fingernails into my eyes and I want to

scratch and scratch and scratch my itch.

But I don't.

But I can't.

[sound: fingertips tapping surface]

A memory may flake off and stick under my nail.

And I won't be able to put it back into my eye.

And then I will forget.

And I can't let that happen.

My memories are all that I have.

[sound: sobbing]

So I look out of my window.

[ten second silence]

And I look onto the sand and I don't *blink*.

And if I stare and stare and stare through the pain.

Then I can see our names.

I see.

ALEX+ANA.

Then I lie flat.

[sound: a body flopping back onto bed]

My back stuck to my red duvet.

My arms and legs a perfectly straight X.

I open myself.

I open all of myself.

Waiting for you to re-enter into my picture.

I know that you'll return.

–Are you there?–

~Can you hear me?~
You're waiting for me to die.
~Are you there?~
You're waiting to see if you've killed me.

[silence]

I am trapped.
I will not leave this black square box.

[sound: pinging of a filament in a light bulb]

When we were students you liked to sing.
I liked to sing too.
You once told me that I had a sweet voice.
~Did you once say that?
I'm not too sure that you did.
I remember one day.
I couldn't tolerate hearing the same sad song over and over.
About the same Indian Girl.
And how she had broken your heart.
So I asked you why you didn't write a new song.
Something about the two of us.
We'd been together for over a year.
~And do you remember what you said to me?~
You said, **I can't write about you**.
You laughed when you said that.

And you said, **the Indian Girl is the only girl that I have ever loved.**

That, **nothing could compare to her**.

I never asked her name.

~Would you even have told me?~

[sound: glass smashing]
